Sidney Sheldon is the author of *The Other Side of Midnight*, *A Stranger in the Mirror*, *Bloodline*, *Rage of Angels*, *Master of the Game*, *If Tomorrow Comes*, *Windmills of the Gods*, *The Sands of Time*, *Memories of Midnight*, *The Doomsday Conspiracy*, *The Stars Shine Down*, *Nothing Lasts Forever*, *Morning, Noon & Night*, *The Best Laid Plans* and *Tell Me Your Dreams*, all number one international bestsellers. His first book, *The Naked Face*, was acclaimed by *The New York Times* as 'the best first mystery novel of the year'. Mr Sheldon has won a Tony Award for Broadway's *Redhead* and an Academy Award for *The Bachelor and the Bobby Soxer*. *Rage of Angels*, *Master of the Game*, *Windmills of the Gods* and *Memories of Midnight* have been made into highly successful television mini-series.

He has written the screenplays for twenty-three motion pictures, including *Easter Parade* (with Judy Garland) and *Annie Get Your Gun*. He also created four long-running television series, including *Hart to Hart* and *I Dream of Jeannie*, which he produced. He was awarded the 1993 Prix Littéraire de Deauville, from the Deauville Film Festival, and is now included in the *Guinness Book of Records* as 'The Most Translated Author'.

For more information about Sidney Sheldon, visit his website at www.sidneysheldon.com

SIDNEY SHELDON

THE SKY IS FALLING

HarperCollins *Publishers*

First published in Great Britain by
HarperCollins *Publishers* 2000

Seventh impression 2009

Copyright © The Sidney Sheldon Family Limited
Partnership 2000

Sidney Sheldon asserts the moral right
to be identified as the author of this work

ISBN 13: 9788172236076

HarperCollins *Publishers*
A-53, Sector 57, NOIDA, Uttar Pradesh – 201301, India
77-85 Fulham Palace Road, London W6 8JB, United Kingdom
Hazelton Lanes, 55 Avenue Road, Suite 2900, Toronto, Ontario M5R 3L2
and 1995 Markham Road, Scarborough, Ontario M1B 5M8, Canada
25 Ryde Road, Pymble, Sydney, NSW 2073, Australia
31 View Road, Glenfield, Auckland 10, New Zealand
10 East 53rd Street, New York NY 10022, USA

Printed and bound at
Thomson Press (India) Ltd.

For Alexandra
The Angel On My Shoulder

The sky is falling! The sky is falling!

—Chicken Little

Show me a hero and I will write you a tragedy.

—F. Scott Fitzgerald

PROLOGUE

There were twelve men in the heavily guarded underground chamber, representing twelve far-flung countries. They were seated in comfortable chairs set in six rows, several feet apart. They listened intently as the speaker addressed them.

'I am happy to inform you that the threat with which we have all been so deeply concerned is about to be eliminated. I need not go into details because the whole world will hear about it within the next twenty-four hours. Rest assured that nothing will stop us. The gates will remain open. We will now begin the auction. Do I have a first bid? Yes. One billion dollars. Do I have two? Two billion. Do I have three?'

One

She was hurrying along Pennsylvania Avenue, a block from the White House, shivering in the cold December wind, when she heard the terrifying, ear-splitting scream of air-raid sirens and then the sound of a bomber plane overhead, ready to unload its cargo of death. She stopped, frozen, engulfed in a red mist of terror.

Suddenly she was back in Sarajevo, and she could hear the shrill whistle of the bombs dropping. She closed her eyes tightly, but it was impossible to shut out the vision of what was happening all around her. The sky was ablaze, and she was deafened by the sounds of automatic-weapons fire, roaring planes, and the *wump* of deadly mortar shells. Nearby buildings erupted into showers of cement, bricks, and dust. Terrified people were running in every direction, trying to outrace death.

From far, far away, a man's voice was saying, 'Are you all right?'

Slowly, warily, she opened her eyes. She was back on Pennsylvania Avenue, in the bleak winter sunlight, listening to the fading sounds of the jet plane and the ambulance siren that had triggered her memories.

'Miss – *are you all right*?'

She forced herself back to the present. 'Yes. I'm – I'm fine, thank you.'

He was staring at her. 'Wait a minute! You're Dana Evans. I'm a big fan of yours. I watch you on WTN every night, and I saw all your broadcasts from Yugoslavia.' His voice was filled with enthusiasm. 'It must have been really exciting for you, covering that war, huh?'

'Yes.' Dana Evans's throat was dry. *Exciting to see people blown to shreds, to see the bodies of babies thrown down wells, bits of human jetsam flowing down a river of red.*

She suddenly felt sick to her stomach. 'Excuse me.' She turned and hurried away.

Dana Evans had returned from Yugoslavia just three months earlier. The memories were still too fresh. It seemed unreal to walk down streets in broad daylight without fear, to hear birds singing and people laughing. There had been no laughter in Sarajevo, only the sounds of exploding mortars and the anguished screams that followed.

John Donne was right, Dana thought. *No man is an*

island. What happens to one, happens to us all, for we are all made of clay and stardust. We share the same moments of time. The universal second hand starts its unforgiving sweep toward the next minute:

In Santiago, a ten-year-old girl is being raped by her grandfather . . .

In New York City, two young lovers are kissing by candlelight . . .

In Flanders, a seventeen-year-old girl is giving birth to a crack baby . . .

In Chicago, a fireman risks his life to save a cat from a burning building . . .

In São Paulo, hundreds of fans are trampled to death at a soccer match as the stands collapse . . .

In Pisa, a mother cries with joy as she watches her baby take its first steps . . .

All this and infinitely more in the space of sixty seconds, Dana thought. *And then time ticks on until it finally sends us into the same unknown eternity.*

Dana Evans, at twenty-seven, was lovely looking, with a slim figure, midnight-black hair, large, intelligent gray eyes, a heart-shaped face, and a warm, contagious laugh. Dana had grown up as an army brat, the daughter of a colonel who traveled from base to base as an armament instructor, and that kind of life had given Dana a taste for adventure. She was vulnerable and at the same time fearless, and the combination was irresistible. During the

5

year that Dana had covered the war in Yugoslavia, people all over the world were spellbound by the beautiful, young, impassioned woman broadcasting in the middle of battle, risking her life to report on the deadly events occurring around her. Now, wherever she went, she was aware of signs and whispers of recognition. Dana Evans was embarrassed by her celebrity.

Hurrying down Pennsylvania Avenue, passing the White House, Dana looked at her watch and thought, *I'm going to be late for the meeting.*

Washington Tribune Enterprises took up an entire block of Sixth Street NW, with four separate buildings: a newspaper printing plant, newspaper staff offices, an executive tower, and a television broadcasting complex. The Washington Tribune Network television studios occupied the sixth floor of building four. The place was always charged with energy, its cubicles humming with people at work on their computers. Wire copy from half a dozen news services constantly spewed out updated news from around the globe. The immensity of the operation never ceased to amaze and excite Dana.

It was there that Dana had met Jeff Connors. An All-Star pitcher until he injured his arm in a skiing accident, Jeff was now an on-air sports reporter for WTN and also wrote a daily column for the Washington Tribune Syndicate. He was in his thirties, tall and lean, with boyish looks and an easy, laid-back charm that attracted people to him. Jeff and Dana had fallen in love, and they had talked about marriage.

In the three months since Dana had returned from Sarajevo, events in Washington had moved swiftly. Leslie Stewart, the former owner of Washington Tribune Enterprises, had sold out and disappeared, and the corporation had been bought by an international media tycoon, Elliot Cromwell.

The morning meeting with Matt Baker and Elliot Cromwell was about to begin. When Dana arrived, she was greeted by Abbe Lasmann, Matt's sexy red-headed assistant.

'The fellows are waiting for you,' Abbe said.

'Thanks, Abbe.' Dana walked into the corner office. 'Matt . . . Elliot . . .'

'You're late,' Matt Baker grumbled.

Baker was a short, gray-haired man in his early fifties, with a gruff, impatient manner fueled by a brilliant, restless mind. He wore rumpled suits that looked as if they had been slept in, and Dana suspected that they had been. He ran WTN, the Washington Tribune Enterprises television operation.

Elliot Cromwell was in his sixties, with a friendly, open manner and a ready smile. He was a billionaire, but there were a dozen different accounts of how he had achieved his vast fortune, some of them not flattering. In the media business, where the object was to disseminate information, Elliot Cromwell was an enigma.

He looked at Dana and said, 'Matt tells me we're beating the competition again. Your ratings keep going up.'

'I'm glad to hear that, Elliot.'

'Dana, I listen to a half-dozen newscasts every night, but yours is different from the others. I'm not exactly sure why, but I like it.'

Dana could have told Elliot Cromwell why. Other newscasters were talking at – not to – audiences of millions, announcing the news. Dana had decided to make it personal. In her mind, she would be talking one night to a lonely widow, the next night to a shut-in, lying helpless in bed, and the next to a solitary salesman somewhere far away from his home and family. Her news reports sounded private and intimate, and viewers loved them and responded to them.

'I understand you're going to have an exciting guest to interview tonight,' Matt Baker said.

Dana nodded. 'Gary Winthrop.'

Gary Winthrop was America's Prince Charming. A member of one of the country's most prominent families, he was young, handsome, charismatic.

'He doesn't like personal publicity,' Cromwell said. 'How did you get him to agree?'

'We have a common hobby,' Dana told him.

Cromwell's brows furled. 'Really?'

'Yes.' Dana smiled. 'I like to look at Monets and van Goghs, and he likes to buy them. Seriously, I've interviewed him before, and we've become friendly. We'll run a tape of his news conference, which we'll cover this afternoon. My interview will be a follow-up.'

'Wonderful.' Cromwell beamed.

They spent the next hour talking about the new show the network was planning, *Crime Line*, an investigative hour that Dana was going to produce and anchor. The objective was twofold: to correct injustices that had been done and to spur interest in solving forgotten crimes.

'There are a lot of other reality shows on the air,' Matt warned, 'so we've got to be better than they are. I want us to start out with a grabber. Something that will capture the audience's attention and –'

The intercom buzzed. Matt Baker flicked down a key. 'I told you, no calls. Why – ?'

Abbe's voice came over the intercom. 'I'm sorry. It's for Miss Evans. It's Kemal's school calling. It sounds urgent.'

Matt Baker looked at Dana. 'First line.'

Dana picked up the phone, her heart pounding. 'Hello . . . Is Kemal all right?' She listened a moment. 'I see . . . I see . . . Yes, I'll be right there.' She replaced the receiver.

'What's wrong?' Matt asked.

Dana said, 'They'd like me to come to the school to pick Kemal up.'

Elliot Cromwell frowned. 'That's the boy you brought back from Sarajevo.'

'Yes.'

'That was quite a story.'

'Yes,' Dana said reluctantly.

'Didn't you find him living in some vacant lot?'

'That's right,' Dana said.

'He had some disease or something?'

'No,' she said firmly, disliking even to talk about those days. 'Kemal lost an arm. It was blown off by a bomb.'

'And you adopted him?'

'Not officially yet, Elliot. I'm going to. For now, I'm his guardian.'

'Well, go get him. We'll discuss *Crime Line* later.'

When Dana arrived at the Theodore Roosevelt Middle School, she went directly to the assistant principal's office. The assistant principal, Vera Kostoff, a harassed-looking, prematurely gray-haired woman in her fifties, was at her desk. Kemal was seated across from her. He was twelve years old, small for his age, thin and sallow, with tousled blond hair and a stubborn chin. Where his right arm should have been was an empty sleeve. His slight body seemed dwarfed by the room.

When Dana walked in, the atmosphere in the office was grim.

'Hello, Mrs Kostoff,' Dana said brightly. 'Kemal.'

Kemal was staring at his shoes.

'I understand there's a problem?' Dana continued.

'Yes, there certainly is, Miss Evans.' She handed Dana a sheet of paper.

Dana stared at it, puzzled. It read: *Vodja, pizda, zbosti, fukati, nezakonski otrok, umreti, tepec.* She looked up. 'I – I don't understand. These are Serbian words, aren't they?'

Mrs Kostoff said tightly, 'Indeed they are. It's Kemal's misfortune that I happen to be Serbian. These are words that Kemal has been using in school.' Her face was flushed. 'Serbian truck drivers don't talk like that, Miss Evans, and I won't have such language coming from the mouth of this young boy. Kemal called me a *pizda*.'

Dana said, 'A *pi* –?'

'I realize that Kemal is new to our country, and I've tried to make allowances, but his – his behavior is reprehensible. He's constantly getting into fights, and when I reprimanded him this morning, he – he insulted me. That was too much.'

Dana said tactfully, 'I'm sure you know how difficult it must be for him, Mrs Kostoff, and –'

'As I told you before, I'm making allowances, but he's trying my patience.'

'I understand.' Dana looked over at Kemal. He was still staring down, his face sullen.

11

'I do hope this will be the last incident,' Mrs Kostoff said.

'So do I.' Dana rose.

'I have Kemal's report card for you.' Mrs Kostoff opened a drawer, took out a card, and handed it to Dana.

'Thank you,' Dana said.

On the way home, Kemal was silent.

'What am I going to do with you?' Dana asked. 'Why are you always getting into fights, and why do you use words like that?'

'I didn't know she spoke Serbian.'

When they reached Dana's apartment, she said, 'I'm going to have to go back to the studio, Kemal. Will you be all right here alone?'

'Word.'

The first time Kemal had said that to her, Dana had thought he had not understood her, but she quickly learned that it was part of the arcane idiom spoken by the young. 'Word' meant 'yes.' 'Phat' described members of the opposite sex: *p*retty *h*ot *a*nd *t*empting. Everything was cool or sweet or tight or rad. If there was something they didn't like, it sucked.

Dana took out the report card that Mrs Kostoff had given her. As she studied it, her lips tightened. History, D. English, D. Science, D. Social Studies, F. Math, A.

Looking at the card, Dana thought, *Oh, Lord, what am I going to do?* 'We'll discuss this another time,' she said. 'I'm late.'

Kemal was an enigma to Dana. When they were together, he behaved beautifully. He was loving and thoughtful and endearing. On weekends, Dana and Jeff turned Washington into a playground for him. They went to the National Zoo, with its spectacular array of wild animals, starring the exotic giant panda. They visited the National Air and Space Museum, where Kemal saw the first Wright brothers plane dangling from the ceiling, and then walked through Skylab and touched moon rocks. They went to the Kennedy Center and the Arena Stage. They introduced Kemal to pizza at Tom Tom, tacos at Mextec, and southern fried chicken at Georgia Brown's. Kemal loved every moment of it. He adored being with Dana and Jeff.

But . . . when Dana had to leave to go to work, Kemal turned into another person. He became hostile and confrontational. It was impossible for Dana to hold on to a housekeeper, and sitters told horror stories about evenings with Kemal.

Jeff and Dana tried reasoning with him, but it had no effect. *Maybe he needs professional help,* Dana thought. She had no idea of the terrible fears that plagued Kemal.

*

The WTN evening news was on the air. Richard Melton, Dana's personable co-anchor, and Jeff Connors were seated beside her.

Dana Evans was saying, '. . . and in foreign news, France and England are still locking horns over mad cow disease. Here is René Linaud reporting from Rheims.'

In the control booth, the director, Anastasia Mann, ordered, 'Go to remote.'

A scene in the French countryside flashed on the television screens.

The studio door opened and a group of men came in and approached the anchor desk.

Everyone looked up. Tom Hawkins, the ambitious young producer of the evening news, said, 'Dana, you know Gary Winthrop.'

'Of course.'

In person, Gary Winthrop was even more handsome than in photographs. He was in his forties, with bright blue eyes, a warm smile, and enormous charm.

'We meet again, Dana. Thanks for inviting me.'

'I appreciate your coming.'

Dana looked around. Half a dozen secretaries had suddenly found urgent reasons to be in the studio. *Gary Winthrop must be used to that*, Dana thought, amused.

'Your segment is coming up in a few minutes. Why don't you sit here next to me? This is Richard

Melton.' The two men shook hands. 'You know Jeff Connors, don't you?'

'You bet I do. You should be out there pitching, Jeff, instead of talking about the game.'

'I wish I could,' Jeff said ruefully.

The remote from France came to an end and they switched to a commercial. Gary Winthrop sat down and watched as the commercial ended.

From the control booth, Anastasia Mann said, 'Stand by. We're going to tape.' She silently counted off with her index finger. 'Three . . . two . . . one . . .'

The scene on the monitor flashed to the exterior of the Georgetown Museum of Art. A commentator was holding a microphone in his hand, braving the cold wind.

'We're standing in front of the Georgetown Museum of Art, where Mr Gary Winthrop is inside at a ceremony marking his fifty-million-dollar gift to the museum. Let's go inside now.'

The scene on the screen changed to the spacious interior of the art museum. Various city officials, dignitaries, and television crews were gathered around Gary Winthrop. The museum's director, Morgan Ormond, was handing him a large plaque.

'Mr Winthrop, on behalf of the museum, the many visitors who come here, and its trustees, we want to thank you for this most generous contribution.'

Camera lights flashed.

Gary Winthrop said, 'I hope this will give young American painters a better chance not only to

15

express themselves but to have their talents recognized around the world.'

There was applause from the group.

The announcer on tape was saying, 'This is Bill Toland at the Georgetown Museum of Art. Back to the studio. Dana?'

The camera's red light came on.

'Thank you, Bill. We're fortunate enough to have Mr Gary Winthrop with us to discuss the purpose of his enormous gift.'

The camera pulled back to a wider angle, revealing Gary Winthrop in the studio.

Dana said, 'This fifty-million-dollar donation, Mr Winthrop, will it be used to buy paintings for the museum?'

'No. It's for a new wing that will be dedicated to young American artists who might not otherwise have a chance to show what they can do. A portion of the fund will be used for scholarships for gifted children in inner cities. Too many youngsters grow up without knowing anything about art. They may hear about the great French impressionists, but I want them to be aware of their own heritage, with American artists like Sargent, Homer, and Remington. This money will be used to encourage young artists to fulfill their talents and for all young people to take an interest in art.'

Dana said, 'There's a rumor that you're planning to run for the Senate, Mr Winthrop. Is there any truth to it?'

Gary Winthrop smiled. 'I'm testing the waters.'

'They're pretty inviting. In the straw polls we've seen, you're way ahead.'

Gary Winthrop nodded. 'My family has had a long record of government service. If I can be of any use to this country, I will do whatever I am called on to do.'

'Thank you for being with us, Mr Winthrop.'

'Thank *you*.'

During the commercial break, Gary Winthrop said good-bye and left the studio.

Jeff Connors, sitting next to Dana, said, 'We need more like him in Congress.'

'Amen.'

'Maybe we could clone him. By the way – how is Kemal?'

Dana winced. 'Jeff – please don't mention Kemal and cloning in the same breath. I can't handle it.'

'Did the problem at school this morning work out?'

'Yes, but that was today. Tomorrow is –'

Anastasia Mann said, 'We're back. Three . . . two . . . one . . .'

The red light flashed on. Dana looked at the Tele-PrompTer. 'It's time for sports now with Jeff Connors.'

Jeff looked into the camera. 'Merlin the Magician was missing from the Washington Bullets tonight. Juwan Howard tried his magic and Gheorghe Muresan and Rasheed Wallace helped stir up the

17

brew, but it was bitter, and they had finally to swallow it along with their pride . . .'

At 2:00 AM, in Gary Winthrop's town house in the elite north-west section of Washington, two men were removing paintings from the walls of the drawing room. One man wore the mask of the Lone Ranger, the other the mask of Captain Midnite. They worked at a leisurely pace, cutting the pictures out of the frames and putting their loot into large burlap sacks.

The Lone Ranger asked, 'What time does the patrol come by again?'

Captain Midnite replied, 'Four AM.'

'It's nice of them to keep to a schedule for us, isn't it?'

'Yeah.'

Captain Midnite removed a painting from the wall and dropped it onto the oak floor with a loud noise. The two men stopped what they were doing and listened. Silence.

The Lone Ranger said, 'Try it again. Louder.'

Captain Midnite took down another painting and threw it heavily against the floor. 'Now let's see what happens.'

In his bedroom upstairs, Gary Winthrop was awakened by the noise. He sat up in bed. Had he heard a sound, or had he dreamed it? He listened a moment longer. Silence. Unsure, he rose and

18

stepped out into the hallway and pressed the light switch. The hallway remained dark.

'Hello. Is anyone down there?' There was no answer. Downstairs, he walked along the corridor until he reached the door of the drawing room. He stopped and stared in disbelief at the two masked men.

'What the hell are you doing?'

The Lone Ranger turned to him and said, 'Hi, Gary. Sorry we woke you up. Go back to sleep.' A Beretta with a silencer appeared in his hand. He pulled the trigger twice and watched Gary Winthrop's chest explode into a red shower. The Lone Ranger and Captain Midnite watched him fall to the floor. Satisfied, they turned and continued to remove the paintings.

Two

Dana Evans was awakened by the relentless ringing of the telephone. She struggled to sit up and looked at the bedside clock, bleary-eyed. It was five o'clock in the morning. She picked up the phone. 'Hello?'

'Dana . . .'

'Matt?'

'See how fast you can get down to the studio.'

'What's happened?'

'I'll fill you in when you get here.'

'I'm on my way.'

Fifteen minutes later, hastily dressed, Dana was knocking on the door of the Whartons' apartment, her next-door neighbors.

Dorothy Wharton opened the door, wearing a robe. She looked at Dana in alarm. 'Dana, what's wrong?'

'I hate to do this to you, Dorothy, but I've been called to the studio on an emergency. Would you mind getting Kemal to school?'

'Why, of course not. I'd be happy to.'

21

'Thank you so much. He has to be there at seven-forty-five, and he'll need breakfast.'

'Don't you worry. I'll take care of it. You run along.'

'Thanks,' Dana said gratefully.

Abbe Lasmann was already in her office, looking sleepy. 'He's waiting for you.'

Dana walked into Matt's office.

'I have some awful news,' he said. 'Gary Winthrop was murdered earlier this morning.'

Dana sank into a chair, stunned. '*What?* Who –?'

'Apparently his house was being robbed. When he confronted the burglars, they killed him.'

'Oh, no! He was so wonderful!' Dana remembered the friendliness and warmth of the attractive philanthropist, and she felt ill.

Matt shook his head in disbelief. 'This makes – my God – the fifth tragedy.'

Dana was puzzled. 'What do you mean, the fifth tragedy?'

Matt looked at her in surprise, then suddenly realized, 'Of course – you were in Sarajevo. I guess over there, with a war going on, what happened to the Winthrops during the last year wouldn't have been such headline news. I'm sure you know about Taylor Winthrop, Gary's father?'

'He was our ambassador to Russia. He and his wife died in a fire last year.'

'Right. Two months later, their older son, Paul, was killed in an automobile accident. And six weeks after that, their daughter, Julie, died in a skiing accident.' Matt paused for a moment. 'And now, this morning, Gary, the last of the family.'

Dana was stunned into silence.

'Dana, the Winthrops are a legend. If this country had a royal family, they would hold the crown. They invented charisma. They were world-famous for their philanthropy and government service. Gary was planning to follow in his father's footsteps and run for the Senate, and he'd have been a shoo-in. Everyone loved him. Now he's gone. In less than one year, one of the most distinguished families in the world has been totally wiped out.'

'I – I don't know what to say.'

'You'd better think of something,' Matt said briskly. 'You're on the air in twenty minutes.'

The news of Gary Winthrop's death sent shock waves around the world. Comments from government leaders flashed onto universal television screens.

'It's like a Greek tragedy . . .'

'Unbelievable . . .'

'An ironic twist of fate . . .'

'The world has sustained a terrible loss . . .'

'The brightest and the best, and they're all gone . . .'

Gary Winthrop's murder seemed to be all that anyone was talking about. A wave of sadness swept over the country. Gary Winthrop's death had brought back the memory of the other tragic deaths in his family.

'It's unreal,' Dana told Jeff. 'The whole family must have been so wonderful.'

'They were. Gary was a real sports fan and a big supporter.' Jeff shook his head. 'It's hard to believe that some two-bit thieves wiped out such a wonderful person.'

Driving to the studio the next morning, Jeff said, 'By the way, Rachel's in town.'

By the way? How casual. Much too casual, Dana thought.

Jeff had been married to Rachel Stevens, a top model. Dana had seen her picture in television ads and on magazine covers. It was hard to believe how beautiful she was. *But she probably doesn't have a working brain cell in her head,* Dana decided. *On the other hand, with that face and body, she doesn't need any brains.*

Dana had discussed Rachel with Jeff. 'What happened to the marriage?'

'It was great in the beginning,' Jeff told her. 'Rachel was so supportive. Even though she hated baseball, she used to come to the games to watch me play. Besides that, we had a lot in common.'

I'll bet you did.

'She's really a wonderful woman, completely unspoiled. She loved to cook. When she was on a shoot, Rachel would cook for the other models.'

Great way to get rid of the competition. They were probably dropping like flies.

'What?'

'I didn't say anything.'

'Anyway, we were married for five years.'

'And then?'

'Rachel was very successful. She was always booked, and her work took her all over the world. Italy . . . England . . . Jamaica . . . Thailand . . . Japan . . . You name it. Meanwhile, I was playing ball around the country. We didn't get together very often. Little by little the magic faded.'

The next question seemed logical because Jeff loved children. 'Why no children?'

Jeff smiled wryly. 'Not good for a model's figure. Then one day Roderick Marshall, one of Hollywood's ace directors, sent for her. Rachel went to Hollywood.' He hesitated. 'She called me a week later to tell me she wanted a divorce. She felt we had drifted too far apart. I had to agree. I gave her the divorce. Shortly after that I broke my arm.'

'And you became a sportscaster.' What about Rachel? She didn't make it in movies?'

Jeff shook his head. 'She wasn't really interested. But she's doing just fine.'

'And you're still friendly?' A loaded question.

'Yes. As a matter of fact, when she called me, I told her about us. She wants to meet you.'

Dana frowned. 'Jeff, I don't think –'

'She's really very nice, honey. Let's all have lunch tomorrow. You'll like her.'

'I'm sure I will,' Dana agreed. *Snowball in hell,* Dana thought. *But I don't get to talk to many airheads.*

The airhead turned out to be even more beautiful than Dana had feared. Rachel Stevens was tall and slender, with lustrous, long blond hair, flawless tanned skin, and striking facial features. Dana hated her on sight.

'Dana Evans, this is Rachel Stevens.'

Dana thought, *Shouldn't it have been 'Rachel Stevens, this is Dana Evans'?*

Rachel Stevens was saying, '. . . your broadcasts from Sarajevo whenever I could. They were incredible. We could all feel your heartbreak and share it.'

How do you respond to a sincere compliment? 'Thank you,' Dana said lamely.

'Where would you like to have lunch?' Jeff asked.

Rachel suggested, 'There's a marvelous restaurant called the Straits of Malaya. It's just two blocks off Dupont Circle.' She turned to Dana and asked, 'Do you like Thai food?'

As if she really cares. 'Yes.'

Jeff smiled. 'Fine. Let's try it.'

Rachel said, 'It's only a few blocks from here. Shall we walk?'

In this freezing weather? 'Sure,' Dana said gamely. *She probably walks naked in the snow.*

They headed for Dupont Circle. Dana felt uglier by the second. She was bitterly sorry she had accepted the invitation.

The restaurant turned out to be packed, with a dozen people at the bar, waiting for tables. The maître d' came bustling up.

'A table for three,' Jeff said.

'Do you have a reservation?'

'No, but we –'

'I'm sorry, but –' He recognized Jeff. 'Mr Connors, it's a pleasure to see you.' He looked at Dana. 'Miss Evans, this is an honor.' He made a small moue. 'I'm afraid there will be a short delay.' His glance moved to Rachel, and his face lit up. 'Miss Stevens! I read that you were doing a layout in China.'

'I was, Somchai. I'm back.'

'Wonderful.' He turned to Dana and Jeff. 'Of course we have a table for you.' He led them to a table in the center of the room.

I hate her, Dana thought. *I truly hate her.*

When they were seated, Jeff said, 'You look great, Rachel. Whatever you're doing agrees with you.'

And we can all guess what that is.

'I've been doing a lot of traveling. I think I'm going to start taking it easy for a while.' She looked into Jeff's eyes. 'Do you remember the night that you and I –'

Dana looked up from the menu. 'What is *udang goreng*?'

Rachel glanced at Dana. 'That's shrimp in coconut milk. It's very good here.' She turned back to Jeff. 'The night you and I decided that we wanted to –'

'What is *laksa*?'

Rachel said patiently, 'That's spicy noodle soup.' She turned back to Jeff. 'You said you wanted to –'

'And *poh pia*?'

Rachel looked at Dana and said sweetly, 'That's jicama stir-fried with vegetables.'

'Really?' Dana decided not to ask what jicama was.

But as the meal went on, Dana was surprised that in spite of herself, she began to like Rachel Stevens. She had a warm and charming personality. Unlike most world-class beauties, Rachel seemed to be completely unself-conscious about her looks and displayed no ego. She was intelligent and articulate, and when she gave the luncheon order to the waiter in Thai, there was no hint of superiority. *How did Jeff ever let this one get away?* Dana wondered.

'How long will you be in Washington?' Dana asked.

'I have to leave tomorrow.'

'Where are you heading for this time?' Jeff wanted to know.

Rachel hesitated. 'Hawaii. But I'm feeling really

tired, Jeff. I was even thinking of canceling this.'

'But you won't,' Jeff said knowingly.

Rachel sighed. 'No, I won't.'

'When will you be back?' Dana asked.

Rachel looked at her for a long moment and then said softly, 'I don't think I'll be coming back to Washington, Dana. I hope you and Jeff will be very happy.' There was an unspoken message in her words.

Outside, after lunch, Dana said, 'I have some errands to do. You two go on ahead.'

Rachel took Dana's hand in hers. 'I'm very glad we met.'

'So am I,' Dana said, and to her surprise she really meant it.

Dana watched Jeff and Rachel start down the street. *A striking couple*, she thought.

Because it was early December, Washington was preparing for the holiday season. The streets of the capital were decorated with Christmas lights and wreaths of holly, and on almost every corner Salvation Army Santa Clauses stood, tolling their bells for coins. The sidewalks were crowded with shoppers braving the icy winds.

The time has come, Dana thought. *I have to get started with my own shopping*. Dana thought about the people for whom she should buy gifts. Her mother; Kemal; Matt, her boss; and, of course, wonderful

Jeff. Dana jumped in a cab and headed for Hecht's, one of Washington's largest department stores. The place was jammed with people celebrating the Christmas spirit by rudely elbowing other shoppers out of the way.

When Dana finished shopping, she headed back to her apartment to drop off her gifts. The apartment was on Calvert Street, in a quiet residential section. Attractively furnished, it consisted of one bedroom, a living room, a kitchen, a bathroom, and a study, where Kemal slept.

Dana put the gifts in a closet, looked around the small apartment, and thought happily, *We'll have to get a larger place when Jeff and I get married*. As she headed for the door to return to the studio, the telephone rang. *Murphy's law*. Dana picked up the phone. 'Hello.'

'Dana, darling.'

It was her mother. 'Hello, Mother. I was just leav –'

'My friends and I listened to your broadcast last night. You were very good.'

'Thank you.'

'Although we thought you could have brightened up the news a bit.'

Dana sighed. 'Brightened up the news?'

'Yes. All the things you talk about are so depressing. Can't you find something cheerful to discuss?'

'I'll certainly see what I can do, Mother.'

'That would be nice. By the way, I'm running just a little short of cash this month. I wonder if you could help me out again?'

Dana's father had disappeared years ago. In time, Dana's mother had moved to Las Vegas. It seemed that she was always short of cash. The monthly allowance Dana gave her mother never seemed to be enough.

'Do you gamble, Mother?'

'Of course not,' Mrs Evans said indignantly. 'Las Vegas is a very expensive city. By the way, when are you going to come out here? I would like to meet Kimbal. You should bring him here.'

'His name is Kemal, Mother. I can't get away right now.'

There was a slight hesitation at the other end. 'You can't? My friends are all saying how fortunate you are to have a job where you only have to work an hour or two a day.'

Dana said, 'I guess I'm just lucky.'

As anchorwoman, Dana arrived at the television studio at nine o'clock every morning and spent much of the day on international conference calls, getting the latest news from London, Paris, Italy, and other foreign locations. The rest of the day was devoted to meetings, putting all the news together, and deciding what would be broadcast and in what order when she went on the air. She did two evening broadcasts.

31

'It's nice that you have such an easy job, darling.'

'Thank you, Mother.'

'You'll come and see me soon, won't you?'

'Yes, I will.'

'I can't wait to meet that darling little boy.'

It will be good for Kemal to meet her, too, Dana thought. *He'll have a grandmother. And when Jeff and I are married, Kemal will have a real family again.*

As Dana stepped out into the corridor of her apartment building, Mrs Wharton appeared.

'I want to thank you for taking care of Kemal the other morning, Dorothy. I really appreciate it.'

'It was my pleasure.'

Dorothy Wharton and her husband, Howard, had moved into the building a year ago. They were Canadians, a delightful middle-aged couple. Howard Wharton was an engineer who repaired monuments.

As he had explained to Dana at dinner one night, 'There's no better city in the world than Washington for my kind of work. Where else could I find opportunities like this?' And he answered his own question. 'Nowhere.'

'Howard and I both love Washington,' Mrs Wharton confided. 'We're never going to leave.'

*

When Dana got back to her office, the latest edition of the *Washington Tribune* was on her desk. The front page was filled with stories and photographs of the Winthrop family. Dana looked at the photographs for a long time, her mind racing. *Five of them all dead in less than a year. Incredible.*

The call was made to a private phone in the executive tower of Washington Tribune Enterprises.

'I just got the instructions.'

'Good. They've been waiting. What do you want them to do with the paintings?'

'Burn them.'

'All of them? They're worth millions of dollars.'

'Everything's gone perfectly. We can't allow any loose ends. Burn them now.'

Dana's secretary, Olivia Watkins, was on the intercom. 'There's a call for you on line three. He's called twice already.'

'Who is it, Olivia?'

'Mr Henry.'

Thomas Henry was the principal of Theodore Roosevelt Middle School.

Dana rubbed her hand against her forehead to wipe away the headache that was about to start. She picked up the telephone. 'Good afternoon, Mr Henry.'

'Good afternoon, Miss Evans. I wonder if you could stop by and see me?'

'Certainly. In an hour or two, I'm –'

'I would suggest *now*, if that's possible.'

'I'll be there.'

Three

School was an unbearable ordeal for Kemal. He was smaller than the other kids in his classes, and to his deep shame, that included the girls. He was nicknamed 'the runt' and 'the shrimp' and 'the minnow'. As far as his studies were concerned, Kemal's only interest was in math and computers, where he invariably got the highest grades of anyone. An offshoot of the class was the chess club, and Kemal dominated it. In the past, he had enjoyed soccer, but when he had gone to try out for the school varsity team, the coach had looked at Kemal's empty sleeve and said, 'Sorry, we can't use you.' It was not said unkindly, but it was a devastating blow.

Kemal's nemesis was Ricky Underwood. At lunchtime some of the students ate in the enclosed patio instead of the cafeteria. Ricky Underwood would wait to see where Kemal was having lunch and then join him.

35

'Hey, orphan boy. When is your wicked step-mother going to send you back where you came from?'

Kemal ignored him.

'I'm talking to you, freak. You don't think she's going to keep you, do you? Everyone knows why she brought you over here, camel face. Because she was a famous war correspondent, and it made her look good to save a cripple.'

'*Fukat!*' Kemal shouted. He got up and leaped at Ricky.

Ricky's fist went into Kemal's stomach, and then crashed into Kemal's face. Kemal fell on the ground, writhing in pain.

Ricky Underwood said, 'Anytime you want more, just tell me. And you better do it fast, because from what I hear, you're history.'

Kemal lived in an agony of doubt. He did not believe the things that Ricky Underwood said and yet . . . What if they were true? *What if Dana does send me back? Ricky is right,* Kemal thought. *I am a freak. Why would someone as wonderful as Dana want me?*

Kemal had believed his life was over when his parents and sister were killed in Sarajevo. He had been sent to the Orphans Institution outside of Paris, and it was a nightmare.

At two o'clock every Friday afternoon, the boys

and girls in the orphanage would line up as prospective foster parents arrived to evaluate them and select one to take home. As each Friday approached, the excitement and tension among the children rose to an almost unbearable pitch. They would wash and dress neatly, and as the adults walked along the line, each child would inwardly pray to be chosen.

Invariably, when the prospective parents saw Kemal, they would whisper, 'Look, he's got only one arm,' and they would move on.

Every Friday was the same, but Kemal would still wait hopefully as the adults examined the line of candidates. But they always picked other children. Standing there, ignored, Kemal would be filled with humiliation. *It will always be someone else*, he thought despairingly. *No one wants me.*

Kemal wished desperately to be part of a family. He tried everything he could think of to make it happen. One Friday he would smile brightly at the adults to let them know what a nice, friendly boy he was. The next Friday he would pretend to be occupied with something, showing them that he didn't really care whether he was chosen or not, and that they would be lucky to have him. At other times, he would look at them appealingly, silently begging them to take him home with them. But week after week, it was always someone else who was chosen and taken away to wonderful homes and happy families.

Miraculously, Dana had changed all that. She was

the one who had found him living homeless on the streets of Sarajevo. After Kemal was airlifted by the Red Cross to the orphanage, Kemal wrote Dana a letter. To his astonishment, she had telephoned the orphanage and said that she wanted Kemal to come live with her in America. That was the happiest moment of Kemal's life. It was an impossible dream come true, and it turned out to be a joy even greater than he had ever imagined.

Kemal's life had changed completely. He was grateful now that no one had chosen him before. He was no longer alone in the world. Someone cared about him. He loved Dana with all his heart and soul, but within him was always the terrible fear that Ricky Underwood had instilled, that someday Dana would change her mind and send him back to the orphanage, to the life of hell he had escaped. He had a recurring dream: He was back in the orphans' asylum, and it was Friday. A line of adults was inspecting the children, and Dana was there. She looked at Kemal and said, *That ugly little boy has only one arm*, and she moved on and picked the boy next to him. Kemal would wake up in tears.

Kemal knew that Dana hated for him to get into fights at school, and he did everything he could to avoid them, but he could not bear to have Ricky Underwood or his friends insult Dana. As soon as they realized that, the insults about Dana increased, and so did the fights.

Ricky would greet Kemal with 'Hey, have you packed your suitcase, shrimp? On the news this morning it said your bitch stepmother is going to send you back to Yugoslavia.'

'*Zbosti!*' Kemal would yell.

And the fight would begin. Kemal would come home with black eyes and bruises, but when Dana asked him what had happened, he could not tell her the truth, for he was terrified that if he put it into words, what Ricky Underwood had said might happen.

Now, as Kemal waited in the principal's office for Dana to arrive, he thought, *When she hears what I've done this time, she is going to send me away.* He sat there miserable, his heart racing.

When Dana entered the office of Thomas Henry, the principal was pacing the floor, looking grim. Kemal sat in a chair across the room.

'Good morning, Miss Evans. Please sit down.'

Dana glanced at Kemal and took a seat.

Thomas Henry picked up a large butcher knife from his desk. 'One of Kemal's teachers took this from him.'

Dana swiveled to look at Kemal, furious. '*Why?*' she asked angrily. 'Why did you bring this to school?'

Kemal looked at Dana and said sullenly, 'I didn't have a gun.'

'Kemal!'

Dana turned to the principal. 'May I speak to you alone, Mr Henry?'

'Yes.' He looked over at Kemal, his jaw tight. 'Wait in the hallway.'

Kemal got to his feet, took one last look at the knife, and left.

Dana began, 'Mr Henry, Kemal is twelve years old. He's lived most of those years going to sleep with the sound of exploding bombs in his ears, the same bombs that killed his mother and father and sister. One of those bombs took off his arm. When I found Kemal in Sarajevo, he was living in a cardboard box in a vacant lot. There were a hundred other homeless boys and girls there, living like animals.' She was remembering, trying to keep her voice steady.

'The bombs have stopped, but the boys and girls are still homeless and helpless. The only way they can defend themselves against their enemies is with a knife or a rock or a gun, if they're lucky enough to get hold of one.' Dana closed her eyes for an instant and took a deep breath. 'These children are scarred. Kemal is scarred, but he's a decent boy. He just needs to learn that he's safe here. That none of us is his enemy. I promise you he won't do this again.'

There was a long silence. When Thomas Henry spoke, he said, 'If I ever need a lawyer, Miss Evans, I'd like you to defend me.'

Dana managed a relieved smile. 'I promise.'

Thomas Henry sighed. 'All right. Have a talk with Kemal. If he does anything like this again, I'm afraid I'll have to –'

'I'll talk to him. Thank you, Mr Henry.'

Kemal was waiting in the hallway.

'Let's go home,' Dana said curtly.

'Did they keep my knife?'

She did not bother to answer.

During the ride home, Kemal said, 'I'm sorry I got you in trouble, Dana.'

'Oh, no trouble. They've decided not to kick me out of school. Look, Kemal –'

'Okay. No more knives.'

When they returned to the apartment, Dana said, 'I have to get back to the studio. The sitter will be here any minute. Tonight you and I are going to have to have a long talk.'

When the evening broadcast was finished, Jeff turned to Dana. 'You look worried, honey.'

'I am. It's Kemal. I don't know what to do about him, Jeff. I had to go see his principal again today, and two more housekeepers have quit because of him.'

'He's a great kid,' Jeff said. 'He just needs warm-up time.'

'Maybe. Jeff?'

'Yes?'

41

'I hope I didn't make a terrible mistake bringing him here.'

When Dana returned to the apartment, Kemal was waiting.

Dana said, 'Sit down. We have to talk. You must start obeying the rules, and these fights at school have to stop. I know the other boys are making it difficult for you, but you've got to come to some understanding with them. If you keep getting into fights, Mr Henry is going to throw you out of school.'

'I don't care.'

'You *have* to care. I want you to have a wonderful future, and that can't happen without an education. Mr Henry is giving you a break, but –'

'Fuck him.'

'Kemal!' Without thinking, Dana slapped him across the face. She was instantly sorry. Kemal stared at her, a look of disbelief on his face, got up, ran into the study, and slammed the door shut.

The telephone rang. Dana picked it up. It was Jeff. 'Dana –'

'Darling, I – I can't talk right now. I'm too upset.'

'What happened?'

'It's Kemal. He's impossible!'

'Dana . . .'

'Yes?'

'Walk in his shoes.'

42

'What?'

'Think about it. Sorry, I'm on a deadline. Love you, and we'll talk later.'

Walk in his shoes? That doesn't make any sense, Dana thought. *How can I know what Kemal is feeling? I'm not a twelve-year-old war orphan with one arm who's gone through what he's gone through.* Dana sat there for a long time, thinking. *Walk in his shoes.* She rose, went into her bedroom, closed the door, and opened her closet door. Before Kemal had arrived, Jeff had spent several nights a week at the apartment and had left some of his clothes there. In the closet were pants, shirts and ties, a sweater, and a sports jacket.

Dana took out some of the clothes and placed them on the bed. She went to a bureau drawer and removed a pair of Jeff's Jockey shorts and socks. Then Dana got completely undressed. She picked up Jeff's Jockey shorts with her left hand and started putting them on. She lost her balance and fell. It took her two more attempts before she could get them on. Next, she picked up one of Jeff's shirts. Using only her left hand, it took three frustrating minutes to slip into it and button it. She had to sit on the bed to don the trousers, and they were difficult to zip up. It took another two minutes to put on Jeff's sweater.

When Dana was finally dressed, she sat down to catch her breath. This was what Kemal had to go through every morning. And that was only the beginning. He had to bathe and brush his teeth and comb his hair. And that was now. What about the past? Living in the horror of war, watching his mother, father, sister, and friends murdered.

Jeff's right, she thought. *I'm expecting too much too soon. He needs more time to adjust. I could never give up on him. My father abandoned my mother and me and I've never really forgiven him for that. There should be a thirteenth commandment: Thou shalt not abandon those who love you.*

Slowly, as Dana got dressed in her own clothes, she thought about the lyrics of the songs that Kemal listened to over and over again. The CDs of Britney Spears, the Backstreet Boys, Limp Bizkit. *'Don't want to lose you,' 'I need you tonight,' 'As long as you love me,' 'I just want to be with you,' 'I need love.'*

All the lyrics were about loneliness and wanting.

Dana picked up Kemal's report card. It was true that he was failing in most of his classes, but he had an A in math. *It's the A that's important*, Dana thought. *That's where he excels. That's where he has a future. We'll work on the other grades.*

When Dana opened the door to the study, Kemal was in bed, with his eyes tightly closed and his pale face stained with tears. Dana looked at him a moment, then leaned over and kissed him on the cheek. 'I'm so sorry, Kemal,' she whispered. 'Forgive me.'

Tomorrow will be a better day.

*

Early the following morning Dana took Kemal to a prominent orthopedic surgeon, Dr William Wilcox. After the examination, Dr Wilcox talked to Dana alone.

'Miss Evans, to fit him with a prosthesis would cost twenty thousand dollars and there's a problem here. Kemal is only twelve years old. His body will keep growing until he's seventeen or eighteen. He could outgrow the prosthesis every few months. I'm afraid financially it's not practical.'

Dana had a sinking feeling. 'I see. Thank you, Doctor.'

Outside, Dana said to Kemal, 'Don't worry, darling. We'll find a way.'

Dana dropped Kemal off at school and then headed for the studio. Half a dozen blocks away, her cell phone rang. She picked it up. 'Hello?'

'It's Matt. There's going to be a press conference on the Winthrop murder at police headquarters at noon. I want you to cover it. I'm sending over a camera crew. The police have really got their asses in a sling. The story is getting bigger every minute, and the cops don't have a clue.'

'I'll be there, Matt.'

Police Chief Dan Burnett was in his office on the telephone when his secretary said, 'The mayor is on line two.'

Burnett snapped, 'Tell him I'm talking to the

governor on line one.' He went back to the phone.

'Yes, Governor. I know that . . . Yes, sir. I think . . . I'm sure we can . . . As soon as we . . . Right. Good-bye, sir.' He slammed the phone down.

'The White House press secretary is on line four.'

The whole morning went like that.

At noon, the conference room in the Municipal Center at 300 Indiana Avenue in downtown Washington was crowded with members of the media. Police Chief Burnett entered and walked to the front of the room.

'Let's have it quiet, please.' He waited until there was silence. 'Before I take your questions, I have a statement to make. The savage murder of Gary Winthrop is a great loss not only to this community, but to the world, and our investigation is going to continue until we apprehend the ones responsible for this terrible crime. I'll take your questions.'

A reporter stood up. 'Chief Burnett, do the police have any leads?'

'At about three AM a witness saw two men loading up a white van in the driveway of Gary Winthrop's house. Their actions looked suspicious, and he took down the license number. The plates were from a stolen truck.'

'Do the police know what was taken from the house?'

'A dozen valuable paintings are missing.'

'Was anything stolen besides the paintings?'

'No.'

'What about cash and jewelry?'

'The jewelry and cash in the house were untouched. The thieves were just after the paintings.'

'Chief Burnett, didn't the house have an alarm system, and if so, was it turned on?'

'According to the butler, it was always turned on at night. The burglars found a way to circumvent it. We're not sure yet how.'

'How did the burglars gain entrance to the house?'

Chief Burnett hesitated. 'That's an interesting question. There were no signs of a break-in. We don't have the answer to that yet.'

'Could it have been an inside job?'

'We don't think so. Gary Winthrop's staff has been with him for many years.'

'Was Gary Winthrop alone in the house?'

'As far as we know, yes. The staff was off.'

Dana called out, 'Do you have a list of the stolen paintings?'

'We do. They're all well known. The list has been circulated to museums, art dealers, and collectors. The minute one of those paintings appears, the case will be solved.'

Dana sat down, puzzled. *The killers must have been aware of that, so they wouldn't dare try to sell the paintings. Then what was the point of stealing them? And committing a murder? And why didn't they take the money and jewelry? Something doesn't add up.*

The funeral services for Gary Winthrop were held at the National Cathedral, the sixth largest in the world. Wisconsin and Massachusetts Avenues had been closed off to traffic. Secret Service men and Washington police were out in full force. Inside, waiting for the service to begin, were the vice president of the United States, a dozen senators and members of Congress, a Supreme Court Justice, two cabinet officers, and a host of dignitaries from around the world. The police and press helicopters beat a tattoo in the sky. On the street outside were hundreds of onlookers who had come either to pay their respects or to get a glimpse of the celebrities inside. People were paying tribute not just to Gary, but to the entire ill-fated Winthrop dynasty.

Dana covered the funeral with two camera crews. Inside, the cathedral was hushed.

'God moves in mysterious ways,' the minister was intoning. 'The Winthrops spent their lives building hopes. They donated billions of dollars to schools and churches and to the homeless and the hungry. But just as important, they selflessly gave of their time and talent. Gary Winthrop carried on the great family tradition. Why this family, with all its achievements and generosity, has been taken from us so cruelly is beyond our knowledge. In one sense,

48

they are not really gone, for their legacy will live on forever. What they have done for us will always make us proud. . . .'

God shouldn't let people like that die those kinds of horrible deaths, Dana thought sadly.

Dana's mother called. 'My friends and I watched you cover the funeral, Dana. For a moment there, when you were talking about the Winthrop family, I thought you were going to cry.'

'So did I, Mother. So did I.'

Dana had difficulty getting to sleep that night. When she finally did fall asleep, her dreams were a wild kaleidoscope of fires and automobile accidents and shootings. In the middle of the night, she awakened suddenly and sat up. *Five members of the same family killed in less than a year? What are the odds?*

Four

'What are you trying to tell me, Dana?'

'Matt, I'm saying that five violent deaths in one family in less than a year is too much of a coincidence.'

'Dana, if I didn't know you better, I'd call a psychiatrist and tell him Chicken Little is in my office saying that the sky is falling. You think we're dealing with some kind of conspiracy? Who's behind it? Fidel Castro? The CIA? Oliver Stone? For God's sake, don't you know that every time someone prominent is killed, there are a hundred different conspiracy theories? A guy came in here last week and said he could prove that Lyndon Johnson killed Abraham Lincoln. Washington is always drowning in conspiracy theories.'

'Matt, we're getting ready to do *Crime Line*. You want to start with a grabber? Well, if I'm right, this could be it.'

51

Matt Baker sat there for a moment, studying her. 'You're wasting your time.'

'Thanks, Matt.'

The *Washington Tribune*'s morgue was in the building's basement, filled with thousands of tapes from earlier news shows, all neatly cataloged.

Laura Lee Hill, an attractive brunette in her forties, was seated behind her desk cataloging tapes. She looked up as Dana entered.

'Hi, Dana. I saw your broadcast of the funeral. I thought you did a great job.'

'Thank you.'

'Wasn't that a terrible tragedy?'

'Terrible,' Dana agreed.

'You just never know,' Laura Lee Hill said somberly. 'Well – what can I do you for?'

'I want to look at some tapes of the Winthrop family.'

'Anything in particular?'

'No. I just want to get a feel of what the family was like.'

'I can tell you what they were like. They were saints.'

'That's what I keep hearing,' Dana said.

Laura Lee Hill rose. 'I hope you have plenty of time, honey. We have tons of coverage on them.'

'Good. I'm in no hurry.'

Laura Lee led Dana to a desk with a television

monitor on it. 'I'll be right back,' she said. She returned five minutes later with a full armload of tapes. 'You can start with these,' she said. 'There are more coming.'

Dana looked at the huge pile of tapes and thought, *Maybe I am Chicken Little. But if I'm right . . .*

Dana put in a tape, and the picture of a stunningly handsome man flashed on the screen. His features were strong and sculpted. He had a mane of dark hair, candid blue eyes, and a strong chin. By his side was a young boy. A commentator said, 'Taylor Winthrop has added another wilderness camp to the ones he has already established for underprivileged children. His son Paul is here with him, ready to join in the fun. This is the tenth in a series of such camps that Taylor Winthrop is building. He plans at least a dozen more.'

Dana pressed a button and the scene changed. An older-looking Taylor Winthrop, with flecks of gray in his hair, was shaking hands with a group of dignitaries. '. . . has just confirmed his appointment as consultant to NATO. Taylor Winthrop will be leaving for Brussels in the next few weeks to . . .'

Dana changed the tape. The scene was the front lawn of the White House. Taylor Winthrop was standing next to the president, who was saying, '. . . and I have appointed him to head up the FRA, the Federal Research Agency. The agency is dedicated to helping developing countries all around the world, and I can think of no one better qualified than Taylor Winthrop to lead that organization . . .'

The monitor flashed onto the next scene, the Leonardo da Vinci airport in Rome, where Taylor Winthrop was debarking from a plane. 'Several heads of state are here to greet Taylor Winthrop as he arrives to negotiate trade deals between Italy and the United States. The fact that Mr Winthrop was selected by the president to handle these negotiations shows how significant they are . . .'

The man had done everything, Dana thought.

She changed tapes. Taylor Winthrop was at the presidential palace in Paris, shaking hands with the president of France. 'A landmark trade agreement with the French has just been completed by Taylor Winthrop . . .'

Another tape. Taylor Winthrop's wife, Madeline, was in front of a compound with a group of boys and girls. 'Madeline Winthrop today dedicated a new care center for abused children, and –'

There was a tape of the Winthrops' own children playing at their estate farm in Manchester, Vermont.

Dana put the next tape in. Taylor Winthrop at the White House. In the background were his wife, his two handsome sons, Gary and Paul, and his beautiful daughter, Julie. The president was presenting Taylor Winthrop with a Medal of Freedom. '. . . and for his selfless devotion to his country and for all his wonderful accomplishments, I am pleased to present Taylor Winthrop with the highest civilian award we can give – the Medal of Freedom.'

There was a tape of Julie skiing . . .

Gary funding a foundation to help young artists . . .

The Oval Office again. The press was out in full force. A gray-haired Taylor Winthrop and his wife were standing next to the president. 'I have just appointed Taylor Winthrop our new ambassador to Russia. I know you are all familiar with Mr Winthrop's innumerable services to our country, and I'm delighted that he has agreed to accept this post instead of spending his days playing golf.' The press laughed.

Taylor Winthrop quipped, 'You haven't seen my golf game, Mr President.'

Another laugh . . .

And then came the series of disasters.

Dana inserted a new tape. The scene outside a burned-out home in Aspen, Colorado. A female newscaster was pointing to the gutted house. 'The chief of police of Aspen has confirmed that Ambassador Winthrop and his wife, Madeline, both perished in the terrible fire. The fire department was alerted in the early hours of this morning and arrived within fifteen minutes, but it was too late to save them. According to Chief Nagel, the fire was caused by an electrical problem. Ambassador and Mrs Winthrop were known worldwide for their philanthropy and dedication to government service.'

Dana put in another tape. The scene was the

Grand Corniche on the French Riviera. A reporter said, 'Here is the curve where Paul Winthrop's car skidded off the road and plummeted down the mountainside. According to the coroner's office, he was killed instantly by the impact. There were no passengers. The police are investigating the cause of the accident. The terrible irony is that only two months ago Paul Winthrop's mother and father died in a fire at their home in Aspen, Colorado.'

Dana reached for another tape. A mountain skiing trail in Juneau, Alaska. A heavily bundled-up newscaster: '. . . and this is the scene of the tragic skiing accident that occurred last evening. Authorities are not sure why Julie Winthrop, a champion skier, was skiing alone at night on this particular trail, which had been closed, but they are investigating. In September, just six weeks ago, Julie's brother Paul was killed in a car accident in France, and in July of this year, her parents, Ambassador Taylor Winthrop and his wife, died in a fire. The president has expressed his sympathy.'

The next tape. Gary Winthrop's home in the northwest section of Washington, DC. Reporters were swarming around the outside of the town house. In front of the house, a newscaster was saying, 'In a tragic, unbelievable turn of events, Gary Winthrop, the last remaining member of the beloved Winthrop family, has been shot and killed by burglars. Early this morning a security guard noticed that the alarm light was off, entered the home, and found Mr Winthrop's body. He had been shot twice. Apparently the thieves were after valuable paintings and were interrupted. Gary Winthrop was the fifth and last member of the family to meet a violent death this year.'

Dana turned off the television monitor and sat there for a long time. *Who would want to wipe out a wonderful family like that? Who? Why?*

Dana arranged an appointment with Senator Perry Leff at the Hart Senate Office Building. Leff was in his early fifties, an earnest and impassioned man.

He rose as Dana was ushered in. 'What can I do for you, Miss Evans?'

'I understand that you worked closely with Taylor Winthrop, Senator?'

'Yes. We were appointed by the president to serve on several committees together.'

'I know what his public image is, Senator Leff, but what was he like as a person?'

Senator Leff studied Dana for a moment. 'I'll be glad to tell you. Taylor Winthrop was one of the finest men I've ever met. What was most remarkable about him was the way he related to people. He really cared. He went out of his way to make this a better world. I'll always miss him, and what's happened to his family is just too goddamn awful to think about.'

*

Dana was talking to Nancy Patchin, one of Taylor Winthrop's secretaries, a woman in her sixties, with a lined face and sad eyes.

'You worked for Mr Winthrop for a long time?'

'Fifteen years.'

'In that period of time, I imagine you got to know Mr Winthrop well.'

'Yes, of course.'

Dana said, 'I'm trying to get a picture of what kind of man he was. Was he –?'

Nancy Patchin interrupted. 'I can tell you exactly what kind of man he was, Miss Evans. When we discovered my son had Lou Gehrig's disease, Taylor Winthrop took him to his own doctors and paid all the medical bills. When my son died, Mr Winthrop paid the funeral expenses and sent me to Europe to recover.' Her eyes filled with tears. 'He was the most wonderful, the most generous gentleman I've ever known.'

Dana arranged for an appointment with General Victor Booster, the director of the FRA, the Federal Research Agency, which Taylor Winthrop had headed. Booster had refused to talk to Dana at first, but when he learned whom she wanted to talk to him about, he agreed to see her.

In midmorning, Dana drove to the Federal Research Agency, near Fort Mead, Maryland. The agency's headquarters were set on eighty-two closely guarded acres. There was no sign of the forest of satellite dishes hidden behind the heavily wooded area.

Dana drove up to an eight-foot-high Cyclone fence topped with barbed wire. She gave her name and showed her driver's license to an armed guard at the sentry booth and was admitted. A minute later she approached a closed electrified gate with a surveillance camera. She spoke her name again and the gate automatically swung open. She followed the driveway to the enormous white administration building.

A man in civilian clothes met Dana outside. 'I'll take you to General Booster's office, Miss Evans.'

They took a private elevator up five floors and walked down a long corridor to a suite of offices at the end of the hall.

They entered a large reception office with two secretaries' desks. One of the secretaries said, 'The general is expecting you, Miss Evans. Go right in, please.' She pressed a button and a door to the inner office clicked open.

Dana found herself in a spacious office, with ceilings and walls heavily soundproofed. She was greeted by a tall, slim, attractive man in his forties. He held out his hand to Dana and said genially, 'I'm Major Jack Stone. I'm General Booster's aide.' He indicated the man seated behind a desk. 'This is General Booster.'

Victor Booster was African-American, with a

chiseled face and hard obsidian eyes. His shaved head gleamed under the ceiling lights.

'Sit down,' he said. His voice was deep and gravelly.

Dana took a seat. 'Thank you for seeing me, General.'

'You said this was about Taylor Winthrop?'

'Yes. I wanted –'

'Are you doing a story on him, Miss Evans?'

'Well, I –'

His voice hardened. 'Can't you fucking journalists let the dead rest? You're all a bunch of muckraking coyotes picking at dead bodies.'

Dana sat there in shock.

Jack Stone looked embarrassed.

Dana controlled her temper. 'General Booster, I assure you I am not interested in muckraking. I know the legend about Taylor Winthrop. I'm trying to get a picture of the man himself. Anything you can tell me would be greatly appreciated.'

General Booster leaned forward. 'I don't know what the hell you're after, but I can tell you one thing. The legend *was* the man. When Taylor Winthrop was head of FRA, I worked under him. He was the best director this organization ever had. Everybody admired him. What's happened to him and his family is a tragedy I can't even begin to comprehend.' His face was tight. 'Frankly, I don't like the press, Miss Evans. I think you people have gotten way out of hand. I watched your coverage in

Sarajevo. Your hearts-and-flowers broadcasts didn't help us any.'

Dana was trying hard to control her anger. 'I wasn't there to help you, General. I was there to report what was happening to the innocent –'

'Whatever. For your information, Taylor Winthrop was as great a statesman as this country has ever had.' His eyes fixed on hers. 'If you intend to tear down his memory, you're going to find yourself with a lot of enemies. Let me give you some advice. Don't go looking for trouble, or you're going to find it. That's a promise. I'm warning you to stay the hell away. Good-bye, Miss Evans.'

Dana stared at him a moment, then rose. 'Thank you very much, General.' She strode out of the office.

Jack Stone hurried after her. 'I'll show you out.'

In the corridor, Dana took a deep breath and said angrily, 'Is he always like that?'

Jack Stone sighed. 'I apologize for him. He can be a little abrupt. He doesn't mean anything by it.'

Dana said tightly, 'Really? I had the feeling he did.'

'Anyway, for what it's worth, I'm sorry,' Jack Stone said. He started to turn away.

Dana touched his sleeve. 'Wait. I'd like to talk to you. It's twelve o'clock. Could we have lunch somewhere?'

61

Jack Stone glanced toward the general's door. 'All right. Sholl's Colonial Cafeteria on K Street in an hour?'

'Great. Thank you.'

'Don't thank me too soon, Miss Evans.'

Dana was waiting for him when he walked into the half-deserted cafeteria. Jack Stone stood in the doorway for a moment making sure there was no one he knew in the restaurant, then he joined Dana at a table.

'General Booster would have my ass if he knew I was talking to you. He's a fine man. He's in a tough, sensitive job, and he's very, very good at what he does.' He hesitated. 'I'm afraid he doesn't like the press.'

'I gathered that,' Dana said dryly.

'I have to make something clear to you, Miss Evans. This conversation is completely off the record.'

'I understand.'

They picked up trays and selected their food. When they sat down again, Jack Stone said, 'I don't want you to get the wrong impression of our organization. We're the good guys. That's why we got into it in the first place. We're working to help underdeveloped countries.'

'I appreciate that,' Dana said.

'What can I tell you about Taylor Winthrop?'

62

Dana said, 'All I've gotten so far are tales of sainthood. The man must have had *some* flaws.'

'He did,' Jack Stone admitted. 'Let me tell you the good things first. More than any man I've ever known, Taylor Winthrop cared about people.' He paused. 'I mean *really* cared. He took notice of birthdays and marriages, and everyone who worked for him adored him. He had a keen, incisive mind, and he was a problem solver. And even though he was so involved in everything he was doing, he was at heart a family man. He loved his wife and he loved his children.' He stopped.

Dana said, 'What's the bad part?'

Jack Stone said reluctantly, 'Taylor Winthrop was a magnet for women. He was charismatic, handsome, rich, and powerful. Women found that hard to resist.' He went on: 'So every once in a while, Taylor . . . slipped. He had a few affairs, but I can assure you that none of them was serious, and he kept them very private. He would never do anything to hurt his family.'

'Major Stone, can you think of anyone who would have had a reason to kill Taylor Winthrop and his family?'

Jack Stone put down his fork. '*What?*'

'Someone with that high a profile must have made *some* enemies down the line.'

'Miss Evans – are you implying that the Winthrops were *murdered*?'

'I'm just asking,' Dana said.

Jack Stone considered it a moment. Then he shook his head. 'No,' he said. 'It doesn't make sense. Taylor Winthrop never harmed anyone in his life. If you've talked to any of his friends or associates, you would know that.'

'Let me tell you what I've learned so far,' Dana said. 'Taylor Winthrop was –'

Jack Stone held up a hand. 'Miss Evans, the less I know, the better. I'm trying to stay outside the loop. I can help you best that way, if you know what I mean.'

Dana looked at him, puzzled. 'I'm not sure exactly.'

'Frankly, for your sake, I wish you would drop this whole matter. If you won't, then be careful.' And he stood up and was gone.

Dana sat there, thinking about what she had just heard. *So Taylor Winthrop had no enemies. Maybe I'm going about this from the wrong angle. What if it wasn't Taylor Winthrop who made a deadly enemy? What if it was one of his children? Or his wife?*

Dana told Jeff about her luncheon with Major Jack Stone.

'That's interesting. What now?'

'I want to talk to some of the people who knew the Winthrop children. Paul Winthrop was engaged to a girl named Harriet Berk. They were together for almost a year.'

'I remember reading about them,' Jeff said. He hesitated. 'Darling, you know I'm behind you one hundred percent . . .'

'Of course, Jeff.'

'But what if you're wrong about this? Accidents do happen. How much time are you going to spend on this?'

'Not much more,' Dana promised. 'I'm just going to do a little more checking.'

Harriet Berk lived in an elegant duplex apartment in northwest Washington. She was a slim blonde in her early thirties, with a nervously engaging smile.

'Thank you for seeing me,' Dana said.

'I'm not exactly sure why I *am* seeing you, Miss Evans. You said it was something about Paul.'

'Yes.' Dana chose her words carefully. 'I don't mean to pry into your personal life, but you and Paul were engaged to be married, and I'm sure you probably knew him better than anyone else.'

'I like to think so.'

'I'd love to know a little more about him, what he was really like.'

Harriet Berk was silent for a moment. When she spoke, her voice was soft. 'Paul was like no other man I've ever known. He had a zest for life. He was kind and thoughtful of others. He could be very funny. He didn't take himself too seriously. He was great fun to be around. We were planning to be married in October.' She stopped. 'When Paul died in the accident, I – I felt as though my life was over.' She looked at Dana and said quietly, 'I still feel that way.'

'I'm so sorry,' Dana said. 'I hate to press this, but do you know if he had any enemies, someone who would have a reason to kill him?'

Harriet Berk looked at her and tears came to her eyes. 'Kill Paul?' Her voice was choked. 'If you had known him, you wouldn't have even asked that.'

Dana's next interview was with Steve Rexford, the butler who had worked for Julie Winthrop. He was a middle-aged, elegant-looking Englishman.

'How may I help you, Miss Evans?'

'I wanted to ask you about Julie Winthrop.'

'Yes, ma'am?'

'How long did you work for her?'

'Four years and nine months.'

'What was she like to work for?'

He smiled reminiscently. 'She was extremely pleasant, a lovely lady in every way. I – I couldn't believe it when I heard the news about her accident.'

'Did Julie Winthrop have any enemies?'

He frowned. 'I beg your pardon?'

'Was Miss Winthrop involved with anyone she

might have . . . jilted? Or someone who might want to harm her or her family?'

Steve Rexford shook his head slowly. 'Miss Julie wasn't that sort of person. She could never hurt anyone. No. She was very generous with her time and with her wealth. Everyone loved her.'

Dana studied him a moment. He meant it. They all meant it. *What the hell am I doing?* Dana wondered. *I feel like Dana Quixote. Only there are no windmills.*

Morgan Ormond, the director of the Georgetown Museum of Art, was next on Dana's list.

'I understand you wanted to ask me about Gary Winthrop?'

'Yes. I wondered –'

'His death was a terrible loss. Our nation has lost its greatest art patron.'

'Mr Ormond, isn't there a great deal of competition in the art world?'

'Competition?'

'Doesn't it sometimes happen that several people might be after the same work of art and get into –'

'Of course. But never with Mr Winthrop. He had a fabulous private collection, yet at the same time he was very generous with museums. Not just with this museum, but with museums all over the world. His ambition was to make great art available to everybody.'

'Did you know of any enemies he –'

'Gary Winthrop? Never, never, never.'

Dana's final meeting was with Rosalind Lopez, who had worked for Madeline Winthrop for fifteen years as her personal maid. She was now working at a catering business she and her husband owned.

'Thank you for seeing me, Miss Lopez,' Dana said. 'I wanted to talk to you about Madeline Winthrop.'

'That poor lady. She – she was the nicest person I've ever known.'

It's beginning to sound like a broken record, Dana thought.

'It was just terrible the awful way she died.'

'Yes,' Dana agreed. 'You were with her a long time.'

'Oh, yes, ma'am.'

'Do you know of anything she might have done that would have offended anybody or made enemies of them?'

Rosalind Lopez looked at Dana in surprise. 'Enemies? No, ma'am. Everyone loved her.'

It *is* a broken record, Dana decided.

On her way back to the office, Dana thought, *I guess I was wrong. In spite of the odds, their deaths must have been coincidental.*

Dana went in to see Matt Baker. She was greeted by Abbe Lasmann.

'Hi, Dana.'

'Is Matt ready for me?'

'Yes. You can go in.'

Matt Baker looked up as Dana walked into his office. 'How's Sherlock Holmes today?'

'It's elementary, my dear Watson. I was wrong. There is no story there.'

Five

The call from Dana's mother, Eileen, came without warning.

'Dana, darling. I have the most exciting news for you!'

'Yes, Mother?'

'I'm getting married.'

Dana was stunned. 'What?'

'Yes. I went up to Westport, Connecticut, to visit a friend, and she introduced me to this lovely, lovely man.'

'I'm – I'm thrilled for you, Mother. That's wonderful.'

'He's – he's so –' She giggled. 'I can't describe him, but he's adorable. You'll love him.'

Dana said cautiously, 'How long have you known him?'

'Long enough, darling. We're perfect for each other. I'm so lucky.'

'Does he have a job?' Dana asked.

'Stop acting like my father. Of course he has a job. He's a very successful insurance salesman. His name is Peter Tomkins. He has a beautiful home in Westport, and I'm dying for you and Kimbal to come up here and meet him. Will you come?'

'Of course we will.'

'Peter is so anxious to meet you. He's told everyone about how famous you are. Are you sure you can make it?'

'Yes.' Dana was off the air weekends, so there would be no problem. 'Kemal and I are looking forward to it.'

When Dana picked Kemal up at school, she said, 'You're going to meet your grandmother. We're going to be a real family, darling.'

'Dope.'

Dana smiled. 'Dope is right.'

Early Saturday morning Dana and Kemal drove to Connecticut. Dana looked forward to the trip to Westport with great anticipation.

'This is going to be wonderful for everyone,' Dana assured Kemal. 'All grandparents need grandchildren to spoil. That's the best part of having children. And you'll be able to stay with them some of the time.'

Kemal said nervously, 'Will you be there, too?'

Dana squeezed his hand. 'I'll be there.'

Peter Tomkins's home was a charming old cottage on Blind Brook Road, with a small stream running alongside it.

'Hey, this is cool,' Kemal said.

Dana ruffled Kemal's hair. 'I'm glad you like it. We'll come here often.'

The front door of the cottage opened, and Eileen Evans stood there. There were still vague traces of beauty left, like clues to what once was, but bitterness had overlaid the past with a harsh brush. It was a Dorian Gray situation. Her beauty had gone into Dana. Standing beside Eileen was a middle-aged, pleasant-faced man wearing a broad smile.

Eileen rushed forward and took Dana in her arms. 'Dana, darling! And there's Kimbal!'

'Mother . . .'

Peter Tomkins said, 'So this is the famous Dana Evans, eh? I've told all my clients about you.' He turned to Kemal. 'And this is the boy.' He noticed Kemal's missing arm. 'Hey, you didn't tell me he was a cripple.'

Dana's blood froze. She saw the shock on Kemal's face.

Peter Tomkins shook his head. 'If he had had insurance with our company before that happened, he'd be a rich kid.' He turned toward the door. 'Come on in. You must be hungry.'

'Not anymore,' Dana said tightly. She turned to Eileen. 'I'm sorry, Mother. Kemal and I are going back to Washington.'

'I'm sorry, Dana. I –'

'So am I. I hope you're not making a big mistake. Have a nice wedding.'

'Dana –'

Dana's mother watched in dismay as Dana and Kemal got into the car and drove away.

Peter Tomkins looked after them in astonishment. 'Hey, what did I say?'

Eileen Evans sighed. 'Nothing, Peter. Nothing.'

Kemal was silent on the ride home. Dana glanced at him from time to time.

'I'm so sorry, darling. Some people are just ignorant.'

'He's right,' Kemal said bitterly. 'I am a cripple.'

'You're *not* a cripple,' Dana said fiercely. 'You don't judge people by how many arms or legs they have. You judge them by what they are.'

'Yeah? And what am I?'

'You're a survivor. And I'm proud of you. You know, Mr Charming was right about one thing – I'm hungry. I guess it wouldn't interest you, but I see a McDonald's ahead.'

Kemal smiled. 'Awesome.'

*

After Kemal went to bed, Dana walked into the living room and sat down to think. She turned on the television set and started surfing the news channels. They were all doing follow-up stories on the Gary Winthrop murder.

'. . . hoping that the stolen van might offer some clues to the identity of the murderers . . .'

'. . . two bullets from a Beretta. Police are checking all gun shops to . . .'

'. . . and the brutal murder of Gary Winthrop in the exclusive northwest area proved that no one is . . .'

There was something at the back of Dana's mind, teasing her. It took her hours to get to sleep. In the morning, when Dana awakened, she suddenly realized what had been bothering her. *Money and jewels were lying in the open. Why hadn't the killers taken them?*

Dana got up and made a pot of coffee while she reviewed what Chief Burnett had said.

Do you have a list of the stolen paintings?

We do. They're all well known. The list is being circulated to museums, art dealers, and collectors. The minute one of those paintings appears, the case will be solved.

The burglars must have known that the paintings couldn't be sold easily, Dana thought, *which could mean that the theft was arranged by a wealthy collector who intends to keep the paintings for himself. But why would a man like that put himself in the hands of two murderous hoodlums?*

*

On Monday morning when Kemal got up, Dana fixed breakfast and dropped him off at school.

'Have a good day, darling.'

'See you, Dana.'

Dana watched Kemal walk into the front door of the school, and then she headed for the police station on Indiana Avenue.

It was snowing again and there was a sadistic wind tearing at everything in its path.

Detective Phoenix Wilson, in charge of the Gary Winthrop murder, was a street-smart misanthrope, with a few scars to show how he had gotten that way. He looked up as Dana walked into his office.

'No interviews,' he growled. 'When there's any new information on the Winthrop murder, you'll hear it at the press conference with everybody else.'

'I didn't come to ask you about that,' Dana said.

He eyed her skeptically. 'Oh, really?'

'Really. I'm interested in the paintings that were stolen. You have a list of them, I assume?'

'So?'

'Could you give me a copy?'

Detective Wilson asked suspiciously, 'Why? What did you have in mind?'

'I'd like to see what the killers took. I might do a segment on the air.'

Detective Wilson studied Dana a moment. 'That's not a bad idea. The more publicity these paintings

76

get, the less chance the killers will have to sell them.' He rose. 'They took twelve paintings and left a lot more. I guess they were too lazy to carry them all. Good help is hard to find these days. I'll get you a copy of that report.'

He was back in a few minutes with two photocopies. He handed them to Dana. 'Here's a list of the ones taken. Here's the other list.'

Dana looked at him, puzzled. 'What other list?'

'All the paintings Gary Winthrop owned, including the paintings the killers left behind.'

'Oh. Thank you. I appreciate it.'

Out in the corridor, Dana examined the two lists. What she was seeing was confusing. Dana walked out into the frigid air and headed for Christie's, the world-famous auction house. It was snowing harder, and the crowds were hurrying to finish their Christmas shopping and get back to their warm homes and offices.

When Dana arrived at Christie's, the manager recognized her immediately. 'Well! This is an honor, Miss Evans. What can we do for you?'

Dana explained, 'I have two lists of paintings here. I would appreciate it if someone could tell me what these paintings are worth.'

'But of course. It would be our pleasure. Come this way, please . . .'

*

Two hours later Dana was in Matt Baker's office.

'There's something very strange going on,' Dana began.

'We're not back to the Chicken Little conspiracy theory again, are we?'

'You tell me.' Dana handed Matt the longer of the two lists. 'This has *all* the artworks Gary Winthrop owned. I just had these paintings appraised at Christie's.'

Matt Baker scanned the list. 'Hey, I see some heavy hitters here. Vincent van Gogh, Hals, Matisse, Monet, Picasso, Manet.' He looked up. 'So?'

'Now look at *this* list,' Dana said. She handed Matt the shorter list, which had the stolen art on it.

Matt read them aloud. 'Camille Pissarro, Marie Laurencin, Paul Klee, Maurice Utrillo, Henry Lebasque. So what's your point?'

Dana said slowly, 'A lot of the paintings on the complete list are worth more than ten million apiece.' She paused. 'Most of the paintings on the shorter list, which were stolen, are worth two hundred thousand apiece or less.'

Matt Baker blinked. 'The burglars took the less valuable paintings?'

'That's right.' Dana leaned forward. 'Matt, if they were professional burglars, they would also have taken the cash and jewelry lying around. We were meant to assume that someone hired them to steal only the more valuable paintings. But according to these lists, they didn't know a thing about art. So

78

why were they really hired? Gary Winthrop wasn't armed. Why did they kill him?'

'Are you saying that the robbery was a cover-up, and the real motive for the break-in was murder?'

'That's the only explanation I can think of.'

Matt swallowed. 'Let's examine this. Suppose that Taylor Winthrop *did* make an enemy and was murdered – why would anyone want to wipe out his entire family?'

'I don't know,' Dana said. 'That's what I want to find out.'

Dr Armand Deutsch was one of Washington's most respected psychiatrists, an imposing-looking man in his seventies, with a broad forehead and appropriately probing blue eyes. He glanced up as Dana entered.

'Miss Evans?'

'Yes. I appreciate your seeing me, Doctor. What I need to see you about is really very important.'

'And what is it that's so very important?'

'You've read about the deaths in the Winthrop family?'

'Of course. Terrible tragedies. So many accidents.'

Dana said, 'What if they weren't accidents?'

'What? What are you saying?'

'That there's a possibility they were all murdered.'

'The Winthrops *murdered*? That seems very far-fetched, Miss Evans. *Very* far-fetched.'

'But possible.'

'What makes you think they might have been murdered?'

'It's – it's just a hunch,' Dana admitted.

'I see. A hunch.' Dr Deutsch sat there, studying her. 'I watched your broadcasts from Sarajevo. You are an excellent reporter.'

'Thank you.'

Dr Deutsch leaned forward on his elbows, his blue eyes fixed on hers. 'So, not long ago, you were in the middle of a terrible war. Yes?'

'Yes.'

'Reporting about people being raped, killed, babies murdered . . .'

Dana was listening, wary.

'You were obviously under great stress.'

Dana said, 'Yes.'

'How long have you been back – five, six months?'

'Three months,' Dana said.

He nodded, satisfied. 'Not much time to get adjusted to civilian life again, is it? You must have nightmares about all the terrible murders you witnessed, and now your subconscious mind imagines –'

Dana interrupted him. 'Doctor, I'm not paranoid. I have no proof, but I have reason to believe the Winthrop deaths were not accidental. I came to see you because I was hoping you could help me.'

'Help you? In what way?'

'I need a motive. What motive could anyone have for wiping out an entire family?'

Dr Deutsch looked at Dana and steepled his fingers. 'There are precedents, of course, for such violent aggression. A vendetta ... vengeance. In Italy, the Mafia has been known to kill entire families. Or it could possibly involve drugs. It might be revenge for some terrible tragedy that the family caused. Or it could be a maniac who might not have any rational motive to –'

'I don't think that's the case here,' Dana said.

'Then, of course, there's one of the oldest motives in the world – money.'

Money. Dana had already thought of that.

Walter Calkin, head of the firm of Calkin, Taylor & Anderson, had been the Winthrops' family lawyer for more than twenty-five years. He was an elderly man, crippled with arthritis, but while his body was frail, his mind was still keen.

He studied Dana a moment. 'You told my secretary that you wanted to talk to me about the Winthrop estate?'

'Yes.'

He sighed. 'It's incredible to me what happened to that wonderful family. Incredible.'

'I understand that you handled their legal and financial affairs,' Dana said.

'Yes.'

'Mr Calkin, in the last year, was there anything unusual about those affairs?'

He was looking at Dana curiously. 'Unusual in what sense?'

Dana said carefully, 'This is awkward, but – would you be aware of it if any member of the family was . . . being blackmailed?'

There was a momentary silence. 'You mean, would I know if they were regularly paying out large sums of money to somebody?'

'Yes.'

'I suppose I would, yes.'

'And *was* there anything like that?' Dana pursued.

'Nothing. I assume you're suggesting some sort of foul play? I must tell you I find that utterly ridiculous.'

'But they are all dead,' Dana said. 'The estate must be worth many billions of dollars. I would very much appreciate it if you could tell me who stands to receive that money.'

She watched the lawyer open a bottle of pills, take one out, and swallow it with a sip of water. 'Miss Evans, we never discuss our clients' affairs.' He hesitated. 'In this instance, however, I see no harm in it, because a press announcement is going to be made tomorrow.'

And then there's always one of the oldest motives in the world – money.

Walter Calkin looked at Dana. 'With the death of

Gary Winthrop, the last surviving member of the family –'

'Yes?' Dana was holding her breath.

'The entire Winthrop fortune goes to charity.'

Six

The staff was getting ready for the evening news.

Dana was in studio A at the anchor desk, going through last-minute changes for the broadcast. The news bulletins that had been coming in all day from wire services and police channels had been studied and selected or rejected.

Seated at the anchor table next to Dana were Jeff Connors and Richard Melton. Anastasia Mann started the countdown and ended 3-2-1 with her extended forefinger. The camera's red light flashed on.

The announcer's voice boomed out, 'This is the eleven o'clock news live on WTN with Dana Evans' – Dana smiled into the camera – 'and Richard Melton.' Melton looked into the camera and nodded. 'Jeff Connors with sports and Marvin Greer with the weather. The eleven o'clock news begins right now.'

Dana looked into the camera. 'Good evening. I'm Dana Evans.'

Richard Melton smiled. 'And I'm Richard Melton.'

Dana read from the TelePrompTer. 'We have a breaking story. A police chase ended earlier this evening after a holdup at a downtown liquor store.'

'Roll tape one.'

The screen flashed to the interior of a helicopter. At the controls of the WTN helicopter was Norman Bronson, a former marine pilot. Next to him sat Alyce Barker. The camera angle changed. On the ground below were three police cars surrounding a sedan that had crashed into a tree.

Alyce Barker said, 'The chase began when two men walked into the Haley Liquor Store on Pennsylvania Avenue and tried to hold up the clerk. He resisted and pressed the alarm button to summon police. The robbers fled, but the police pursued them for four miles until the suspects' car crashed into a tree.'

The chase was covered by the station's news helicopter. Dana looked at the picture and thought: *The best thing Matt ever did was to get Elliot to buy that new helicopter. It makes a big difference to our coverage.*

There were three more segments, and the director signaled for a break. 'We'll be right back after this,' Dana said.

A commercial came on.

Richard Melton turned to Dana. 'Have you looked outside? It's a bitch out there.'

'I know.' Dana laughed. 'Our poor weatherman is going to get a lot of hate mail.'

The red camera light flashed on. The TelePrompTer was blank for a moment, then began to roll again. Dana started to read, 'On New Year's Eve I'd like – ' She stopped, stunned, as she looked at the rest of the words. They read: ... *us to get married. We'll have a double reason to celebrate every New Year's Eve.*

Jeff was standing next to the TelePrompTer, grinning.

Dana looked into the camera and said awkwardly, 'We'll – we'll pause for another brief commercial.' The red light went off.

Dana stood up. 'Jeff!'

They moved toward each other and embraced. 'What do you say?' he asked.

She held him tightly and whispered, 'I say yes.'

The studio echoed with cheers from the crew.

When the broadcast was over and they were alone, Jeff said, 'What would you like, honey? Big wedding, small wedding, medium wedding?'

Dana had thought about her wedding from the time she was a little girl. She had visualized herself in a beautiful, lacy white gown with a long, long train. In the movies she had seen, there was the frantic excitement of getting ready for the wedding ... the guest list to prepare ... the caterer to choose

... the bridesmaids ... the church ... All her friends would be there, and her mother. It was going to be the most wonderful day of her life. And now it was a reality.

Jeff said, 'Dana ... ?' He was waiting for her answer.

If I have a big wedding, Dana thought, *I would have to invite Mother and her husband. I can't do that to Kemal.*

'Let's elope,' Dana said.

Jeff nodded, surprised. 'If that's what you want, then it's what I want.'

Kemal was thrilled when he heard the news. 'You mean Jeff is going to live with us?'

'That's right. We'll all be together. You'll have a real family, darling.' Dana sat at Kemal's bedside for the next hour, excitedly discussing their future. The three of them were going to live together, vacation together, and just be together. *That magic word.*

When Kemal was asleep, Dana went into her bedroom and turned on the computer. *Apartments. Apartments. We'll need two bedrooms, two baths, a living room, kitchen, dining area, and maybe an office and a study. That shouldn't be too difficult.* Dana thought of Gary Winthrop's town house sitting empty, and her mind began to wander. *What had really happened that night? And who had turned off the alarm? If there were no signs of a break-in, then how had the burglars gotten in?* Almost involuntarily her fingers typed in 'Winthrop' on the keyboard. *What the devil is the matter with me?* Dana saw the same familiar information she had seen earlier.

Regional > US States > Washington DC > Government > Politics > Federal Research Agency
* *Winthrop, Taylor* – served as Ambassador to Russia and negotiated an important trade agreement with Italy . . .
* *Winthrop, Taylor* – self-made billionaire Taylor Winthrop devoted himself to serving his country . . .
* *Winthrop, Taylor* – Winthrop family set up philanthropic trusts to help schools, libraries, and inner-city programs . . .

There were fifty-four Web sites for the Winthrop family. Dana was about to change the search to *Apartments* when a random entry caught her eye.

* *Winthrop, Taylor* – Lawsuit. Joan Sinisi, former secretary to Taylor Winthrop, filed a lawsuit and later dropped it.

Dana read the item again. *What kind of lawsuit?* Dana wondered.

She switched to several more Winthrop Web sites, but there was no further mention of any lawsuit.

Dana typed in the name *Joan Sinisi*. Nothing came up.

'Is this a secure line?'

'Yes.'

'I want a report on the Web sites the subject is checking.'

'We will take care of it immediately.'

The following morning, when Dana arrived at her office after dropping Kemal off at school, she looked through the Washington telephone directory. No Joan Sinisi. She tried the Maryland directory ... Virginia ... No luck. *She's probably moved away*, Dana decided.

Tom Hawkins, the show's producer, walked into Dana's office. 'We beat the competition again last night.'

'Great.' Dana was thoughtful for a moment. 'Tom, do you know anyone at the telephone company?'

'Sure. You need a telephone?'

'No. I want to see if someone has an unlisted number. Do you think you could check it out?'

'What's the name?'

'Sinisi. Joan Sinisi.'

He frowned. 'Why is that name familiar?'

'She was involved in a lawsuit with Taylor Winthrop.'

'Ah, yes. I remember now. That was about a year ago. You were in Yugoslavia. I thought there was going to be a juicy story there, but it got hushed up pretty quickly. She's probably living somewhere in Europe, but I'll try to find out.'

Fifteen minutes later Olivia Watkins said, 'Tom is on the line for you.'

'Tom?'

'Joan Sinisi is still living in Washington. I have her unlisted number for you, if you want it.'

'Wonderful,' Dana said. She picked up a pen. 'Go ahead.'

'Five-five-five-two-six-nine-zero.'

'Thank you.'

'Forget the thanks. Make it a lunch.'

'You've got it.'

The office door opened and Dean Ulrich, Robert Fenwick, and Maria Toboso, three writers who worked on the television news, came in.

Robert Fenwick said, 'It's going to be a bloody newscast tonight. We have two train wrecks, a plane crash, and a major landslide.'

The four of them began to read through the incoming news bulletins. Two hours later, when the meeting was over, Dana picked up the piece of paper with Joan Sinisi's number on it and called it.

A woman answered. 'Miss Sinisi's residence.'

'Could I talk to Miss Sinisi, please? This is Dana Evans.'

The woman said, 'I'll see if she's available. Just a moment, please.'

Dana waited. Another woman's voice came on the phone, soft and hesitant. 'Hello . . .'

'Miss Sinisi?'

'Yes.'

'This is Dana Evans. I wondered if –'

'*The* Dana Evans?'

'Er – yes.'

'Oh! I watch your broadcast every night. I'm a tremendous fan of yours.'

'Thank you,' Dana said. 'That's very flattering. I wonder if you could spare a few minutes of your time. Miss Sinisi. I'd like to talk to you.'

'You would?' There was a happily surprised note in her voice.

'Yes. Could we meet somewhere?'

'Well, certainly. Would you like to come here?'

'That would be fine. When would be convenient for you?'

There was a brief hesitation. 'Any time. I'm here all day.'

'What about tomorrow afternoon, say around two o'clock?'

'All right.' She gave Dana the address.

'I'll see you tomorrow,' Dana said. She replaced the receiver. *Why am I going on with this? Well, this will be the end of it.*

*

At two o'clock the following afternoon, Dana drove up in front of Joan Sinisi's high-rise apartment building on Prince Street. A uniformed doorman stood in front of the building. Dana looked at the imposing structure and thought, *How can a secretary afford to live here?* She parked the car and went inside to the lobby. There was a receptionist at the desk.

'May I help you?'

'I have an appointment to see Miss Sinisi. Dana Evans.'

'Yes, Miss Evans. She's expecting you. Just take the elevator to the penthouse. It's apartment A.'

The penthouse?

When Dana arrived at the top floor, she got out of the elevator and rang the doorbell of apartment A. The door was opened by a uniformed maid.

'Miss Evans?'

'Yes.'

'Come in, please.'

Joan Sinisi lived in a twelve-room apartment with a huge terrace overlooking the city. The maid led Dana through a long hallway into a large drawing room done in white and beautifully decorated. A small, slender woman was seated on the couch. She rose as Dana entered.

Joan Sinisi was a surprise. Dana had not known what to anticipate, but the woman who got up to greet her was the last thing she would have expected. Joan Sinisi was small and plain looking, with dull brown eyes hidden behind thick glasses. Her voice was shy and almost inaudible.

'It's a real pleasure to meet you in person, Miss Evans.'

'Thank you for seeing me,' Dana said. She joined Joan Sinisi on a large white couch near the terrace.

'I was just about to have some tea. Would you care for some?'

'Thank you.'

Joan Sinisi turned to the maid and said almost diffidently, 'Greta, would you mind bringing us some tea?'

'Yes, ma'am.'

'Thank you, Greta.'

There was a feeling of unreality about this. Dana thought, *Joan Sinisi and the penthouse don't fit together at all. How could she afford to live here? What kind of settlement had Taylor Winthrop made? And what had the lawsuit been about?*

'. . . and I never miss your broadcasts,' Joan Sinisi was saying softly. 'I think you're wonderful.'

'Thank you.'

'I remember when you were broadcasting from Sarajevo with all those terrible bombs and guns going off. I was always afraid something was going to happen to you.'

'To be honest, so was I.'

'It must have been a horrible experience.'

94

'Yes, in one way it was.'

Greta came in with a tray of tea and cakes. She set it on the table in front of the two women.

'I'll pour,' Joan Sinisi said.

Dana watched as she poured the tea.

'Would you like a cake?'

'No, thanks.'

Joan Sinisi handed Dana a cup of tea, then poured a cup for herself. 'As I said, I'm really delighted to meet you, but I – I can't imagine what you want to talk to me about.'

'I wanted to talk to you about Taylor Winthrop.'

Joan Sinisi gave a start and some of the tea spilled on her lap. Her face had gone white.

'Are you all right?'

'Yes, I'm – I'm fine.' She dabbed at her skirt with a napkin. 'I – I didn't know that you wanted . . .' Her voice trailed off.

The atmosphere had suddenly changed. Dana said, 'You were Taylor Winthrop's secretary, weren't you?'

Joan Sinisi said carefully, 'Yes. But I left Mr Winthrop's employ a year ago. I'm afraid I can't help you.' The woman was almost trembling.

Dana said soothingly, 'I've heard such good things about Taylor Winthrop. I just wondered if you could add to them?'

Joan Sinisi looked relieved. 'Oh, yes, of course I can. Mr Winthrop was a great man.'

'How long did you work for him?'

'Almost three years.'

Dana smiled. 'It must have been a wonderful experience.'

'Yes, yes, it was, Miss Evans.' She sounded much more relaxed.

'But you brought a lawsuit against him.'

The fear was back in Joan Sinisi's eyes. 'No – I mean yes. But it was a mistake, you see. I made a mistake.'

'What kind of mistake?'

Joan Sinisi swallowed. 'I – I misunderstood something Mr Winthrop said to someone. I behaved very foolishly. I'm ashamed of myself.'

'You sued, but you didn't take him to court?'

'No. He – we settled the lawsuit. It was nothing.'

Dana glanced around the penthouse. 'I see. Can you tell me what the settlement was?'

'No, I'm afraid I can't,' Joan Sinisi said. 'It's all very confidential.'

Dana wondered what it could have been that made this timid woman bring a lawsuit against a titan like Taylor Winthrop and why she was terrified to talk about it. What was she afraid of?

There was a long silence. Joan Sinisi was watching Dana, and Dana had the feeling that she wanted to say something.

'Miss Sinisi –'

Joan Sinisi rose. 'I'm sorry I can't be more – if there's nothing else, Miss Evans . . .'

'I understand,' Dana said.
I wish I did.

He put the tape into the machine and pressed the start button.

I – I misunderstood something Mr Winthrop said to someone. I behaved very foolishly. I'm ashamed of myself.
You sued, but you didn't take him to court?
No. He – we settled the lawsuit. It was nothing.
I see. Can you tell me what the settlement was?
No, I'm afraid I can't. It's all very confidential.
Miss Sinisi –
I'm sorry I can't be more – if there's nothing else, Miss Evans . . .
I understand.

Tape ends.

It had begun.

Dana had made arrangements for a real estate broker to show her apartments, but it was a wasted morning. Dana and the broker covered George-town, Dupont Circle, and the Adams-Morgan district. The apartments were too small, or too large, or too expensive. By noon, Dana was ready to give up.

'Don't worry,' the real estate agent said reassuringly. 'We'll find exactly what you're looking for.'

'I hope so,' Dana said. *And soon.*

Dana could not get Joan Sinisi out of her mind. What did she have on Taylor Winthrop that would make him pay her off with a penthouse and God only knew what else? *She wanted to tell me something,* Dana thought. *I'm sure of it. I have to talk to her again.*

Dana telephoned Joan Sinisi's apartment. Greta answered: 'Good afternoon.'

'Greta, this is Dana Evans. I'd like to speak to Miss Sinisi, please.'

'I'm sorry. Miss Sinisi is not taking any calls.'

'Well, would you tell her that it's Dana Evans, and I need –'

'I'm sorry, Miss Evans. Miss Sinisi is not available.' The line went dead.

The following morning Dana dropped Kemal off at school. In a frozen sky, a pale sun was trying to come out. On street corners all over the city, the same faux Santa Clauses were ringing their charity bells.

I must find an apartment for the three of us before New Year's Eve, Dana thought.

When Dana got to the studio, she spent the morning in a conference with the news staff, discussing which stories to go with and the locations they needed to have taped. There was a story of a particularly brutal unsolved murder, and Dana thought of the Winthrops.

She called Joan Sinisi's number again.

'Good afternoon.'

'Greta, it's very important that I talk to Miss Sinisi. Tell her that Dana Evans –'

'She won't talk to you, Miss Evans.' The line went dead.

What is going on? Dana wondered.

Dana went in to see Matt Baker. Abbe Lasmann greeted her.

'Congratulations! I understand the wedding date is all set.'

Dana smiled. 'Yes.'

Abbe sighed. 'What a romantic proposal.'

'That's my fella.'

'Dana, our Advice to the Lovelorn columnist said that after the wedding, you should go out and buy a couple bags of canned groceries and stash them in the trunk of your car.'

'Why on earth . . . ?'

'She says that one day down the road, you might decide to have a little extracurricular fun and get home late. When Jeff asks where you've been, you just show him the bags and say, "Shopping." He'll—'

'Thank you, Abbe dear. Is Matt available?'

'I'll tell him you're here.'

Moments later, Dana was in Matt Baker's office.

'Sit down, Dana. Good news. We just got the latest Nielsens. We clobbered the opposition again last night.'

'Great. Matt, I talked to an ex-secretary of Taylor Winthrop's and she –'

He grinned. 'You Virgos never let go, do you? You told me that you –'

'I know, but listen to this. When she was working for Taylor Winthrop, she filed a lawsuit against him. It never came to trial because he settled with her. She's living in an enormous penthouse she couldn't possibly have afforded on a secretary's salary, so the settlement must have been really heavy. When I mentioned Winthrop's name, this woman was terrified, absolutely terrified. She acted as though she were in fear for her life.'

Matt Baker said patiently, 'Did she say she was in fear for her life?'

'No.'

'Did she say she was in fear of Taylor Winthrop?'

'No, but –'

'So for all you know, she might be afraid of a boyfriend who beats her up or burglars under her bed. You have absolutely nothing to go on, do you?'

'Well, I –' Dana saw the expression on his face. 'Nothing concrete.'

'Right. About the Nielsens . . .'

*

Joan Sinisi was watching the evening news on WTN. Dana was saying, '. . . and in local news, according to the latest report, the crime rate in the United States has gone down twenty-seven percent in the last twelve months. The largest decreases in crime have been in Los Angeles, San Francisco, and Detroit . . .'

Joan Sinisi was studying Dana's face, looking into her eyes, trying to come to a decision. She watched the entire newscast, and by the time it was over, she had made her decision.

Seven

When Dana walked into her office on Monday morning, Olivia said, 'Good morning. You've had three calls from some woman who won't leave her name.'

'Did she leave a number?'

'No. She said she would call back.'

Thirty minutes later Olivia said, 'That woman's on the line again. Do you want to talk to her?'

'All right.' Dana picked up the phone. 'Hello, this is Dana Evans. Who is –'

'This is Joan Sinisi.'

Dana's heart quickened. 'Yes, Miss Sinisi . . .'

'Do you still want to talk to me?' She sounded nervous.

'Yes. Very much.'

'All right.'

'I can be at your apartment in –'

'No!' Panic was in her voice. 'We must meet

103

somewhere else. I – I think I'm being watched.'

'Wherever you say. Where?'

'The aviary section at the zoo in the park. Can you be there in an hour?'

'I'll be there.'

The park was virtually deserted. The icy December winds that swept through the city were keeping the usual crowds away. Dana stood in front of the aviary waiting for Joan Sinisi, shivering in the cold. Dana looked at her watch. She had been there for over an hour. *I'll give her another fifteen minutes.*

Fifteen minutes later Dana told herself, *Another half hour, and that's it.* Thirty minutes later she thought, *Damn it! She's changed her mind.*

Dana returned to her office, chilled and wet. 'Any calls?' she asked Olivia hopefully.

'Half a dozen. They're on your desk.'

Dana looked at the list. Joan Sinisi's name was not on it. Dana called Joan Sinisi's number. She listened to the phone ring a dozen times before she hung up. *Maybe she'll change her mind again.* Dana tried twice more, but there was no answer. She debated whether to go back to the apartment but decided against it. *I'll have to wait until she comes to me*, Dana decided.

There was no further word from Joan Sinisi.

*

At six o'clock the following morning, Dana was watching the news while she got dressed. '... and the situation in Chechnya has worsened. A dozen more Russian bodies have been found, and in spite of the Russian government's assurance that the rebels have been defeated, the fighting is still going on ... In local news, a woman fell to her death from her thirtieth-floor penthouse apartment. The victim, Joan Sinisi, was a former secretary to Ambassador Taylor Winthrop. The police are investigating the accident.'

Dana stood there, paralyzed.

'Matt, remember the woman I told you I went to see – Joan Sinisi, Taylor Winthrop's former secretary?'

'Yes. What about her?'

'She was on the news this morning. She's dead.'

'*What?*'

'Yesterday morning she called and made an urgent appointment to meet me. She said she had something very important to tell me. I waited for her at the zoo for more than an hour. She never showed up.'

Matt was staring at her.

'When I talked to her on the phone, she said she thought she was being watched.'

Matt Baker sat there, scratching his chin. 'Jesus. What the hell have we got here?'

'I don't know. I want to talk to Joan Sinisi's maid.'

'Dana . . .'

'Yes?'

'Be careful. Be very careful.'

When Dana walked into the lobby of the apartment building, there was a different doorman on duty.

'May I help you?'

'I'm Dana Evans. I came about Miss Sinisi's death. It was a terrible tragedy.'

The doorman's face grew sad. 'Yes, it was. She was a lovely lady. Always quiet and kept to herself.'

'Did she have many visitors?' Dana asked casually.

'No, not really. She was very private.'

'Were you on duty yesterday when the' – Dana's tongue tripped on the word – 'accident happened?'

'No, ma'am.'

'So you don't know whether anyone was with her?'

'No, ma'am.'

'But someone was on duty here?'

'Oh, yes. Dennis. The police questioned him. He was out on an errand when poor Miss Sinisi fell.'

'I'd like to talk to Greta, Miss Sinisi's maid.'

'I'm afraid that's impossible.'

'Impossible? Why?'

'She's gone.'

'Where?'

'She said she was going home. She was terribly upset.'

'Where is her home?'

The doorman shook his head. 'I have no idea.'

'Is anyone up in the apartment now?'

'No, ma'am.'

Dana thought fast. 'My boss would like me to do a story for WTN on Miss Sinisi's death. I wonder if I might see the apartment again? I was here a few days ago.'

He thought for a moment, then shrugged. 'I don't see any problem. I'll have to go up with you.'

'That's fine,' Dana said.

They rode up to the penthouse in silence. When they reached the thirtieth floor, the doorman took out a passkey and opened the door to apartment A.

Dana stepped inside. The apartment was exactly as Dana had last seen it. *Except that Joan Sinisi is missing.*

'Did you want to see anything in particular, Miss Evans?'

'No,' Dana lied. 'I just wanted to refresh my memory.'

She walked down the hallway to the living room and moved toward the terrace.

'That's where the poor lady fell off,' the doorman said.

Dana stepped out onto the huge terrace and walked over to the edge. A four-foot wall ran completely around the terrace. There was no possible

107

way anyone could have accidentally fallen over it.

Dana looked down at the street below, bustling with Christmas traffic, and thought, *Who could be ruthless enough to do a thing like that?* She shuddered.

The doorman was at her side. 'Are you all right?'

Dana took a deep breath. 'Yes, fine. Thank you.'

'Did you want to see anything else?'

'No, I've seen enough.'

The lobby of the downtown police precinct was crowded with felons, drunks, prostitutes, and desperate tourists whose wallets had mysteriously disappeared.

'I'm here to see Detective Marcus Abrams,' Dana told the desk sergeant.

'Third door on the right.'

'Thank you.' Dana walked down the corridor.

Detective Abrams's door was open.

'Detective Abrams?'

He was at the filing cabinet, a big man with a paunch and tired brown eyes. He looked over at Dana. 'Yes?' He recognized her. 'Dana Evans. What can I do for you?'

'I'm told that you're handling the Joan Sinisi' – again that word – 'accident.'

'That's right.'

'Can you tell me anything about it?'

He walked over to his desk carrying a handful of

108

papers and sat down. 'There's not much to tell. It was either an accident or suicide. Sit down.'

Dana took a chair. 'Was anyone with her when it happened?'

'Just the maid. She was in the kitchen at the time. She said no one else was there.'

'Do you have any idea where I can reach the maid?' Dana asked.

He thought it over. 'She's going to be on the news tonight, eh?'

Dana smiled at him. 'Right.'

Detective Abrams walked back to the filing cabinet and searched through some papers. He took out a card. 'Here we are. Greta Miller. Eleven-eighty Connecticut Avenue. That do it?'

Twenty minutes later Dana was driving on Connecticut Avenue, looking at the house numbers: 1170 ... 1172 ... 1174 ... 1176 ... 1178 ...

Number 1180 was a parking lot.

'You really believe the Sinisi woman was thrown from the terrace?' Jeff asked.

'Jeff, you don't call to make an urgent appointment and then commit suicide. Someone didn't want her to tell me something. It's frustrating. It's like the Hound of the Baskervilles. No one heard the dog bark. No one knows anything.'

Jeff said, 'This is getting scary. I'm not sure you should go on with it.'

'I can't stop now. I have to find out.'

'If you're right, Dana, six people have been murdered.'

Dana swallowed. 'I know.'

'. . . and the maid gave the police a phony address and disappeared,' Dana was saying to Matt Baker. 'When I talked to Joan Sinisi, she seemed nervous, but she certainly didn't strike me as being suicidal. Someone helped her off that balcony.'

'But we have no proof.'

'No. But I know I'm right. When I first met with her, Joan Sinisi was fine until the second I mentioned Taylor Winthrop's name. That's when she panicked. This is the first time I've seen a crack in the wonderful legend that Taylor Winthrop has built up. A man like Winthrop didn't pay off a secretary unless she had something really big on him. It had to be blackmail. There's something weird going on. Matt, do you know anyone who worked with Taylor Winthrop who might have had a problem with him, someone who's not afraid to speak up?'

Matt Baker was thoughtful for a moment. 'You might go see Roger Hudson. He was the majority leader in the Senate before he retired, and he worked with Taylor Winthrop on a committee or two. He might know something. He's a man who's not afraid of anybody.'

'Could you arrange a meeting for me?'

'I'll see what I can do.'

An hour later, Matt Baker was on the line. 'You have an appointment to see Roger Hudson Thursday at noon at his home in Georgetown.'

'Thanks, Matt. I appreciate it.'

'I have to warn you, Dana . . .'

'Yes?'

'Hudson can be pretty prickly.'

'I'll try not to get too close.'

Matt Baker was about to leave his office when Elliot Cromwell came in.

'I want to talk to you about Dana.'

'Any problem?'

'No, and I don't want there to be. This Taylor Winthrop thing she's investigating –'

'Yes.'

'She's ruffling a few feathers, and I think she's wasting her time. I knew Taylor Winthrop and his family. They were all wonderful people.'

Matt Baker said, 'Good. Then there's no harm in Dana going ahead.'

Elliot Cromwell looked at Matt a moment, then shrugged. 'Keep me informed.'

'Is this a secure line?'

'Yes, sir.'

'Good. We're counting heavily on the information from WTN. Are you certain your information is reliable?'

'Absolutely. It's coming right from the executive tower.'

Eight

Wednesday morning, as Dana was preparing breakfast, she heard loud sounds outside. She looked out the window and was surprised to see a moving van in front of the apartment building, with men loading furniture onto it.

Who could be moving out? Dana wondered. Every apartment was occupied, and they were all on long-term leases.

Dana was putting the cereal on the table when there was a knock at the door. It was Dorothy Wharton.

'Dana, I have some news for you,' she said excitedly. 'Howard and I are moving to Rome today.'

Dana stared at her in astonishment. *'Rome? Today?'*

'Isn't it *incredible*? Last week a man came to see Howard. It was very hush-hush. Howard told me I couldn't say anything. Well, last night the man called and offered Howard a job with his company in Italy at three times Howard's present salary.' Dorothy was beaming.

'Well, that's – that's wonderful,' Dana said. 'We're going to miss you.'

'We're going to miss you, too.'

Howard came to the door. 'I guess Dorothy told you the news?'

'Yes. I'm delighted for you. But I thought you were set here for life? And suddenly –'

Howard just kept on talking. 'I can't believe it. Right out of the blue. It's a great company, too. Italiano Ripristino. They're one of the biggest conglomerates in Italy. They have a subsidiary that's into restoration of ruins. I don't know how they heard about me, but they flew a man all the way here just to make a deal with me. There are lots of monuments in Rome that need repairs. They're even paying the rest of our rent here for the year and we get back our deposit. The only thing is, we have to be in Rome by tomorrow. That means we have to be out of the apartment today.'

Dana said tentatively, 'That's very unusual, isn't it?'

'I guess they're in a big hurry.'

'Do you need help packing?'

Dorothy shook her head. 'No. We've been up all night. Most of the stuff's going to Goodwill. On Howard's new salary, we can afford much better.'

114

Dana laughed. 'Keep in touch, Dorothy.'

One hour later the Whartons had left their apartment and were on their way to Rome.

When Dana got to her office, she said to Olivia, 'Would you check out a company for me?'

'Certainly.'

'It's called Italiano Ripristino. I believe its headquarters are in Rome.'

'Right.'

Thirty minutes later Olivia handed a paper to Dana. 'Here it is. It's one of the largest companies in Europe.'

Dana felt a sense of deep relief. 'Good. I'm glad to hear that.'

'By the way,' Olivia said, 'it's not a private company.'

'Oh?'

'No. It's owned by the Italian government.'

When Dana brought Kemal home from school that afternoon, a bespectacled middle-aged man was moving into the Wharton apartment.

Thursday, the day of Dana's appointment with Roger Hudson, started out hellishly.

At the first television meeting, Robert Fenwick

said, 'It looks like we're in trouble on tonight's broadcast.'

'Give it to me,' Dana said.

'You know the crew that we sent to Ireland? We were going to use their film tonight?'

'Yes?'

'They've been arrested. All their equipment has been confiscated.'

'Are you serious?'

'I never joke about the Irish.' He handed Dana a sheet of paper. 'Here's our lead story about the Washington banker who's being charged with fraud.'

'It's a good story,' Dana said. 'And it's our exclusive.'

'Our legal department just killed it.'

'*What?*'

'They're afraid of being sued.'

'Wonderful,' Dana said bitterly.

'I'm not through. The witness in the murder case that we scheduled for a live interview tonight –'

'Yes . . .'

'He's changed his mind. He's a no-show.'

Dana groaned. It was not even ten o'clock in the morning. The only thing Dana had to look forward to on this day was her meeting with Roger Hudson.

When Dana returned from the news meeting, Olivia said, 'It's eleven o'clock, Miss Evans. With this weather, you probably ought to be leaving now for your appointment with Mr Hudson.'

'Thanks, Olivia. I should be back in two or three hours.' Dana looked out the window. It was beginning to snow again. She put on her coat and scarf and started for the door. The phone rang.

'Miss Evans . . .'

Dana turned.

'There's a call for you on line three.'

'Not now,' Dana said. 'I have to go.'

'It's someone from Kemal's school.'

'What?' Dana hurried back to her desk. 'Hello?'

'Miss Evans?'

'Yes.'

'This is Thomas Henry.'

'Yes, Mr Henry. Is Kemal all right?'

'I really don't know how to answer that. I'm very sorry to tell you this, but Kemal is being expelled.'

Dana stood there in shock. *Expelled*. Why? What has he done?'

'Perhaps we should discuss it in person. I would appreciate it if you would come and pick him up.'

'Mr Henry –'

'I'll explain when you get here, Miss Evans. Thank you.'

Dana replaced the receiver, stunned. *What could have happened?*

Olivia asked, 'Is everything all right?'

'Great.' Dana groaned. 'This makes the morning just about perfect.'

'Can I do anything?'

'Say an extra prayer for me.'

Earlier in the morning, when Dana had dropped Kemal off at school, waved good-bye, and driven away, Ricky Underwood was watching.

As Kemal started to walk past him, Ricky said, 'Hey, it's the war hero. Your mom must be real frustrated. You only have one arm, so now when you play stinky finger with her –'

Kemal's movements were almost too swift to be seen. His foot slammed hard into Ricky's groin, and as Ricky screamed and started to double over, Kemal's left knee shot up and broke his nose. Blood spurted into the air.

Kemal leaned over the moaning figure on the ground. 'Next time I'll kill you.'

Dana drove as fast as she could to Theodore Roosevelt Middle School, wondering what could have happened. *Whatever it is, I have to talk Henry into keeping Kemal in school.*

Thomas Henry was waiting for Dana in his office. Kemal was seated in a chair opposite him. As Dana walked in, she had a sense of déjà vu.

'Miss Evans.'

Dana said, 'What happened?'

'Your son broke a boy's nose and cheekbone. An

ambulance had to take him to the emergency room.'

Dana looked at him in disbelief. 'How – how could that have happened? Kemal has only one arm.'

'Yes,' Thomas Henry said tightly. 'But he has two legs. He broke the boy's nose with his knee.'

Kemal was studying the ceiling.

Dana turned to him. 'Kemal, how could you do that?'

He looked down. 'It was easy.'

'You see what I mean, Miss Evans,' Thomas Henry said. 'His whole attitude is – I – I don't know how to describe it. I'm afraid we can no longer put up with Kemal's behavior. I suggest you find a more suitable school for him.'

Dana said earnestly, 'Mr Henry, Kemal doesn't pick fights. I'm sure that if he got into a fight, he had a good reason for it. You can't –'

Mr Henry said firmly, 'We've made our decision, Miss Evans.' There was finality in his tone.

Dana took a deep breath. 'All right. We'll look for a school that's more understanding. Come on, Kemal.'

Kemal got up, glared at Mr Henry, and followed Dana out of the office. They walked toward the curb in silence. Dana looked at her watch. She was now late for her appointment, and she had no place to put Kemal. *I'll have to take him with me.*

When they got into the car, Dana said, 'All right, Kemal. What happened?'

There was no way he would ever tell her what

119

Ricky Underwood had said. 'I'm very sorry, Dana. It was my fault.'

Rad, Dana thought.

The Hudson estate was nestled on five acres of ground in an exclusive area of Georgetown. The house, invisible from the street, was a three-story Georgian-style mansion on a hill. It had a white exterior and a long, sweeping driveway leading up to the front entrance.

Dana stopped the car in front of the house. She looked at Kemal. 'You're coming in with me.'

'Why?'

'Because it's cold out here. Come on.'

Dana went to the front door and Kemal reluctantly followed her.

Dana turned to him. 'Kemal, I'm here to do a very important interview. I want you to be quiet and polite. Okay?'

'Okay.'

Dana rang the bell. The door was opened by a pleasant-faced giant of a man in the uniform of a butler. 'Miss Evans?'

'Yes.'

'I am Cesar. Mr Hudson is expecting you.' He looked at Kemal, then back at Dana. 'May I have your coats?' A moment later he was hanging them up in the front hall guest closet. Kemal kept staring up at Cesar, who towered above him.

'How tall are you?'

Dana said, 'Kemal! Don't be rude.'

'Oh, it's all right, Miss Evans. I'm quite used to it.'

'Are you bigger than Michael Jordan?' Kemal asked.

'I'm afraid so.' The butler smiled. 'I'm seven feet one. Come this way, please.'

The entry was enormous, a long hall with a hardwood floor, antique mirrors, and marble tables. Along the walls were shelves of precious Ming Dynasty figurines and Chihuly blown-glass statues.

Dana and Kemal followed Cesar down the long hallway to a step-down living room, with pale yellow walls and white woodwork. The room was furnished with comfortable sofas, Queen Anne end tables, and Sheraton wing chairs covered in pale yellow silk.

Senator Roger Hudson and his wife, Pamela, were seated at a backgammon table. They rose as Dana and Kemal were announced by Cesar.

Roger Hudson was a stern-looking man in his late fifties, with cold gray eyes and a wary smile. There was a cautious aloofness about him.

Pamela Hudson was a beauty, slightly younger than her husband. She seemed warm and open and down to earth. She had ash-blond hair and a trace of gray that she had not bothered to disguise.

'I'm so sorry I'm late,' Dana apologized. 'I'm Dana Evans. This is my son, Kemal.'

'I'm Roger Hudson. This is my wife, Pamela.'

Dana had looked up Roger Hudson on the Internet. His father had owned a small steel company, Hudson Industries, and Roger Hudson had built it into a worldwide conglomerate. He was a billionaire, had been the Senate majority leader, and at one time had headed the Armed Services Committee. He had retired from business and was now a political adviser to the White House. Twenty-five years earlier he had married a society beauty, Pamela Donnelly. The two of them were prominent in Washington society and influential in politics.

Dana said, 'Kemal, this is Mr and Mrs Hudson.' She looked at Roger. 'I apologize for bringing him with me, but –'

'That's perfectly all right,' Pamela Hudson said. 'We know all about Kemal.'

Dana looked at her in surprise. 'You do?'

'Yes. A great deal has been written about you, Miss Evans. You rescued Kemal from Sarajevo. It was a wonderful thing to do.'

Roger Hudson stood there, silent.

'What can we get you?' Pamela Hudson asked.

'Nothing for me, thank you,' Dana said.

They looked at Kemal. He shook his head.

'Sit down, please.' Roger Hudson and his wife took seats on the couch. Dana and Kemal sat in the two easy chairs across from them.

Roger Hudson said curtly, 'I'm not sure why

you're here, Miss Evans. Matt Baker asked me to see you. What is it I can do for you?'

'I wanted to talk to you about Taylor Winthrop.'

Roger Hudson frowned. 'What about him?'

'I understand that you knew him?'

'Yes. I met Taylor when he was our ambassador to Russia. At the time, I was head of the Armed Services Committee. I went to Russia to evaluate their weapon capabilities. Taylor spent two or three days with our committee.'

'What did you think of him, Mr Hudson?'

There was a thoughtful pause. 'To be quite candid, Miss Evans, I was not overly impressed by all that charm. But I must say, I thought the man was very capable.'

Kemal, bored, looked around, got up, and wandered into the next room.

'Do you know if Ambassador Winthrop got in any trouble when he was in Russia?'

Roger Hudson gave her a puzzled look. 'I'm not sure I understand. What kind of trouble?'

'Something . . . something where he would have made enemies. I mean, really deadly enemies.'

Roger Hudson shook his head slowly. 'Miss Evans, if anything like that had happened, not only would I have known about it, the whole world would have known. Taylor Winthrop lived a very public life. May I ask where these questions are leading?'

Dana said awkwardly, 'I thought possibly Taylor

Winthrop might have done something to someone that was bad enough to be a motive to want to kill him and his family.'

The Hudsons were both staring at her.

Dana went on quickly. 'I know it sounds far-fetched, but so is their all dying violent deaths in less than a year.'

Roger Hudson said brusquely, 'Miss Evans, I've lived long enough to know that *anything* is possible, but this – what do you base it on?'

'If you mean hard evidence, I have none.'

'I'm not surprised.' He hesitated. 'I did hear that . . .' His voice trailed off. 'Never mind.'

The two women were looking at him.

Pamela said gently, 'That's not fair to Miss Evans, darling. What were you going to say?'

He shrugged. 'It is not important.' He turned to Dana. 'When I was in Moscow, there was a rumor that Winthrop was involved in some type of private deal with the Russians. But I don't deal in rumors, and I'm sure that you don't, Miss Evans.' His tone was almost a reproach.

Before Dana could respond, there was a loud crash from the adjoining library.

Pamela Hudson rose and hurried toward the sound. Roger and Dana followed. They stopped at the door. In the library, a blue Ming vase had fallen to the floor and shattered. Kemal stood next to it.

'Oh, my God,' Dana said, horrified. 'I'm *so* sorry. Kemal, how could you – ?'

'It was an accident.'

Dana turned to the Hudsons, her face flushed with embarrassment. 'I'm terribly sorry. I'll pay for it, of course. I –'

'Please don't worry about it,' Pamela Hudson said with a nice smile. 'Our dogs do much worse.'

Roger Hudson's face was grim. He started to say something, but a look from his wife stopped him.

Dana looked down at the remains of the vase. *It was probably worth about ten years of my salary*, she thought.

'Why don't we go back to the living room,' Pamela Hudson suggested.

Dana followed the Hudsons with Kemal at her side. 'Stay with me,' she muttered, furious. They sat down again.

Roger Hudson looked at Kemal. 'How did you lose your arm, son?'

Dana was surprised at the bluntness of the question, but Kemal answered readily.

'A bomb.'

'I see. What about your parents, Kemal?'

'They were both killed in an air raid along with my sister.'

Roger Hudson grunted. 'Goddamn wars.'

At that moment, Cesar came into the room. 'Luncheon is served.'

*

The luncheon was delicious. Dana found Pamela warm and charming and Roger Hudson withdrawn.

'What are you working on now?' Pamela Hudson asked Dana.

'We're talking about a new show to be called *Crime Line*. We're going to expose some of the people who have gotten away with committing crimes, and we'll try to help people in prison who are innocent.'

Roger Hudson said, 'Washington is a great place to start. It's full of holier-than-thou phonies in high places who have gotten away with every crime you can think of.'

'Roger's on several government-reform committees,' Pamela Hudson said proudly.

'And a lot of good it does,' her husband grumbled. 'The difference between right and wrong seems to have gotten blurred. It should be taught at home. Our schools certainly don't teach it.'

Pamela Hudson looked at Dana. 'By the way, Roger and I are giving a little dinner party Saturday night. Would you be free to join us?'

Dana smiled. 'Why, thank you. I'd love to.'

'Do you have a young man?'

'Yes. Jeff Connors.'

Roger Hudson said, 'The sports reporter on your station?'

'Yes.'

'He's not bad. I watch him sometimes,' he said. 'I'd like to meet him.'

126

Dana smiled. 'I'm sure Jeff would love to come.'

As Dana and Kemal were leaving, Roger Hudson took Dana aside.

'In all candor, Miss Evans, I find your conspiracy theory about the Winthrops in the realm of fantasy. But for Matt Baker's sake, I'm willing to check around and see if I can find anything that could possibly substantiate it.'

'Thank you.'

In all candor, Miss Evans, I find your conspiracy theory about the Winthrops in the realm of fantasy. But for Matt Baker's sake, I'm willing to check around and see if I can find anything that could possibly substantiate it.

Thank you.

Tape ends.

Nine

They were in the middle of their morning meeting about *Crime Line*, and Dana was in the conference room with half a dozen staff reporters and researchers.

Olivia poked her head in. 'Mr Baker would like to see you.'

'Tell him I'll be there in a minute.'

'The boss is waiting for you.'

'Thanks, Abbe. You're looking cheerful.'

Abbe nodded. 'I finally got a good night's sleep. For the last –'

'Dana? Come in here,' Matt yelled.

'To be continued,' Abbe said.

Dana walked into Matt's office. 'How did the meeting with Roger Hudson go?'

'I have a feeling he wasn't very interested. He thinks my theory is crazy.'

'I told you he's not Mr Warmth.'

'He does take a little getting used to. His wife is lovely. You should hear her on the subject of Washington society madness. Talk about wickedness.'

'I know. She's a wonderful lady.'

Dana ran into Elliot Cromwell in the executive dining room.

'Join me,' Elliot Cromwell said.

'Thank you.' Dana sat down.

'How's Kemal?'

Dana hesitated. 'At the moment, I'm afraid there's a problem.'

'Oh? What kind of problem?'

'Kemal was expelled from school.'

'Why?'

'He got in a fight and sent a boy to the hospital.'

'That would do it.'

'I'm sure the fight wasn't Kemal's fault,' Dana said defensively. 'He gets teased a lot because he has only one arm.'

Elliot Cromwell said, 'I suppose it's really difficult for him.'

'It is. I'm trying to get him a prosthesis. There seem to be problems.'

'What grade is Kemal in?'

'Seventh.'

Elliot Cromwell was thoughtful. 'Are you familiar with the Lincoln Preparatory School?'

'Oh, yes. But I understand it's very difficult to get into.' She added, 'And I'm afraid Kemal's grades aren't very good.'

'I have a few contacts there. Would you like me to speak to someone?'

'I – that's very kind of you.'

'It will be my pleasure.'

Later that day Elliot Cromwell sent for Dana.

'I have good news for you. I spoke to the principal at the Lincoln Preparatory School, and she's agreed to have Kemal enrolled there on a trial basis. Could you take him over tomorrow morning?'

'Of course. I –' It took Dana a moment to let it sink in. 'Oh, that's wonderful! I'm so pleased. Thank you so much. I really appreciate it, Elliot.'

'I want you to know that I appreciate *you*, Dana. I think it was wonderful of you to have brought Kemal to this country. You're a very special person.'

'I – thank you.'

When Dana left the office, she thought, *That took a lot of clout. And a lot of kindness.*

Lincoln Preparatory School was an imposing complex consisting of a large Edwardian building, three smaller annexes, spacious, well-tended grounds, and extensive, manicured playing fields.

Standing in front of the entrance, Dana said,

'Kemal, this is the best school in Washington. You can learn a lot here, but you have to have a positive attitude about it. Do you understand?'

'Sweet.'

'And you can't get into any fights.'

Kemal did not answer.

Dana and Kemal were ushered into the office of Rowana Trott, the school's principal. She was an attractive woman with a friendly manner.

'Welcome,' she said. She turned to Kemal. 'I've heard a great deal about you, young man. We're all looking forward to having you here.'

Dana waited for Kemal to say something. When he was silent, she said, 'Kemal is looking forward to being here.'

'Good. I think you're going to make some very nice friends at our school.'

Kemal stood there without answering.

An older woman came into the office. Mrs Trott said, 'This is Becky. Becky, this is Kemal. Why don't you show Kemal around? Let him become acquainted with some of his teachers.'

'Certainly. This way, Kemal.'

Kemal looked at Dana beseechingly, then turned and followed Becky out the door.

'I want to explain about Kemal,' Dana began. 'He –'

Mrs Trott said, 'You don't have to, Miss Evans. Elliot Cromwell told me about the situation and about Kemal's background. I understand he's been

132

through more than any child should ever have to go through, and we're prepared to make allowances for that.'

'Thank you,' Dana said.

'I have a transcript of his grades from Theodore Roosevelt Middle School. We're going to see if we can't better them.'

Dana nodded. 'Kemal's a very bright boy.'

'I'm sure he is. His grades in math prove that. We're going to try to give him an incentive to excel in all his other subjects.'

'The fact that he has only one arm is very traumatic for him,' Dana said. 'I hope to be able to solve that.'

Mrs Trott nodded understandingly. 'Of course.'

When Kemal was through with his tour of the school and he and Dana were walking back to the car, Dana said, 'I know you're going to like it here.'

Kemal was silent.

'It's a beautiful school, isn't it?'

Kemal said, 'It sucks.'

Dana stopped. 'Why?'

Kemal's voice was choked. 'They have tennis courts and a football field and I can't –' His eyes filled with tears.

Dana wrapped her arms around him. 'I'm sorry, darling.' And she thought to herself, *I've got to do something about this.*

*

133

The dinner party at the Hudsons' on Saturday night was a glamorous, black-tie affair. The beautiful rooms were filled with the movers and shakers of the nation's capital, including the Secretary of Defense, several members of Congress, the head of the Federal Reserve, and the ambassador from Germany.

Roger and Pamela were standing at the door when Dana and Jeff arrived. Dana introduced Jeff.

'I enjoy your sports column and broadcasts,' Roger Hudson said.

'Thank you.'

Pamela said, 'Let me introduce you to some of our guests.'

Many of the faces were familiar, and the greetings were cordial. It seemed that most of the guests were fans of either Dana or Jeff or both of them.

When they were alone for a moment, Dana said, 'My God. The guest list here reads like *Who's Who*.'

Jeff took her hand. '*You're* the biggest celebrity here, darling.'

'No way,' Dana said. 'I'm just –'

At that moment, Dana saw General Victor Booster and Jack Stone heading toward them.

'Good evening, General,' Dana said.

Booster looked at her and said rudely, 'What the hell are you doing here?'

Dana flushed.

'This is a social evening,' the general snapped. 'I didn't know the media was invited.'

Jeff looked at General Booster, furious. 'Hold it!' he said. 'We have as much right –'

Victor Booster ignored him. He leaned close to Dana. 'Remember what I promised you if you go looking for trouble.' He walked away.

Jeff looked after him disbelievingly. 'Jesus. What was that all about?'

Jack Stone stood there, red-faced. 'I'm – I'm terribly sorry. The general gets that way sometimes. He isn't always tactful.'

'We noticed,' Jeff said icily.

The dinner itself was fantastic. In front of each couple was a beautifully handwritten menu:

Russian blini with beluga caviar and light vodka cream cheese

Ambassador pheasant broth with white truffle essence and green asparagus

Bismarck foie gras with Boston lettuce, peppercorns, and Xeres vinegar dressing

Maine lobster thermidor glazed with Mornay champagne sauce

Fillet of beef Wellington with roasted potato Orloff and sautéed vegetables

Warm chocolate soufflé with orange zest liqueur and chocolate morsels, served with nougatine sauce

It was a Lucullan banquet.

To Dana's surprise, she found that she had been seated next to Roger Hudson. *Pamela's doing*, she thought.

'Pamela mentioned that Kemal is enrolled in the Lincoln Preparatory School.'

Dana smiled. 'Yes. Elliot Cromwell arranged it. He's a remarkable man.'

Roger Hudson nodded. 'So I've heard.'

He hesitated a moment. 'This may mean nothing, but it seems that shortly before Taylor Winthrop became our ambassador to Russia, he told close friends that he had definitely retired from public life.'

Dana frowned. 'And then he accepted the ambassadorship to Russia?'

'Yes.'

Strange.

On the way home, Jeff asked Dana, 'What did you do to make such a fan of General Booster?'

'He doesn't want me investigating the deaths in the Winthrop family.'

'Why not?'

'He doesn't explain. He just barks.'

Jeff said slowly, 'His bite is worse than his bark, Dana. He's a bad enemy to have.'

She looked at Jeff curiously. 'Why?'

'He's head of FRA, the Federal Research Agency.'

'I know. They develop technology to help under-developed countries learn modern production and –'

Jeff said dryly, 'And there really is a Santa Claus.'

Dana looked at him, puzzled. 'What are you talking about?'

'The agency is a cover-up. The real function of FRA is to spy on foreign intelligence agencies and intercept their communications. It's ironic. "Frater" means brother in Latin – only this is Big Brother, and Big Brother sure as hell is watching everybody. They're more secretive than even the NSA.'

Dana said thoughtfully, 'Taylor Winthrop was once the head of FRA. That's interesting.'

'I would advise you to stay as far away as you can from General Booster.'

'I intend to.'

'I know you have a sitter problem tonight, honey, so if you have to get home –'

Dana nestled against him. 'No way. The sitter can wait. I can't. Let's go to your place.'

Jeff grinned. 'I thought you'd never ask.'

*

Jeff lived in a small apartment in a four-story building on Madison Street. Jeff led Dana into the bedroom.

'I'll be glad when we move into a bigger apartment,' Jeff said. 'Kemal has to have his own room. Why don't we –?'

'Why don't we stop talking?' Dana suggested.

Jeff took her in his arms. 'Great idea.' He reached behind her and curved his hands around her hips, stroking her softly and gently. He started to undress her.

'Do you know you have a great body?'

'All the fellows tell me that,' Dana said. 'It's the talk of the town. Are you planning to get undressed?'

'I'm thinking it over.'

Dana moved up against him and started to unbutton his shirt.

'Do you know you're a hussy?'

She smiled. 'You bet.'

When Jeff finished undressing, Dana was in bed waiting for him. She warmed herself in the summer of his arms. He was a wonderful lover, sensual and caring.

'I love you so much,' Dana whispered.

'I love you, my darling.'

As Jeff reached for her, a cell phone rang.

'Yours or mine?'

They laughed. It rang again.

'Mine,' Jeff said. 'Let it ring.'

'It might be important,' Dana said.

'Oh, all right.' Jeff sat up, disgruntled. He picked up the phone. 'Hello?' His voice changed. 'No, it's all right ... Go ahead ... Of course ... I'm sure there's nothing to worry about. It's probably just stress.'

The conversation went on for five minutes. 'Right ... So take it easy ... Fine ... Good night, Rachel.' He clicked the phone off.

Isn't it awfully late at night for Rachel to be calling? 'Is anything wrong, Jeff?'

'Not really. Rachel's been doing too much. She just needs a rest. She'll be fine.' He took Dana in his arms and said softly, 'Where were we?' He pulled her naked body to his and the magic began.

Dana forgot about the problems with the Winthrops and Joan Sinisi and generals and house-keepers and Kemal and schools, and life became a joyous, passionate celebration.

Later, Dana said reluctantly, 'I'm afraid it's time for Cinderella to turn into a pumpkin, darling.'

'And what a pumpkin! I'll get my carriage ready.'

She looked down at him. 'I think it's ready. One more time?'

When Dana got home, the woman from the sitter service was impatiently waiting to leave.

'It's one-thirty,' she said accusingly.

'I'm sorry. I got tied up.' Dana gave the woman

139

some extra money. 'Take a taxi,' she said. 'It's dangerous out there. I'll see you tomorrow night.'

The sitter said, 'Miss Evans, I think you should know . . .'

'Yes?'

'All evening Kemal kept pestering me about when you were coming home. That child is very insecure.'

'Thank you. Good night.'

Dana went into Kemal's room. He was awake, playing a computer game.

'Hi, Dana.'

'You're supposed to be asleep, pal.'

'I was waiting for you to come home. Did you have a good time?'

'It was lovely, but I missed you, darling.'

Kemal turned off the computer. 'Are you going to go away every night?'

Dana thought about all the emotions behind the question. 'I'll try to spend more time with you, darling.'

Ten

The call came out of the blue on Monday morning.

'Dana Evans?'

'Yes.'

'This is Dr Joel Hirschberg. I'm with the Children's Foundation.'

Dana listened, puzzled. 'Yes?'

'Elliot Cromwell mentioned to me that you told him you're having a problem getting a prosthetic arm for your son.'

Dana had to think a moment. 'Yes, I guess I did.'

'Mr Cromwell gave me the background. This foundation has been set up to help children from war-torn countries. From what Mr Cromwell told me, your son certainly comes under that heading. I wonder if you would like to bring him in to see me?'

'Well, I – well, yes, of course.' They made the appointment for later that day.

When Kemal got home from school, Dana

said excitedly, 'You and I are going to see a doctor about getting a new arm for you. Would you like that?'

Kemal thought about it. 'I don't know. It won't be a real arm.'

'It will be as close to a real arm as we can get. Okay, pal?'

'Cool.'

Dr Joel Hirschberg was in his late forties, an attractive, earnest-looking man with an air of quiet competence.

When Dana and Kemal exchanged hellos, Dana said, 'Doctor, I want to explain up front that we'd have to work out some kind of financial arrangement, because I was told that because Kemal is growing, a new arm would be outdated every –'

Dr Hirschberg interrupted. 'As I told you over the phone, Miss Evans, the Children's Foundation has been set up especially to help children from war-torn countries. We'll take care of the expenses.'

Dana felt a surge of relief. 'That's wonderful.' She said a silent prayer. *God bless Elliot Cromwell.*

Dr Hirschberg turned to Kemal again. 'Now, let's take a look at you, young man.'

Thirty minutes later Dr Hirschberg said to Dana, 'I think we can fix him up almost as good as new.' He pulled down a chart on the wall. 'We have two kinds of prostheses, myoelectric, which is state-of-the-art, and a cable-operated arm. As you can see here, the myoelectric arm is made of plastics and covered with a handlike glove.' He smiled at Kemal. 'It looks as good as the original.'

Kemal asked, 'Does it move?'

Dr Hirschberg said, 'Kemal, do you ever think about moving your hand? I mean the hand that isn't there any longer.'

'Yes,' Kemal said.

Dr Hirschberg leaned forward. 'Well, now, whenever you think about that phantom hand, the muscles that used to work there will contract and automatically generate a myoelectric signal. In other words, you'll be able to open and close your hand just by thinking about it.'

Kemal's face lit up. 'I will? How – how do I put the arm on and take it off?'

'It's really very simple, Kemal. You'll just pull on the new arm. It's a suction fit. There will be a thin nylon sock over the arm. You can't swim with it, but you can do just about anything else. It's like a pair of shoes. You take it off at night and put it on in the morning.'

'How much does it weigh?' Dana asked.

'Anywhere from six ounces to a pound.'

Dana turned to Kemal. 'What do you think, sport? Should we try it?'

Kemal was trying to conceal his excitement. 'Will it look real?'

143

Dr Hirschberg smiled. 'It will look real.'

'It sounds rad.'

'You've had to become left-handed, so you're going to have to unlearn that. That will take time, Kemal. We can get you fitted immediately, but you'll have to see a therapist for a little while to learn how to make this a part of you and how to control the myoelectric signals.'

Kemal took a deep breath. 'Cool.'

Dana hugged Kemal tightly. 'It's going to be wonderful,' she said. She was fighting back tears.

Dr Hirschberg watched them a moment, then smiled. 'Let's go to work.'

When Dana returned to the office, she went in to see Elliot Cromwell.

'Elliot, we just left Dr Hirschberg.'

'Good. I hope he can help Kemal.'

'It looks as though he can. I can't tell you how very, very much I appreciate this.'

'Dana, there's nothing to appreciate. I'm glad I could be helpful. Just let me know how it goes.'

'I will.' *Bless you.*

'Flowers!' Olivia walked into the office with a large bouquet of flowers.

'They're beautiful!' Dana exclaimed.

She opened the envelope and read the card. *Dear*

Miss Evans, Our friend's bark is worse than his bite. Enjoy the flowers. Jack Stone.

Dana studied the card a moment. *That's interesting,* she thought. *Jeff said his bite is worse than his bark. Which one is right?* Dana had the feeling that Jack Stone hated his job. And hated his boss. *I'll remember that.*

Dana telephoned Jack Stone at FRA.

'Mr Stone? I just wanted to thank you for the beautiful –'

'Are you at your office?'

'Yes. I –'

'I'll call back.' Dial tone.

Three minutes later Jack Stone called.

'Miss Evans, it would be better for us both if a mutual friend didn't know we were talking. I've tried to change his attitude, but he's a stubborn man. If you ever need me – I mean *really need me* – I'm going to give you my private cell phone number. It will reach me anytime.'

'Thank you.' Dana wrote down the number.

'Miss Evans –'

'Yes.'

'Never mind. Be careful.'

When Jack Stone had gotten in that morning, General Booster had been waiting for him.

'Jack, I have a feeling that Evans bitch is a trouble-maker. I want you to start a file on her. And keep me in the loop.'

'I'll take care of it.' *Only there's not going to be any loop.* And he had sent Dana flowers.

Dana and Jeff were in the television station's exec-utive dining room talking about Kemal's prosthesis.

Dana said, 'I'm so excited, darling. This is going to make all the difference in the world. He's been belligerent because he feels inferior. This is going to change all that.'

'He must be thrilled,' Jeff said. 'I know I am.'

'And the wonder is that the Children's Founda-tion is going to pay for all of it. If we can –'

Jeff's cell phone rang. 'Excuse me, honey.' He pressed a button and talked into the phone. 'Hello? . . . Oh . . .' He glanced at Dana. 'No . . . It's all right . . . Go ahead . . .'

Dana sat there, trying not to listen.

'Yes . . . I see . . . Right . . . It's probably nothing serious, but maybe you should see a doctor. Where are you now? Brazil? They have some good doctors there. Of course . . . I understand . . . No . . .' The conversation seemed to go on and on. Jeff finally said, 'Take care. Good-bye.' He put the phone down.

Dana said, 'Rachel?'

'Yes. She's having some physical problems. She

canceled her shoot in Rio. She's never done anything like that before.'

'Why is she calling you, Jeff?'

'She has no one else, honey. She's all alone.'

'Good-bye, Jeff.'

Rachel hung up reluctantly, hating to let go. She
looked out the window at Sugarloaf in the distance
and Ipanema Beach far below. She walked into her
bedroom and lay down, exhausted, the day reeling
tipsily through her mind. It had started off well.
That morning she had been shooting a commercial
for American Express, posing on the beach.

Around noon the director said, 'That last one was
great, Rachel. But let's do one more.'

She started to say yes and then heard herself saying, 'No. I'm sorry. I can't.'

He had looked at her in surprise. 'What?'

'I'm very tired. You'll have to excuse me.' She
had turned and fled to the hotel, through the lobby,
into the safety of her room. She was trembling and
felt nauseated. *What is the matter with me?* Her forehead was feverish.

She picked up the telephone and called Jeff. The
very sound of his voice made her feel better. *Bless
him. He is always there for me, my lifeline.* When the
conversation was over, Rachel lay in bed, thinking.
*We had some good times. He was always fun. We enjoyed
doing the same things, and we loved sharing things. How*

could I have let him go? She made herself remember how the marriage had ended.

It had started with a telephone call.

'Rachel Stevens?'

'Yes.'

'Roderick Marshall is calling.' *One of the most important directors in Hollywood.*

A moment later he was on the line. 'Miss Stevens?'

'Yes?'

'Roderick Marshall. Do you know who I am?'

She had seen several of his movies. 'Of course I do, Mr Marshall.'

'I've been looking at photographs of you. We need you here at Fox. Would you be willing to come to Hollywood to do a screen test?'

Rachel hesitated about it for a moment. 'I don't know. I mean, I don't know if I can act. I've never –'

'Don't worry. I'll take care of that. We'll pay all your expenses, of course. I'll direct the test myself. How soon can you be out here?'

Rachel thought about her schedule. 'In three weeks.'

'Good. The studio will make all of the arrangements.'

When Rachel hung up she realized she had not consulted Jeff.

He won't mind, she thought. *We're seldom together anyway.*

*

'Hollywood?' Jeff had repeated.

'It will be a lark, Jeff.'

He nodded. 'All right. Go for it. You'll probably be great.'

'Can you come with me?'

'Honey, we're playing in Cleveland on Monday, then we're going on to Washington and then to Chicago. We still have a lot of games left on the schedule. I think the team would notice if one of their starting pitchers was missing.'

'Too bad.' She tried to sound casual. 'Our lives never seem to come together, do they, Jeff?'

'Not often enough.'

Rachel started to say something more, but she thought, *This isn't the time.*

Rachel was picked up at Los Angeles airport by a studio employee in a stretch limousine.

'My name is Henry Ford.' He chuckled. 'No relation. They call me Hank.'

The limousine glided out into traffic. On the way, he gave Rachel a running commentary.

'First time in Hollywood, Miss Stevens?'

'No. I've been here many times. The last time was two years ago.'

'Well, it's sure changed. It's bigger and better than ever. If you're into glamour, you're going to love it.'

If I'm into glamour.

'The studio booked you at the Chateau Marmont. That's where all the celebrities stay.'

Rachel pretended to be impressed. *'Really?'*

'Oh, yes. John Belushi died there, you know, after overdosing.'

'My.'

'Gable used to stay there, Paul Newman, Marilyn Monroe.' The name-dropping went on and on. Rachel had stopped listening.

The Chateau Marmont was just north of the Sunset Strip, looking like a castle from a movie set.

Henry Ford said, 'I'll pick you up at two o'clock to take you to the studio. You'll meet Roderick Marshall there.'

'I'll be ready.'

Two hours later Rachel was in the office of Roderick Marshall. He was in his forties, small and compact, with the energy of a dynamo.

'You'll be glad you came,' he said. 'I'm going to make you a big star. We'll shoot your test tomorrow. I'll have one of my assistants take you over to wardrobe to choose something nice for you. You're going to do a test scene from one of our big pictures, *End of a Dream.* Tomorrow morning at seven o'clock we'll do makeup and hair. I guess that's nothing new to you, huh?'

Rachel said tonelessly, 'No.'

'Are you alone here, Rachel?'

'Yes.'

'Why don't we have dinner together tonight?'

Rachel thought about it for a moment. 'Fine.'

'I'll pick you up at eight o'clock.'

Dinner turned out to be a whirlwind evening on the town.

'If you know where to go – and you can get in,' Roderick Marshall told Rachel, 'LA has some of the hottest clubs in the world.'

The evening's rounds began at the Standard, a trendy bar, restaurant, and hotel on Sunset Boulevard. As they passed the front desk, Rachel stopped to stare. Next to the desk, behind a frosted glass window, was a live human painting, a nude model.

'Isn't that great?'

'Unbelievable,' Rachel said.

There was a montage of noisy, crowded clubs, and by the end of the evening, Rachel was exhausted.

Roderick Marshall dropped her off at the hotel. 'Sleep well. Tomorrow's going to change your whole life.'

At 7:00 AM, Rachel was in the makeup room. Bob Van Dusen, the makeup man, looked at her appreciatively and said, 'And they're paying me for this?'

She laughed.

'You don't need much makeup. Nature took care of that.'

'Thank you.'

When Rachel was ready, a wardrobe woman helped her into the dress they had fitted the afternoon before. An assistant director took her to the huge soundstage.

Roderick Marshall and the crew were waiting. The director studied Rachel a moment and said, 'Perfect. We're going to do a two-part test, Rachel. You're going to sit in this chair and I'll ask you some questions off-camera. Just be yourself.'

'Right. And the second part?'

'The short test scene I mentioned.'

Rachel sat down and the cameraman set his focus. Roderick Marshall was standing off-camera. 'Are you ready?'

'Yes.'

'Good. Just relax. You're going to be wonderful. Camera. Action. Good morning.'

'Good morning.'

'I hear you're a model.'

Rachel smiled. 'Yes.'

'How did you get started?'

'I was fifteen. The owner of a model agency saw me in a restaurant with my mother, went up and talked to her, and a few days later I was a model.'

The interview went on for fifteen easy minutes, and Rachel's intelligence and poise shone through.

'Cut! Wonderful!' Roderick Marshall handed her

a short test scene. 'We're going to take a break. Read this. When you're ready, tell me, and we'll shoot it. You're a cinch, Rachel.'

Rachel read the scene. It was about a wife asking her husband for a divorce. Rachel read it again.

'I'm ready.'

Rachel was introduced to Kevin Webster, who was going to play opposite her – a handsome young man in the Hollywood mold.

'All right,' Roderick Marshall said. 'Let's shoot it. Camera. Action.'

Rachel looked at Kevin Webster. 'I talked to a divorce lawyer this morning, Cliff.'

'I heard about it. Shouldn't you have talked to me first?'

'I did talk to you about it. I've talked to you about it for the last year. We don't have a marriage anymore. You just weren't listening, Jeff.'

'Cut,' Roderick said. 'Rachel, his name is Cliff.'

Rachel said, embarrassed, 'I'm so sorry.'

'Let's go again. Take two.'

The scene really is about Jeff and me, Rachel thought. *We don't have a marriage anymore. How could we? We live separate lives. We hardly see each other. We both meet attractive people, but we can't get involved because of a contract that no longer means anything.*

'Rachel!'

'Sorry.'

The scene began again.

*

By the time Rachel finished the test, she had made two decisions: She did not belong in Hollywood.

And she wanted a divorce . . .

Now, lying in bed in Rio, feeling ill and exhausted, Rachel thought, *I made a mistake. I never should have divorced Jeff.*

Tuesday when Kemal finished school, Dana took him to the therapist who was working with Kemal and his new arm. The artificial arm looked real and functioned well, but it was difficult for Kemal to get used to it, both physically and psychologically.

'It will feel like he's attached to a foreign object,' the therapist had explained to Dana. 'Our job is to get him to accept it as a part of his own body. He has to get used to being ambidextrous again. There's usually a two- to three-month learning period. I must warn you that it can be a very difficult time.'

'We can handle it,' Dana assured him.

It was not that easy. The following morning Kemal walked out of the study without his prosthesis. 'I'm ready.'

Dana looked at him in surprise. 'Where's your arm, Kemal?'

Kemal raised his left hand defiantly. 'Here it is.'

'You know what I mean. Where's your prosthesis?'

'It's freak. I won't wear it anymore.'

'You'll get used to it, darling. I promise. You have
to give it a chance. I'll help you to –'

'No one can help me. I'm a *fukati* cripple . . .'

Dana went to see Detective Marcus Abrams again.
When Dana walked in, Abrams was at his desk
busily filling out reports. He looked up, scowling.

'You know what I hate about this damned job?'
He indicated the pile of papers. '*This*, I could be out
on the street having fun shooting perps. Oh, I forgot.
You're a reporter, aren't you? Don't quote me.'

'Too late.'

'And what can I do for you today, Miss Evans?'

'I came to ask about the Sinisi case. Has there
been an autopsy?'

'Pro forma.' He took out some papers from his
desk drawer.

'Was there anything suspicious in the report?'

She watched Detective Abrams scan the paper.
'No alcohol . . . no drugs . . . No.' He looked up. 'It
looks like the lady was depressed and just decided
to end it all. That it?'

'That's it,' Dana said.

Dana's next stop was Detective Phoenix Wilson's
office.

'Good morning, Detective Wilson.'

'And what brings you to my humble office?'

'I wondered whether there was any news on Gary Winthrop's murder.'

Detective Wilson sighed and scratched the side of his nose. 'Not one damn thing. I would have thought that by now one of those paintings would have turned up. That's what we've been counting on.'

Dana wanted to say, *I wouldn't if I were you*, but she held her tongue. 'No clues of any kind?'

'Not a thing. The bastards got away clean as a whistle. We don't have too many art thefts, but the MO is almost always the same. That's what's so surprising.'

'Surprising?'

'Yeah. This one is different.'

'Different . . . how?'

'Art thieves don't kill unarmed people, and there was no reason for these guys to shoot down Gary Winthrop in cold blood.' He stopped. 'Do you have any special interest in this case?'

'No,' Dana lied. 'Not at all. Just curious. I –'

'Right,' Detective Wilson said. 'Keep in touch.'

At the end of a meeting in General Booster's office at the secluded FRA headquarters, the general turned to Jack Stone and asked, 'What's happening with the Evans woman?'

'She's going around asking questions, but I think it's harmless. She's not getting anywhere.'

'I don't like her snooping around. Kick it up to a code three.'

'When do you want it to start?'

'Yesterday.'

Dana was in the middle of preparing for the next broadcast when Matt Baker walked into her office and sank into a chair.

'I just got a phone call about you.'

Dana said lightly, 'My fans can't get enough of me, can they?'

'This one's had enough of you.'

'Oh?'

'The call was from the FRA. They're asking you to stop your investigation of Taylor Winthrop. Nothing official. Just what they called a friendly suggestion. Looks like they want you to mind your own business.'

'It does, doesn't it?' Dana said. She locked eyes with Matt. 'It makes you wonder why, doesn't it? I'm not backing away from the story because some government agency wants me to. It started in Aspen, where Taylor and his wife were killed in the fire. I'm going there first. And if there's something there, it should be a great kickoff story for *Crime Line*.'

'How much time do you need?'

'It shouldn't take more than a day or two.'

'Go for it.'

Eleven

It was an effort for Rachel to move. Just walking from room to room in her Florida home was exhausting. She could not remember when she had ever been so tired. *I probably have a flu of some kind. Jeff was right. I should see a doctor. A hot bath will relax me . . .*

It was while Rachel was stretched out in the soothing warm water that her hand went to her breast and felt the lump.

Her first reaction was shock. Then denial. *It's nothing. It's not cancer. I don't smoke. I exercise and take care of my body. There is no cancer in my family. I'm fine. I'll have a doctor look at it, but it's not cancer.*

Rachel got out of the tub, dried herself, and made a telephone call.

'Betty Richman Model Agency.'

'I'd like to speak to Betty Richman. Please tell her it's Rachel Stevens.'

A moment later Betty Richman was on the line.

'Rachel! It's great to hear from you. Are you all right?'

'Of course I am. Why do you ask?'

'Well, you cut the Rio shoot short, and I thought that maybe –'

Rachel laughed. 'No, no. I was just tired, Betty. I'm eager to go to work again.'

'That's great news. Everyone's been trying to book you.'

'Well, I'm ready. What's on the agenda?'

'Hold on a moment.'

A minute later Betty Richman was back on the line. 'The next shoot is in Aruba. It starts next week. That gives you plenty of time. They've been asking for you.'

'I love Aruba. Book me for it.'

'You've got it. I'm glad you're feeling better.'

'I feel great.'

'I'll send all the details.'

At two o'clock the following afternoon, Rachel had an appointment with Dr Graham Elgin.

'Good afternoon, Dr Elgin.'

'And what can I do for you?'

'I have a small cyst in my right breast and –'

'Oh, you've seen a doctor?'

'No, but I know what it is. It's just a little cyst. I know my body. I'd like you to use microsurgery to get it out.' She smiled. 'I'm a model. I can't afford to have a scar. With just a tiny blemish, I can cover it with makeup. I'm leaving next week for Aruba, so would it be possible to schedule the operation tomorrow or the next day?'

Dr Elgin was studying her. Considering the situation, she seemed unnaturally calm. 'Let me examine you first, then I'll have to do a biopsy. But yes, we can schedule the operation within the week, if necessary.'

Rachel was beaming. 'Wonderful.'

Dr Elgin stood up. 'Let's go into the other room, shall we? I'll have the nurse bring you a hospital gown.'

Fifteen minutes later, with a nurse looking on, Dr Elgin was palpating the lump in Rachel's breast.

'I told you, Doctor, it's just a cyst.'

'Well, to be certain, Miss Stevens, I'd like to do the biopsy. I can do it right here.'

Rachel tried not to wince as Dr Elgin inserted a thin needle into the side of her breast to draw out tissue.

'All finished. That wasn't too bad, was it?'

'No. How soon . . . ?'

'I'll send this in to the lab, and I can have a preliminary cytology report tomorrow morning.'

Rachel smiled. 'Good. I'm going home to pack for Aruba.'

*

When Rachel got home, the first thing she did was take out two suitcases and lay them on the bed. She went to the closet and started collecting clothes to take to Aruba.

Jeanette Rhodes, her cleaning woman, came into the bedroom.

'Miss Stevens, are you going away again?'

'Yes.'

'Where are you going this time?'

'To Aruba.'

'Where's that?'

'It's a beautiful island in the Caribbean Sea, just north of Venezuela. It's a paradise. Great beaches, beautiful hotels, and wonderful food.'

'Sounds great.'

'By the way, Jeanette, while I'm gone, I'd like you to come in three times a week.'

'Of course.'

At nine o'clock the following morning, the phone rang.

'Miss Stevens?'

'Yes.'

'This is Dr Elgin.'

'Hello, Doctor. Were you able to schedule the operation?'

'Miss Stevens, I just got the cytology report. I'd like you to come into the office so we can –'

'No. I want to hear it now, Doctor.'

There was a slight hesitation. 'I don't like to discuss this sort of thing on the phone, but I'm afraid the preliminary report shows you do have cancer.'

Jeff was in the middle of writing his sports column when the phone rang. He picked it up. 'Hello?'

'Jeff . . .' She was crying.

'Rachel, is that you? What's the matter? What's happened?'

'I – I have breast cancer.'

'Oh, my God. How serious is it?'

'I don't know yet. I have to have a mammogram. Jeff, I can't face this alone. I know I'm asking a lot, but could you come down here?'

'Rachel, I – I'm afraid I –'

'Just for a day. Just till I . . . know.' She was crying again.

'Rachel . . .' He was torn. 'I'll try. I'll call you later.'

She was sobbing too hard to speak.

When Dana returned from a production meeting, she said, 'Olivia, make a reservation for me on a morning plane to Aspen, Colorado. Get me into a hotel. Oh, and I'll want a car rental.'

'Right. Mr Connors is waiting for you in your office.'

'Thanks.' Dana walked inside. Jeff was standing there looking out the window. 'Hi, darling.'

He turned around. 'Hi, Dana.'

There was a strange expression on his face. Dana looked at him, concerned. 'Are you all right?'

'That's a two-part question,' he said heavily. 'Yes and no.'

'Sit down,' Dana said. She took a chair opposite him. 'What's wrong?'

He let out a deep breath. 'Rachel has breast cancer.'

She felt a little shock. 'I – I'm so sorry. Is she going to be all right?'

'She called this morning. They're going to let her know how serious it is. She's panicky. She wants me to come to Florida to help her face the news. I wanted to talk to you first.'

Dana walked over to Jeff and put her arms around him. 'Of course you must go.' Dana remembered the luncheon with Rachel and how wonderful she had been.

'I'll be back in a day or two.'

Jeff was in Matt Baker's office.

'I have an emergency situation, Matt. I have to leave for a few days.'

'Are you okay, Jeff?'

'Yes. It's Rachel.'

'Your ex?'

Jeff nodded. 'She just learned she has cancer.'

'I'm sorry.'

'Anyway, she needs a little moral support. I want to fly to Florida this afternoon.'

'You go ahead. I'll have Maury Falstein fill in for you. Let me know how it goes.'

'I will. Thanks, Matt.'

Two hours later Jeff was on an airplane to Miami.

Dana's most immediate problem was Kemal. *I can't go to Aspen without having someone reliable here to take care of him*, Dana thought. *But who can handle cleaning and laundry and the most ornery little boy in the world?*

She telephoned Pamela Hudson. 'I'm so sorry to bother you, Pamela, but I have to leave town for a little while, and I need someone to stay with Kemal. Would you happen to know of a good housekeeper with the patience of a saint?'

There was a moment's silence. 'It just so happens that I do. Her name is Mary Rowane Daley, and she worked for us years ago. She's a treasure. Let me find her and have her call you.'

'Thanks,' Dana said.

An hour later Olivia said, 'Dana, there's a Mary Daley on the phone for you.'

Dana picked up the phone. 'Mrs Daley?'

'Yes. This is herself.' The warm voice had a rich Irish brogue. 'Mrs Hudson said you might be needing someone to take care of your son.'

'That's right,' Dana said. 'I have to go out of town for a day or two. I wonder if you could drop by early tomorrow morning – say, seven o'clock – so we can talk?'

'It's sure I can. As luck would have it, I'm free at the moment.'

Dana gave Mrs Daley her address.

'I'll be there, Miss Evans.'

Mary Daley arrived the next morning promptly at seven. She appeared to be in her fifties, a dumpling of a woman, with a cheery manner and a bright smile. She shook hands with Dana.

'I'm very glad to meet you, Miss Evans. I watch you on the TV when I can.'

'Thank you.'

'And where's the young lad of the house?'

Dana called out, 'Kemal.'

A moment later Kemal came out of his room. He looked at Mrs Daley and his expression said *Freak*.

Mrs Daley smiled. 'Kemal, is it? I've never met anyone named Kemal before. You look like a young devil.' She walked over to him. 'You must tell me all the favorite things you like to eat. I'm a grand cook. We're going to have a good time together, Kemal.'

I hope so, Dana thought prayerfully. 'Mrs Daley, will you be able to stay here with Kemal while I'm away?'

'Certainly, Miss Evans.'

'That's wonderful,' Dana said gratefully. 'I'm afraid there isn't too much room. The sleeping accommodations are –'

Mrs Daley smiled. 'Don't you worry. That fold-out couch will do nicely.'

Dana breathed a sigh of relief. She looked at her watch. 'Why don't you come with me to drop Kemal off at school? Then you can pick him up at one-forty-five.'

'That will be fine.'

Kemal turned to Dana. 'You're going to come back, aren't you, Dana?'

Dana put her arms around him. 'Of course I'm going to come back to you, darling.'

'When?'

'I'll be back in a few days.' *With some answers.*

When Dana arrived at the studio, on her desk was a small, beautifully wrapped package. She looked at it, curious, and opened it. Inside was a lovely gold pen. The card read 'Dear Dana, have a safe trip.' It was signed *The Gang.*

Thoughtful. Dana put it into her purse.

*

At the same time Dana was boarding a plane, a man in a workman's outfit rang the bell of the Whartons' former apartment. The door opened and the new tenant looked at him, nodded, and closed the door. The man moved on to Dana's apartment and rang the bell.

Mrs Daley opened the door. 'Yes?'

'Miss Evans sent me to repair her TV set.'

'Very well. Come in.'

Mrs Daley watched the man go to the television set and start to work.

Twelve

Rachel Stevens was at Miami International Airport to meet Jeff when his plane arrived.

My God, she's so beautiful, Jeff thought. *I can't believe she's sick.*

Rachel threw her arms around him. 'Oh, Jeff! Thank you for coming.'

'You look amazing,' Jeff assured her. They walked toward a waiting limousine.

'All this will turn out to be nothing. You'll see.'

'Of course.'

On the drive home, Rachel asked, 'How is Dana?'

He hesitated. With Rachel so ill, he didn't want to parade his own happiness. 'She's fine.'

'You're lucky to have her. Did you know I'm scheduled to do a shoot in Aruba next week?'

'*Aruba?*'

'Yes.' She went on, 'Do you know why I accepted that job? Because we honeymooned there. What was the name of the hotel we stayed at?'

'The Oranjestad.'

'It was beautiful, wasn't it? And what was the name of that mountain we climbed?'

'The Hooiberg.'

Rachel smiled and said softly, 'You haven't forgotten, have you?'

'People don't usually forget their honeymoon, Rachel.'

She put her hand on Jeff's arm. 'It was heaven, wasn't it? I've never seen such incredible white beaches.'

Jeff smiled. 'And you were afraid to get a tan. You wrapped yourself up like a mummy.'

There was a moment of silence. 'That's one of my deepest regrets, Jeff.'

He looked at her, not understanding. 'What?'

'Our not having a – never mind.' She looked at him and said quietly, 'I loved being with you in Aruba.'

Jeff said evasively, 'It's a great place. Fishing, windsurfing, snorkeling, tennis, golf . . .'

'And we didn't have time for any of them, did we?'

Jeff laughed. 'No.'

'I'm having a mammogram in the morning. I don't want to be alone when they do it. Will you come with me?'

'Of course, Rachel.'

When they arrived at Rachel's home, Jeff carried his bags into the spacious living room and looked around. 'Nice. Very nice.'

She put her arms around him. 'Thanks, Jeff.'
He could feel her trembling.

The mammogram took place at Tower Imaging in downtown Miami. Jeff stayed in the waiting area while a nurse took Rachel to a room to change into a hospital gown and then escorted her to an examination room for X rays.

'This will take about fifteen minutes, Miss Stevens. Are you ready?'

'Yes. How soon can I get the results?'

'That will have to come from your oncologist. He should have them tomorrow.'

Tomorrow.

The oncologist's name was Scott Young. Jeff and Rachel walked into his office and sat down.

The doctor looked at Rachel a moment and said, 'I'm sorry to say I have bad news for you, Miss Stevens.'

Rachel gripped Jeff's hand. 'Oh?'

'The results of your biopsy and mammogram show that you have an invasive carcinoma.'

Rachel's face turned white. 'What – what does that mean?'

'I'm afraid it means you need a mastectomy.'

'No!' It came out instinctively. 'You can't – I mean, there must be some other way.'

171

'I'm afraid,' Dr Young said gently, 'it's gone too far.'

Rachel was silent for a moment. 'I can't do it right away. You see, I'm scheduled to do a photographic shoot in Aruba next week. I can do it after that.'

Jeff was studying the worried expression on the doctor's face. 'When would you suggest she have it, Dr Young?'

He turned to Jeff. 'As soon as possible.'

Jeff looked at Rachel. She was trying hard not to cry. When she spoke, her voice was trembling. 'I'd like a second opinion.'

'Of course.'

Dr Aaron Cameron said, 'I'm afraid I've come to the same conclusion as Dr Young. I'd recommend a mastectomy.'

Rachel tried to keep her voice level. 'Thank you, Doctor.' She took Jeff's hand and squeezed it. 'I guess that's it, isn't it?'

Dr Young was waiting for them.

'It looks like you were right,' Rachel said. 'I just can't –' There was a long, sad silence. Finally Rachel whispered, 'All right. If you're sure it's – it's necessary.'

'We'll make you as comfortable as possible,' Dr Young said. 'Before I operate, I'll bring in a plastic surgeon to discuss the reconstruction of your breast with you. We can do miracles today.'

Jeff put his arms around her as Rachel burst into tears.

There were no direct flights from Washington, DC, to Aspen. Dana boarded a Delta Airlines flight to Denver, where she changed to a United Express plane. Later, she had no memory of the journey. Her mind was filled with thoughts of Rachel and the torment she must be going through. *I'm glad that Jeff will be there to make it easier for her*. And Dana was worried about Kemal. *What if Mrs Daley quits before I come back? I have* –

The flight attendant's voice came over the loud-speaker. 'We will be landing in Aspen in just a few minutes. Please see that your seat belt is fastened and return your seat back to the upright position.'

Dana began to concentrate on what lay ahead of her.

Elliot Cromwell walked into Matt Baker's office.

'I understand Dana's not doing the broadcasts tonight.'

'That's right. She's in Aspen.'

'Following up on her Taylor Winthrop theory?'

'Yeah.'

'I want you to keep me informed.'

'Right.' Matt watched Cromwell leave and thought, *He's really taken an interest in Dana.*

When Dana disembarked, she headed for the car-rental counter. Inside the terminal, Dr Carl Ramsey was saying to the clerk behind the counter, 'But I reserved a car a week ago.'

The clerk said apologetically, 'I know, Dr Ramsey, but I'm afraid there's been a mix-up. We don't have a single car available. There's an airport bus outside, or I can call a taxi for –'

'Never mind,' the doctor said, and stormed out.

Dana entered the airport lobby and walked up to the rental desk. 'I have a reservation,' she said. 'Dana Evans.'

The clerk smiled. 'Yes, Miss Evans. We've been expecting you.' He gave her a form to sign and handed her some keys. 'It's a white Lexus in parking space one.'

'Thank you. Can you tell me how to get to the Little Nell Hotel?'

'You can't miss it. It's right in the middle of town. Six-seventy-five East Durant Avenue. I'm sure you'll enjoy it.'

'Thank you,' Dana said.

The clerk watched her walk out the door. *What the hell is going on?* he wondered.

*

The Little Nell Hotel was built in an elegant chalet style, nestled at the base of the picturesque Aspen mountains. The lobby had a floor-to-ceiling fireplace with a cheery fire constantly burning in the winter, and large windows with views of the snow-capped Rockies. Guests in ski clothes were sitting around on couches and oversize chairs, relaxing. Dana looked around and thought, *Jeff would love this. Maybe we'll come up here . . .*

When Dana had finished signing in, she said to the clerk, 'Do you happen to know where the Taylor Winthrop home is?'

He looked at her strangely. 'The Taylor Winthrop home? It's not there anymore. It burned to the ground.'

Dana said, 'I know. I just wanted to see –'

'There's nothing up there now but a lot of ashes, but if you want to see it, you go out east to Conundrum Creek Valley. That's about six miles from here.'

'Thank you,' Dana said. 'Would you have my bags taken to my room, please?'

'Certainly, Miss Evans.'

Dana headed back to the car.

The site of the Taylor Winthrop home in Conundrum Creek Valley was surrounded by National Forest lands. The house had been a one-story dwelling made of native stone and redwood, set in a lovely, secluded location with a large beaver pond and a creek running through the property. The view was spectacular. And in the midst of all that beauty, like an obscene scar, were the burned-out remnants of the house in which two people had died.

Dana strolled around the grounds, visualizing what had once been there. It had obviously been a very large one-story house. There must have been many doors and windows at ground level.

And yet the Winthrops had not been able to escape through any of them. *I think I'd better visit the fire department.*

As Dana walked into the fire station, a man approached her. He was in his thirties, tall, tan, and athletic looking. *He probably lives on the ski slopes,* Dana thought.

'Can I help you, ma'am?'

Dana said, 'I read about the Taylor Winthrop house burning down and I was curious about it.'

'Yeah. That was a year ago. Probably the worst thing that ever happened in this town.'

'What time of day did it happen?'

If he thought her question odd, he gave no sign. 'It was the middle of the night. We got the call at three AM. Our trucks were out there by three-fifteen, but it was too late. The house was burning like a torch. We didn't know anybody was inside until later when we put down the fire and found

176

the two bodies. That was a heartbreaking moment, let me tell you.'

'Do you have any idea what started the fire?'

He nodded. 'Oh, yeah. It was an electrical problem.'

'What kind of electrical problem?'

'We don't know exactly, but the day before the fire, someone called an electrician to the house to fix it.'

'But you don't know what the problem was?'

'I think there was something wrong with the fire alarm system.'

Dana tried to sound casual. 'The electrician who went out to fix it – would you happen to have his name?'

'No. I guess the police would have it.'

'Thanks.'

He looked at Dana curiously. 'Why are you so interested in this?'

Dana said earnestly, 'I'm writing an article about ski-resort fires around the country.'

The Aspen police station was a redbrick one-story building, half a dozen blocks from Dana's hotel.

The officer at his desk looked up and exclaimed, 'You're Dana Evans, the TV lady?'

'Yes.'

'I'm Captain Turner. What can I do for you, Miss Evans?'

'I'm curious about the fire that killed Taylor Winthrop and his wife.'

'My God, what a tragedy that was. The folks here are still in shock.'

'I can understand that.'

'Yep. Too bad they weren't able to save them.'

'I understand the fire started from some kind of electrical problem?'

'That's right.'

'Could it have been arson?'

Captain Turner frowned. 'Arson? No, no. It was electrical failure.'

'I'd like to talk to the electrician who went out there the day before the fire. Do you have his name?'

'I'm sure it's here in our files. Want me to check it out?'

'I'd appreciate it.'

Captain Turner picked up the phone and spoke into it briefly, then turned back to Dana. 'First time in Aspen?'

'Yes.'

'Great place. Do you ski?'

'No.' *But Jeff does. When we come up here . . .*

A clerk walked up and handed Captain Turner a sheet of paper. He passed it on to Dana. It read: *Al Larson Electrical Company, Bill Kelly.*

'They're just down the street.'

'Thank you so much, Captain Turner.'

'My pleasure.'

As Dana left the building, a man across the street turned away and spoke into a cell phone.

The Al Larson Electrical Company was in a small gray cement building. A clone of the man at the fire department, tanned and athletic looking, was seated at a desk. He stood up as Dana came in. 'Morning.'

'Morning,' Dana said. 'I'd like to talk to Bill Kelly.'

The man grunted. 'So would I.'

'I beg your pardon?'

'Kelly. He disappeared almost a year ago.'

'Disappeared?'

'Yeah, just left. Didn't say a word. Didn't even stop to pick up his pay.'

Dana said slowly, 'Do you remember exactly when that was?'

'Sure do. It was the morning of that fire. The big one. You know, the one the Winthrops died in.'

Dana felt a chill. 'I see. And you have no idea where Mr Kelly is?'

'Nope. Like I said, he just disappeared.'

The remote island at the tip of South America had been buzzing all morning with the arrival of jet planes. Now it was time for the meeting, and the twenty-odd participants were seated in a guarded, newly built structure that was scheduled to be demolished as soon as the meeting was over. The speaker stepped to the front of the room.

'Welcome. I am happy to see many familiar faces here and some new friends. Before we begin our business, some of you are concerned about a problem that has arisen. A traitor is among us, threatening to expose us. We do not know who it is yet. But I assure you that he will be caught quickly, and that he will suffer the fate of all traitors. Nothing and no one can stand in our way.'

There were murmurs of surprise from the crowd.

'Now. Let us begin our silent bid. There are sixteen packages today. Let's start with two billion. Do I have the first bid? Yes. Two billion dollars. Do I have three?'

Thirteen

That evening when Dana returned to her room, she stopped in sudden alarm. Everything looked the same, and yet . . . she had a feeling something was different. Had her things been moved? *It's Chicken Little time,* Dana thought wryly. She picked up the telephone and called home.

Mrs Daley answered the phone. 'The Evans residence.'

Thank God she was still there. 'Mrs Daley?'

'Miss Evans!'

'Good evening. How is Kemal?'

'Well, he can be a bit of a devil, but I can handle him. My boys were like that.'

'Then everything is . . . all right?'

'Oh, yes.'

Dana's sigh was of pure relief. 'Could I speak to him?'

'Certainly.' Dana heard her call, 'Kemal, it's your mother.'

A moment later Kemal was on the phone. 'Hi, Dana.'

'Hi, Kemal. How are you doing, pal?'

'Cool.'

'How was school?'

'It was okay.'

'And are you getting along all right with Mrs Daley?'

'Yes, she's rad.'

She's more than rad, Dana thought. *She's a miracle.*

'When are you coming home, Dana?'

'I'll be home tomorrow. Have you had your dinner?'

'Yes. It wasn't too bad, actually.'

Dana was almost tempted to say, *Is that you, Kemal?* She was thrilled at the change in him.

'All right, darling. I'll see you tomorrow. Good night.'

'Good night, Dana.'

As Dana was getting ready for bed, her cell phone rang. She picked it up. 'Hello.'

'Dana?'

She felt a surge of joy. 'Jeff! Oh, Jeff!' She blessed the day she had purchased the international cell phone.

'I had to call you to tell you I miss you like bloody hell.'

'I miss you, too. Are you in Florida?'

'Yes.'

'How are things there?'

'Not good.' She heard the hesitation in his voice. 'In fact, it's pretty bad. Tomorrow Rachel is scheduled to have a mastectomy.'

'Oh, no!'

'She's not handling it well.'

'I'm so sorry.'

'I know. It's rotten luck. Darling, I can't wait to get back to you. Did I ever tell you I'm mad about you?'

'I'm mad about you, darling.'

'Is there anything you need, Dana?'

You. 'No.'

'How's Kemal?'

'He's getting along fine. I have a new housekeeper he likes.'

'That's good news. I can't wait until we're all together again.'

'Neither can I.'

'You take care of yourself.'

'I will. And I can't tell you how sorry I am about Rachel.'

'I'll tell her. Good night, baby.'

'Good night.'

Dana opened her suitcase and took out a shirt of Jeff's that she had taken from the apartment. She put it on under her night-gown and hugged it to her. *Good night, darling.*

*

Early the following morning Dana flew back to Washington. She stopped at the apartment before going to the office and was greeted by a cheerful Mrs Daley.

'It's grand to see you back, Miss Evans. That boy of yours is wearing me out.' But it was said with a twinkle.

'I hope he isn't giving you too much trouble.'

'Trouble? Not one bit. I'm pleased at how well he's doing with his new arm.'

Dana looked at her in surprise. 'He's *wearing* it?'

'Of course. He wears it to school.'

'That's wonderful. I'm very pleased.' She looked at her watch. 'I have to get to the studio. I'll be back this afternoon to see Kemal.'

'He'll be so glad to see you. He misses you, you know. You go on ahead. I'll unpack your bags for you.'

'Thank you, Mrs Daley.'

Dana was in Matt's office telling him what she had learned in Aspen.

He was looking at her incredulously. 'The day after the fire, the electrician just goddamn *disappeared*?'

'Without collecting his paycheck.'

'And he was at the Winthrop house the day before the fire happened.'

'Yes.'

184

Matt shook his head. 'It's like *Alice in Wonderland*. This gets curiouser and curiouser.'

'Matt, Paul Winthrop was the next one in the family to die. He was killed in France not long after the fire. I'd like to go there. I want to see if there were any witnesses to his automobile accident.'

'Right.' Then Matt added, 'Elliot Cromwell has been asking about you. He wants you to take care of yourself.'

'That's two of us,' Dana replied.

When Kemal arrived home from school, Dana was waiting for him. Kemal was wearing his new arm, and it seemed to Dana that he appeared to be much calmer.

'You're back.' He gave her a hug.

'Hello, darling. I've missed you. How was school?'

'Not bad. How was your trip?'

'It was fine. I brought something back for you.' She handed Kemal a Native American handwoven satchel and a pair of leather moccasins she had picked up in Aspen. The next part was difficult. 'Kemal, I'm afraid I'm going to have to go away again for a few days.'

Dana braced herself for his reaction, but all Kemal said was 'Okay.'

No sign of an outburst.

'I'll bring you back a nice present.'

'One for every day you're away?'

Dana smiled. 'You're supposed to be in seventh grade, not law school.'

He was comfortably settled in an armchair, with the television set on and a scotch in his hand. On the screen, Dana and Kemal were at the dinner table and Mrs Daley was serving what looked like an Irish stew.

'This is delicious,' Dana said.

'Thank you. I'm glad you like it.'

'I told you she was a good cook,' Kemal said.

It was like being in the same room with them, he thought, instead of watching them from the apartment next door.

'Tell me about school,' Dana said.

'I like my new teachers. My math teacher is tight . . .'

'That's great.'

'The boys are a lot nicer at this school. They think my new arm is rad.'

'I'll bet they do.'

'One of the girls in my class is really pretty. I think she likes me. Her name is Lizzy.'

'Do you like her, darling?'

'Yeah. She's phat.'

He's growing up, Dana thought with an unexpected pang. When it was time, Kemal went to bed and Dana walked into the kitchen to see Mrs Daley.

'Kemal seems so . . . so peaceful. I can't tell you how appreciative I am,' Dana said.

'You're doing *me* a favor.' Mrs Daley smiled. 'It's like having one of my own children back. They're all grown now, you know. Kemal and I are having a grand time.'

'I'm glad.'

Dana waited up until midnight, and when Jeff still had not called, she went to bed. She lay there wondering what Jeff was doing, whether he was making love to Rachel, and she was ashamed of herself for her thoughts.

The man in the next apartment reported in. 'All quiet.'

Her cell phone rang.

'Jeff, darling. Where are you?'

'I'm at Doctors Hospital in Florida. The mastectomy is over. The oncologist is still running tests.'

'Oh, Jeff! I hope it hasn't spread.'

'I hope so, too. Rachel wants me to stay with her for a few days. I wanted to ask you if –'

'Of course. You must.'

'It will only be for a little while. I'll call Matt and tell him. Anything exciting going on there?'

For an instant Dana was tempted to tell Jeff about Aspen and that she was going ahead with the investigation. *He has enough on his mind.* 'No,' Dana said. 'All quiet.'

'Give my love to Kemal. The rest is for you.'

Jeff replaced the receiver. A nurse came up to him.

'Mr Connors? Dr Young would like to see you.'

'The operation went well,' Dr Young told Jeff, 'but she will need a lot of emotional support. She is going to feel less of a woman. When she wakes up, she'll be panicky. You have to let her know that it's all right to be afraid.'

'I understand,' Jeff said.

'And her fear and depression are going to start all over again when we begin radiation treatments to try to stop the spread of the cancer. That can be very traumatic.'

Jeff sat there, thinking about what lay ahead.

'Does she have someone to take care of her?'

'Me.' And as Jeff said it, he realized he was the only one Rachel had.

The Air France flight to Nice was uneventful. Dana turned on her laptop computer to reexamine the information she had collected so far. Provocative, but certainly not conclusive. *Proof*, Dana thought. *There is no story without proof. If I can –*

'Nice flight, isn't it?'

Dana turned to the man seated next to her. He

was tall and attractive and had a French accent.

'Yes, it is.'

'Have you been to France before?'

'No,' Dana said. 'This is my first time.'

He smiled. 'Ah, you are in for a treat. It is a magical country.' He smiled soulfully and leaned close to her. 'Do you have friends to show you around?'

'I'm meeting my husband and three children,' Dana said.

'*Dommage.*' He nodded, turned away, and picked up his copy of *France-Soir*.

Dana went back to her computer. An article caught her eye. Paul Winthrop, who had died in an automobile accident, had had a hobby.

Racing cars.

When the Air France plane landed at the Nice airport, Dana went into the busy terminal to the car-rental office. 'My name is Dana Evans. I have a –'

The clerk looked up. 'Ah! Miss Evans. Your car is ready.' He handed her a form. 'Just sign this.'

Now that's real service, Dana thought. 'I'll need a map of the south of France. Would you happen to –?'

'Of course, *mademoiselle*.' He reached behind the counter and selected a map. '*Voilà.*' He stood there watching Dana leave.

*

In the executive tower of WTN, Elliot Cromwell was saying, 'Where is Dana now, Matt?'

'She's in France.'

'Is she making any progress?'

'It's too early.'

'I worry about her. I think maybe she's traveling too much. Today travel can be dangerous.' He hesitated. 'Very dangerous.'

The air in Nice was cold and crisp, and Dana wondered what the weather had been like on the day Paul Winthrop was killed. She got into the Citroën waiting for her and started driving up the Grande Corniche, passing picturesque little villages along the way.

The accident had happened just north of Beausoleil, on the highway at Roquebrune-Cap-Martin, a resort that overlooked the Mediterranean Sea.

As Dana approached the village, she slowed down, observing the sharp, precipitous curves, wondering which one Paul Winthrop had gone over. What had Paul Winthrop been doing here? Was he meeting someone? Was he taking part in a race? Was he on vacation? Business?

Roquebrune-Cap-Martin is a medieval village with an ancient castle, church, historic caves, and luxurious villas that dot the landscape. Dana drove to the center, parked the car, and went to look for the police station. She stopped a man coming out of a shop.

'Excuse me, can you tell me where the police station is?'

'Je ne parle pas anglais, j'ai peur de ne pouvoir vous aider, mais –'

'Police. Police.'

'Ah, oui.' He pointed. 'La deuxième rue à gauche.'

'Merci.'

'De rien.'

The police station was in an old, crumbling, white-walled building. Inside a middle-aged, uniformed policeman sat behind a desk. He looked up as Dana walked in.

'Bonjour, madame.'

'Bonjour.'

'Comment puis-je vous aider?'

'Do you speak English?'

He thought about it. 'Yes,' he said reluctantly.

'I would like to speak to whoever is in charge here.'

He looked at her a moment, a puzzled expression on his face. Then he suddenly smiled. 'Ah, Commandant Frasier. Oui. One moment.' He picked up a telephone and spoke into it. He nodded and turned to Dana. He pointed down the corridor. 'La première porte.'

'Thank you.' Dana walked down the corridor until she reached the first door. Commandant

Frasier's office was small and neat. The commandant was a dapper man with a little mustache and inquisitive brown eyes. He stood up as Dana entered.

'Good afternoon, Commandant.'

'*Bonjour, mademoiselle*. In what manner can I be of assistance?'

'I'm Dana Evans. I'm doing a story for station WTN in Washington, DC, about the Winthrop family. I understand that Paul Winthrop was killed in an accident around here?'

'*Oui. Terrible! Terrible*. One must be so careful driving the Grande Corniche. It can be *très dangereux*.'

'I heard that Paul Winthrop was killed during a race and –'

'*Non*. There was no race that day.'

'There wasn't?'

'*Non, mademoiselle*. I myself was personally on duty when the accident occurred.'

'I see. Was Mr Winthrop in his car alone?'

'*Oui*.'

'Commandant Frasier, did they do an autopsy?'

'*Oui*. Of course.'

'Was there any alcohol in Paul Winthrop's blood?'

Commandant Frasier shook his head. '*Non*.'

'Drugs?'

'*Non*.'

'Do you remember what the weather was like that day?'

'*Oui. Il pleuvait.* It made rain.'

Dana had one last question, but she asked it without any hope. 'I don't suppose there were any witnesses?'

'*Mais oui, il y en avait.*'

Dana was staring at him, her pulse quickening. 'There were?'

'One witness. He was driving behind Winthrop's car and saw the accident happen.'

Dana felt a quick sense of excitement. 'I would appreciate it very much if you would give me the witness's name,' Dana said. 'I want to talk to him.'

He nodded. 'I see no harm.' He called out, 'Alexandre!' and a moment later his assistant came hurrying in.

'*Oui, Commandant?*'

'*Apportez-moi le dossier de l'accident Winthrop.*'

'*Tout de suite.*' He hurried out of the room.

Commandant Frasier turned to Dana. 'Such an unfortunate family. Life is *très fragile.*' He looked at Dana and smiled. 'One must take one's pleasure when he can.' He added subtly, 'Or when *she* can. Are you alone here, *mademoiselle*?'

'No, my husband and children are waiting for me.'

'*Dommage.*'

Commandant Frasier's assistant returned with a sheaf of papers and the commandant scanned the papers, nodded, and looked up at Dana.

'The witness to the accident was an American

tourist, Ralph Benjamin. According to his statement, he was driving behind Paul Winthrop when he saw a *chien* – a dog – run in front of Winthrop's car. Winthrop turned the wheel to not hit him, went into a big skid, and plunged off the cliff and crashed into the sea. According to the coroner's report, Winthrop died instantly.'

'Do you have Mr Benjamin's address?' Dana asked hopefully.

'*Oui.*' He glanced at the paper again. 'He lives in America. Richfield, Utah. Four-twenty Turk Street.' Commandant Frasier wrote the address down and handed it to Dana.

She tried hard to control her excitement. 'Thank you so much.'

'*Avec plaisir.*' He looked at Dana's bare ring finger. 'And, *madame*?'

'Yes?'

'Say hello to your husband and children for me.'

Dana telephoned Matt.

'Matt,' she said excitedly. 'I found a witness to Paul Winthrop's accident. I'm going to interview him.'

'That's great. Where is he?'

'In Utah. Richfield. I should be back in Washington right after that.'

'All right. By the way, Jeff called.'

'Yes?'

'You know he's in Florida with his ex-wife.' He sounded disapproving.

'I know. She's very ill.'

'If Jeff stays away much longer, I'm going to have to ask him to take a leave of absence.'

'I'm sure he'll be back very soon.' She wished she believed it.

'Right. Good luck with the witness.'

'Thanks, Matt.'

Dana's next call was to Kemal. Mrs Daley answered the phone.

'Miss Evans's residence.'

'Good evening, Mrs Daley. Is everything all right there?' Dana was holding her breath.

'Well, your son almost burned down the kitchen helping me cook dinner last night.' She laughed. 'But other than that, he's fine.'

Dana said a silent prayer of thanks. 'That's great.' *The woman really is a miracle worker*, Dana thought.

'Will you be coming home now? I can prepare dinner and –'

'I have to make one more stop,' Dana said. 'I'll be home in two days. May I talk to Kemal?'

'He's asleep. Shall I wake him up?'

'No, no.' Dana looked at her watch. It was only four o'clock in Washington. 'He's taking a nap?'

She heard Mrs Daley's warm laugh. 'Yes. The lad

has had a long day. He's working hard, and he's playing hard.'

'You give him my love. I'll see him soon.'

I have to make one more stop. I'll be home in two days.

May I talk to Kemal?

He's asleep. Shall I wake him up?

No, no. He's taking a nap?

Yes. The lad has had a long day. He's working hard, and he's playing hard.

You give him my love. I'll see him soon.

Tape ends.

Richfield, Utah, is a comfortable, residential town set in a bowl in the middle of the Monroe mountain range. Dana stopped at a filling station and got directions to the address Commandant Frasier had given her.

Ralph Benjamin's home was a weatherbeaten one-story house that stood in the middle of a block of identical houses.

Dana parked the rental car, walked up to the front door, and rang the doorbell. The door opened and a middle-aged white-haired woman in an apron stood there. 'Can I help you?'

'I would like to see Ralph Benjamin,' Dana said.

The woman studied Dana curiously. 'Is he expecting you?'

'No. I – I just happened to be passing by, and I thought I'd drop in for a moment. Is he here?'

'Yes. Come in.'

'Thank you.' Dana stepped inside and followed the woman into the living room.

'Ralph, you have a visitor.'

Ralph Benjamin rose from a rocking chair and moved toward Dana. 'Hello? Do I know you?'

Dana stood there, frozen. Ralph Benjamin was blind.

Fourteen

Dana and Matt Baker were in the conference room at WTN.

'Ralph Benjamin was in France visiting his son,' Dana was explaining. 'One day his briefcase disappeared from his hotel room. It reappeared the next day, but his passport was missing. Matt, the man who stole it and took Benjamin's identity and told the police he was a witness to the accident is the man who murdered Paul Winthrop.'

Matt Baker was silent for a long time. When he spoke he said, 'It's time to call the police in on this, Dana. If you're right, we're looking for someone who cold-bloodedly murdered six people. I don't want you to be number seven. Elliot is worried about you, too. He thinks you're getting in too deep.'

'We can't bring the police in yet,' Dana protested. 'Everything is circumstantial. We have no proof. We have no idea who the killer is, and we have no motive.'

'I have a bad feeling about this. It's getting too dangerous. I don't want anything to happen to you.'

'I don't either,' Dana said earnestly.

'What's your next step?'

'Finding out what really happened to Julie Winthrop.'

'The operation was a success.'

Rachel opened her eyes slowly. She was lying in a sterile white hospital bed. Her eyes focused blearily on Jeff. 'Is it gone?'

'Rachel –'

'I'm afraid to feel.' She was fighting back tears. 'I'm not a woman anymore. No man will ever love me.'

He took her trembling hands in his. 'You're wrong. I never loved you because of your breasts, Rachel. I loved you because of who you are, a warm, wonderful human being.'

Rachel managed a tiny smile. 'We really did love each other, didn't we, Jeff?'

'Yes.'

'I wish . . .' She looked down at her chest, and her face constricted.

'We'll talk about this later.'

She squeezed his hand harder. 'I don't want to be alone, Jeff. Not until this is all over. Please don't leave me.'

'Rachel, I have to –'

'Not yet. I don't know what I'll do if you leave.'

A nurse came into the hospital room. 'Would you excuse us, Mr Connors?'

Rachel did not want to let go of Jeff's hand. 'Don't go.'

'I'll be back.'

Late that evening Dana's cell phone rang. She rushed across the room to pick it up. 'Dana.' It was Jeff.

She felt a little thrill when she heard his voice. 'Hello. How are you, darling?'

'I'm fine.'

'How is Rachel?'

'The operation went well, but Rachel's suicidal.'

'Jeff – a woman can't judge herself by her breasts or –'

'I know, but Rachel is not your average woman. She's been judged by her looks since she was fifteen. She's one of the highest-paid models in the world. Now she thinks all that is over for her. She feels like a freak. She believes she has nothing more to live for.'

'What are you going to do?'

'I'll stay with her for a few more days and help her get settled in her home. I talked to the doctor. He's still waiting for the test results to see whether they got it all. They think they'll need to follow up with chemotherapy treatments.'

There was nothing Dana could say.

'I miss you,' Jeff said.

'I miss you, my dearest. I have some Christmas presents for you.'

'Hold them for me.'

'I will.'

'Are you wiped out from all the traveling?'

'Not yet.'

'Make sure you leave your cell phone turned on,' Jeff said. 'I plan to make some obscene phone calls.'

Dana smiled. 'Promise?'

'Promise. Take care of yourself, darling.'

'You, too.' The conversation was over. Dana hung up and sat there for a long time, thinking about Jeff and Rachel. She got up and went into the kitchen.

Mrs Daley was saying to Kemal, 'More pancakes, darlin'?'

'Yes, thank you.'

Dana stood there watching the two of them. In the short time Mrs Daley had been there, Kemal had changed so much. He was calm and relaxed and happy. Dana felt a sharp pang of jealousy. *Maybe I'm the wrong person for him.* Guiltily, she remembered her long days and late nights at the television studio. *Maybe someone like Mrs Daley should have adopted him.* She shook herself out of it. *What's the matter with me? Kemal loves me.*

Dana sat down at the table. 'Still enjoying the new school?'

'It's cool.'

Dana took his hand. 'Kemal, I'm afraid I'm going to have to go away again.'

He said indifferently, 'That's okay.'

The pang of jealousy came back.

'Where are you off to now, Miss Evans?' Mrs Daley asked.

'Alaska.'

Mrs Daley was thoughtful for a moment. 'Watch out for those grizzly bears,' she advised.

The flight from Washington to Juneau, Alaska, took nine hours, with a stopover in Seattle. Inside the Juneau airport, Dana walked over to the car-rental counter.

'My name is Dana Evans. I –'

'Yes, Miss Evans. We have a nice Land Rover for you. Stall ten. Just sign here.'

The clerk handed her the keys and Dana walked around to the lot in back of the building. There were a dozen cars in numbered stalls. Dana walked over to stall ten. A man was kneeling in back of the car, working on the tailpipe of a white Land Rover. He looked up as Dana approached.

'Just tightening the tailpipe, miss. You're all set.' He rose.

'Thank you,' Dana said.

He watched her drive away.

In the basement of a government building, a man was looking at a digital map on a computer.

He watched the white Land Rover make a right turn.

'The subject is heading for Starr Hill.'

Juneau was a surprise to Dana. At first sight, it appeared to be a large city, but the narrow, winding streets gave Alaska's capital city the small-town atmosphere of a village nestled in the middle of an ice-age wilderness.

Dana checked into the popular Inn at the Waterfront, a former brothel located in the center of town.

'You're in time for some great skiing,' the hotel desk man told her. 'We're having a good snow season. Bring your own skis?'

'No, I –'

'Well, there's a ski shop right next door. I'm sure they can fix you up with anything you'd like.'

'Thank you,' Dana said. *It's a good place to start.* Dana unpacked and went into the ski shop.

The clerk in the shop was a nonstop talker. The moment Dana walked in he said, 'Hi. I'm Chad Donohoe. Well, you've sure come to the right place.' He indicated a batch of skis. 'We just got these Freeriders in. These babies can really handle the bumps and jumps.' He pointed to another section. 'Or – these are the Salomon X-Scream 9s. They're in big demand. Last year we ran out and couldn't get any more.' He saw the impatient expression on Dana's face and hurried over to the next group. 'If you prefer, we have the Vocal Vertigo G30 or the Atomic 10.20.' He looked at Dana expectantly. 'Which would you – ?'

'I came for some information.'

A disappointed look crossed his face. 'Information?'

'Yes. Did Julie Winthrop get her skis here?'

He studied Dana more closely. 'Yes. As a matter of fact, she used the top-of-the-line Volant Ti power skis. Loved them. Terrible thing that happened to her up at Eaglecrest.'

'Was Miss Winthrop a good skier?'

'Good? She was the best. She had a trophy case full of prizes.'

'Do you know if she was alone here?'

'Far as I know, she was.' He shook his head. 'What's so surprising is that she knew Eaglecrest like the back of her hand. Used to ski here every year. You'd think an accident like that couldn't happen to her, wouldn't you?'

Dana said slowly, 'Yes, I would.'

The Juneau Police Department was two blocks from the Inn at the Waterfront.

Dana stepped into a small reception office that contained the Alaska state flag, the Juneau flag, and the Stars and Stripes. There was a blue carpet, a blue couch, and a blue chair.

A uniformed officer asked, 'May I help you?'

'I'd like some information about Julie Winthrop's death.'

He frowned. 'The man you want to talk to is Bruce Bowler. He's head of Sea Dog Rescue. He has an office upstairs, but he's not in right now.'

'Do you know where I can find him?'

The officer looked at his watch. 'Right now you should be able to catch him at Hanger on the Wharf. That's down two blocks on Marine Way.'

'Thank you very much.'

Hanger on the Wharf was a large restaurant crowded with noontime diners.

The hostess said to Dana, 'I'm sorry, we don't have a table right now. There will be a twenty-minute wait if –'

'I'm looking for Mr Bruce Bowler. Do you –?'

The hostess nodded. 'Bruce? He's over at that table.'

Dana looked. There was a pleasant-faced, rugged-looking man in his early forties, seated alone.

'Thank you.' Dana made her way to the table. 'Mr Bowler?'

He looked up. 'Yes.'

'I'm Dana Evans. I need your help.'

He smiled. 'You're in luck. We have one room available. I'll call Judy.'

Dana looked at him, puzzled. 'I beg your pardon?'

'Aren't you asking about Cozy Log, our bed-and-breakfast inn?'

'No. I wanted to talk to you about Julie Winthrop.'

'Oh.' He was embarrassed. 'Sorry. Please sit down. Judy and I own a small inn outside of town. I thought you were looking for a room. Have you had lunch?'

'No, I –'

'Join me.' He had a nice smile.

'Thank you,' Dana said.

When Dana had ordered, Bruce Bowler said, 'What do you want to know about Julie Winthrop?'

'It's about her death. Was there any chance that it was not an accident?'

Bruce Bowler frowned. 'Are you asking if she could have committed suicide?'

'No. I'm asking if . . . if someone could have murdered her.'

He blinked. 'Murdered Julie? Not a chance. It was an accident.'

'Can you tell me what happened?'

'Sure.' Bruce Bowler was thoughtful for a moment, wondering where to begin. 'We have three different sets of slopes here. There's the beginners' slopes, the Muskeg, Dolly Varden, and Sourdough . . . There's the more difficult ones, Sluice Box, Mother Lode, and Sundance . . . There's the really tough ones, Insane, Spruce Chute, Hang Ten . . . And then there's Steep Chutes. That's the toughest.'

'And Julie Winthrop was skiing . . . ?'

'Steep Chutes.'

'So she was an expert skier?'

'She sure was,' Bruce Bowler said. He hesitated. 'That's what was so unusual.'

'What was?'

'Well, we have night skiing every Thursday from four PM to nine PM. There were a lot of skiers out there that night. They were all back by nine o'clock except Julie. We went looking for her. We found her body at the bottom of Steep Chutes. She had slammed into a tree. Had to have killed her instantly.'

Dana closed her eyes for an instant, feeling the horror and pain of it. 'So – so she was alone when the accident happened?'

'Yeah. Skiers usually travel together, but sometimes the best ones like to hotdog it by themselves. We have an area boundary marked here, and anyone who skis outside it does so at his own risk. Julie Winthrop was skiing outside that boundary, on a closed trail. Took us a good while to find her body.'

'Mr Bowler, what is the procedure when a skier is lost?'

'As soon as someone's reported missing, we start with a bastard search.'

'A bastard search?'

'We telephone friends to see if the skier is with them. We'll call a few bars. It's a quick-and-dirty search. That's to save our crews the trouble of conducting an all-out search for some drunk who's sitting stoned in a bar.'

'And if someone is really lost?' Dana asked.

'We get a physical description of the missing skier, his or her skiing ability, and the last-seen location. We always ask if they had a camera.'

'Why?'

'If they did, it gives us a clue to the scenic areas they might have gone to. We check to see what plans the skier might have had for transportation back to town. If our sweep doesn't turn anything up, then we assume that the missing skier is located outside the ski-area boundary. We notify the Alaska state troopers for search and rescue and they put a helicopter in the air. There are four people in each search party, and the civil air patrol joins in.'

'That's a lot of manpower.'

'Sure is. But remember, we have six hundred and thirty acres of skiing area around here, and we average forty searches a year. Most of them are successful.' Bruce Bowler looked out the window at the cold slate sky. 'I sure wish this one had been.' He turned back to Dana. 'Anyway, the ski patrol does a sweep every day after the lifts close.'

Dana said, 'I was told that Julie Winthrop was used to skiing the top of Eaglecrest.'

He nodded. 'That's right. But that's still no guarantee. Clouds can come in, you can get disoriented, or you can get plain unlucky. Poor Miss Winthrop got unlucky.'

'How did you find her body?'

'Mayday found her.'

'Mayday?'

'That's our top dog. The ski patrol works with black Labradors and shepherds. The dogs are pretty incredible. They work downwind, pick up a human scent, go up to the edge of the scent zone, and work the grid up and back. We sent up a bombardier to the scene of the accident, and when –'

'A bombardier?'

'Our snow machine. We brought Julie Winthrop's body back on a Stokes litter. The three-man ambulance crew checked her out with an EKG monitor and then took photographs and called a mortician. They took her body to Bartlett Regional Hospital.'

'And no one knows how the accident happened?'

He shrugged. 'All we know is she met an unfriendly giant spruce. I saw it. It wasn't a pretty sight.'

Dana looked at Bruce Bowler a moment. 'Would it be possible for me to see the top of Eaglecrest?'

'Why not? Let's finish lunch, and I'll take you up myself.'

They drove in a Jeep to the two-story lodge at the base of the mountain.

Bruce Bowler told Dana, 'This building is where we meet to make our search-and-rescue plans. We carry ski-rental equipment here and we have ski instructors for those who want them. We'll take this lift up to the top of the mountain.'

They slid onto the Ptarmigan chairlift, heading for the top of Eaglecrest. Dana was shivering.

'I should have warned you. For this kind of weather, you need propylene clothing, long underwear, and you have to dress in layers.'

Dana shivered. 'I'll r-remember.'

'This is the chairlift Julie Winthrop came up in. She had her backpack with her.'

'Her backpack?'

'Yes. They contain an avalanche shovel, a beacon that transmits up to fifty yards, and a probe pole.' He sighed. 'Of course, that doesn't help any when you slam into a tree.'

They were nearing the summit. As they reached the platform and they gingerly stepped off the chairs, a man at the top greeted them.

'What brings you up here, Bruce? Someone lost?'

'No. I'm just showing a friend the sights. This is Miss Evans.'

They exchanged hellos. Dana looked around. There was a warming hut that was almost lost in the heavy clouds. *Had Julie Winthrop gone in there before she went skiing? And was someone following her? Someone who was planning to kill her?*

Bruce Bowler turned to Dana. 'Ptarmigan here is top of the mountain. It's all downhill from here.'

Dana turned and looked at the unforgiving ground far, far below and shuddered.

'You look chilly, Miss Evans. I'd better take you down.'

'Thank you.'

Dana had just returned to the Inn at the Waterfront when there was a knock at her door. Dana opened it. A large, pale-faced man stood there.

'Miss Evans?'

'Yes.'

'Hi. My name is Nicholas Verdun. I'm from the *Juneau Empire* newspaper.'

'Yes?'

'I understand you're investigating the Julie Winthrop death? We'd like to do a story on that.'

An alarm sounded in Dana's mind. 'I'm afraid you're mistaken. I'm not doing any investigation.'

The man looked at her skeptically. 'I heard –'

'We're doing a show on around-the-world skiing. This is just one stop.'

He stood there a moment. 'I see. Sorry to have bothered you.'

Dana watched him leave. *How would he know what I'm doing here?* Dana telephoned the *Juneau Empire*. 'Hello. I wanted to talk to one of your reporters, Nicholas Verdun . . .' She listened a moment. 'You don't have anyone there by that name? I see. Thank you.'

It took Dana ten minutes to pack. *I've got to get out of here and find another place.* She suddenly remembered. *Aren't you asking about Cozy Log, our bed-and-breakfast inn? You're in luck. We have one room available.* Dana went down to the lobby to check out. The clerk gave her directions to the inn and drew a small map.

In the basement of the government building, the man looking at the digital map on the computer said, 'The subject is leaving the downtown area, heading west.'

The Cozy Log Bed-and-Breakfast Inn was a neat one-story Alaskan log house, half an hour away from downtown Juneau. *Perfect.* Dana rang the front doorbell and the door was opened by an attractive, cheerful woman in her thirties.

'Hello. Can I help you?'

'Yes. I met your husband, and he mentioned that you had a room available.'

'Indeed we do. I'm Judy Bowler.'

'Dana Evans.'

'Come in.'

Dana stepped inside and looked around. The inn consisted of a large, comfortable living room with a stone fireplace, a dining room where the boarders ate, and two bedrooms with bathrooms.

213

'I do all the cooking here,' Judy Bowler said. 'It's pretty good.'

Dana smiled warmly. 'I'm looking forward to it.'

Judy Bowler showed Dana to her room. It was clean and homey looking. Dana unpacked.

There was one other couple boarding there, and the conversation was casual. Neither of them recognized Dana.

After lunch, Dana drove back into town. She walked into the bar of the Cliff House and ordered a drink. All the employees looked tan and healthy. *Of course.*

'Beautiful weather,' Dana said to the young blond bartender.

'Yeah. Great skiing weather.'

'Do you ski a lot?'

He smiled. 'Whenever I can steal time off.'

'Too dangerous for me.' Dana sighed. 'A friend of mine got killed here a few months ago.'

He put down the glass he was polishing. 'Killed?'

'Yes. Julie Winthrop.'

His expression clouded. 'She used to come in here. Nice lady.'

Dana leaned forward. 'I heard it wasn't an accident.'

His eyes widened. 'What do you mean?'

'I heard she was murdered.'

'Murdered?' he said incredulously. 'Not a chance. It was an accident.'

Twenty minutes later Dana was talking to the bartender at the Prospector Hotel.

'Beautiful weather.'

'Good skiing weather,' the bartender said.

Dana shook her head. 'Too dangerous for me. A friend of mine got killed here skiing. You might have met her. Julie Winthrop.'

'Oh, sure. I liked her a lot. I mean, she didn't put on airs, like some people. She was real down-to-earth.'

Dana leaned forward. 'I heard her death wasn't an accident.'

The expression on the bartender's face changed. He lowered his voice. 'I know damn well it wasn't.'

Dana's heart quickened. 'You do?'

'You bet.' He leaned forward conspiratorially. 'Those damn Martians . . .'

She was at the top of Ptarmigan Mountain on skis, and she could feel the cold wind biting at her. She looked down at the valley below, trying to decide whether to return, when suddenly she felt a push from behind, and she was hurtling down the slopes, faster and faster, heading toward a huge tree. Just before she hit the tree, she woke up, screaming.

Dana sat up in bed, trembling. *Is that what had happened to Julie Winthrop? Who pushed her to her death?*

*

215

Elliot Cromwell was impatient.

'Matt, when the hell is Jeff Connors coming back? We need him.'

'Soon. He keeps in touch.'

'And what about Dana?'

'She's in Alaska, Elliot. Why?'

'I would like to see her back here. The ratings on our evening broadcasts have gone down.'

And Matt Baker looked at him and wondered if that was the real reason for Elliot Cromwell's concern.

In the morning, Dana dressed and drove back into the center of town.

At the airport, waiting for her flight to be called, Dana noticed a man sitting in a corner looking at her from time to time. He looked strangely familiar. He was dressed in a dark gray suit, and he reminded her of someone. And Dana remembered who it was. A different man at the Aspen airport. He had also worn a dark gray suit. But it was not the clothes that triggered Dana's memory. It was something in their bearing. Both of them had an unpleasant aura of arrogance. He was watching her with a look that almost bordered on contempt. She felt a chill.

After Dana boarded the flight, he spoke into a cell phone and left the airport.

Fifteen

When Dana arrived home, she found a beautiful little Christmas tree that Mrs Daley had bought and decorated.

'Look at this ornament,' Mrs Daley said proudly. 'Kemal made it himself.'

The tenant next door was watching the scene on his television set.

Dana kissed the older woman's cheek. 'I love you, Mrs Daley.'

Mrs Daley blushed. 'Oh, what a fuss over nothing.'

'Where is Kemal?'

'He's in his room. There are two messages for you, Miss Evans. You're to call Mrs Hudson. I put the number on your dresser. And your mother called.'

'Thank you.'

When Dana walked into the study, Kemal was at his computer.

He looked up. 'Hey, you're back.'

'I'm back,' Dana said.

'That's dope. I was hoping you'd be here for Christmas.'

Dana hugged him. 'You bet. I wouldn't have missed it for the world. How are you getting along here?'

'Rad.'

Good. 'You like Mrs Daley?'

He nodded. 'She's cool.'

Dana smiled. 'I know. I have a couple of calls to make. I'll be back.'

Bad news first, Dana thought. She called her mother's number. She had not spoken to her since the incident in Westport. *How could she have married a man like that?* Dana listened to the phone ring several times, then her mother's recorded voice came on.

'We're not home right now, but if you leave a message, we will call you back. Wait for the tone.'

Dana waited. 'Merry Christmas, Mother.' She hung up.

The next call was to Pamela.

'Dana, I'm so glad you're back!' Pamela Hudson exclaimed. 'We heard on the news that Jeff is away, but Roger and I are having a few people over for an early Christmas dinner tomorrow, and we want you and Kemal here. Please don't tell me you have other plans.'

'No,' Dana said. 'As a matter of fact, I don't.

218

And we would love to come. Thank you, Pamela.'

'Wonderful. We'll expect you at five o'clock. Casual.' She paused. 'How are things going?'

'I don't know,' Dana said frankly. 'I don't know if they're going anywhere.'

'Well, forget about everything for now. Get some rest. We'll see you both tomorrow.'

When Dana and Kemal arrived at the Hudsons' on Christmas Day, they were greeted at the door by Cesar. His face lit up when he saw Dana.

'Miss Evans! I'm so pleased to see you.' He smiled at Kemal. 'And Master Kemal.'

'Hi, Cesar,' Kemal said.

Dana handed Cesar a brightly wrapped package. 'Merry Christmas, Cesar.'

'I don't know what –' He was stammering. 'I didn't – you're too kind, Miss Evans!'

The gentle giant, as Dana thought of him, was blushing. Dana handed him two more packages. 'These are for Mr and Mrs Hudson.'

'Yes, Miss Evans. I will put them under the tree. Mr and Mrs Hudson are in the drawing room.' Cesar led the way.

Pamela said, 'You're here! We're so glad you two could make it.'

'So are we,' Dana assured her.

Pamela was looking at Kemal's right arm. 'Dana, Kemal has a – that's wonderful!'

Dana grinned. 'Isn't it? Courtesy of my boss. He's quite a fellow. I think it's changed Kemal's whole life.'

'I can't tell you how pleased I am.'

Roger nodded. 'Congratulations, Kemal.'

'Thank you, Mr Hudson.'

Roger Hudson said to Dana, 'Before the other guests arrive, there's something I should mention. Remember I said that Taylor Winthrop told friends he had retired from public life and then became ambassador to Russia?'

'Yes. I suppose the president pressured him to –'

'That's what I thought. But it seems that it was Winthrop who pressured the president to appoint him ambassador. The question is, why?'

The other guests began to arrive. There were only twelve other people at the dinner, and the evening was warm and festive.

After dessert, everyone went into the drawing room. In front of the fireplace was a huge Christmas tree. There were gifts for everyone, but Kemal got the lion's share: computer games, Rollerblades, a sweater, gloves, and videotapes.

The time passed swiftly. The joy of being with such friendly people, after the stress of the last few days, was immense. *I just wish Jeff were here.*

*

Dana Evans was sitting at the anchor desk, waiting for the eleven o'clock news to begin. Beside her was coanchor, Richard Melton. Maury Falstein was seated in the chair usually occupied by Jeff. Dana tried not to think about that.

Richard Melton was saying to Dana, 'I miss you when you're away.'

Dana smiled. 'Thanks, Richard. Miss you, too.'

'You've been gone quite a bit. Is everything all right?'

'Everything's fine.'

'Let's go for a bite afterward.'

'I have to see that Kemal's all right first.'

'We can meet somewhere.'

We must meet somewhere else. I think I'm being watched. The aviary section at the zoo.

Melton continued. 'They say that you're checking out some big story. Want to talk about it?'

'There's nothing to talk about yet, Richard.'

'I heard on the grapevine that Cromwell isn't too happy that you're away so much. I hope you don't get into trouble with him.'

Let me give you some advice. Don't go looking for trouble, or you're going to find it. That's a promise. Dana was finding it hard to concentrate on what Richard Melton was saying.

'He likes to fire people,' Melton said.

Bill Kelly disappeared the day after the fire. He didn't pick up his check, just left.

Richard Melton kept talking. 'As God is my

221

witness, I don't want to work with a new anchor.'

The witness to the accident was an American tourist, Ralph Benjamin. A blind man.

'Five – four – three – two . . .' Anastasia Mann pointed a finger at Dana. The camera's red light flashed on.

The announcer's voice boomed out, 'This is the eleven o'clock news on WTN with Dana Evans and Richard Melton.'

Dana smiled into the camera. 'Good evening. I'm Dana Evans.'

'And I'm Richard Melton.'

They were back on the air.

'Today in Arlington, three students at Wilson High School were arrested after police searched their lockers and found seven ounces of marijuana and various weapons, including a stolen handgun. Holly Rapp has more on this story.'

Back to tape.

We don't have too many art thefts, and the MO is always the same. This is different.

The broadcast was over. Richard Melton looked at Dana.

'Do we meet later?'

'Not tonight, Richard. There's something I have to do.'

He rose. 'Okay.' Dana had a feeling he wanted to ask her about Jeff. Instead he said, 'See you tomorrow.'

Dana stood up. 'Good night, everybody.'

Dana walked out of the studio and went to her office. She sat down, turned on her computer, logged on to the Internet, and began searching again through the myriad articles about Taylor Winthrop. On one of the Web sites, Dana came across an item about Marcel Falcon, a French government official who had been ambassador to NATO. The article mentioned Marcel Falcon negotiating a trade agreement with Taylor Winthrop. In the middle of negotiations, Falcon had given up his government post and retired. *In the middle of a government negotiation? What could have happened?*

Dana tried other Web sites, but there was no further information on Marcel Falcon. *Very strange. I have to look into that*, Dana decided.

By the time Dana was finished, it was two AM. Too early to telephone Europe. She went back to the apartment. Mrs Daley was waiting up for her.

'I'm sorry I'm so late,' Dana said. 'I –'

'No problem. I saw your broadcast tonight. I thought it was wonderful as always, Miss Evans.'

'Thank you.'

Mrs Daley sighed. 'I just wish all the news wasn't so dreadful. What kind of world are we living in?'

'That's a good question. How is Kemal?'

'The little devil's fine. I let him beat me at rummy.'

Dana smiled. 'Good. Thank you, Mrs Daley. If you want to come in late tomorrow –'

'No, no. I'll be here bright and early to get you all off to school and work.'

Dana watched Mrs Daley leave. *A gem*, she thought gratefully. Her cell phone rang. She ran to pick it up. 'Jeff?'

'Merry Christmas, dearest.' His voice washed through her body. 'Am I calling too late?'

'Never too late. Tell me about Rachel.'

'She's back home.'

Jeff means she's back at her house.

'There's a nurse here, but Rachel will only let her stay until tomorrow.'

Dana hated to ask. 'And then?'

'The test results indicate that the cancer has spread. Rachel doesn't want me to leave yet.'

'I see. I don't mean to sound selfish, but isn't there someone else who –?'

'She has no one, darling. She's all alone and panicky. She won't have anyone else here. I honestly don't know what Rachel would do if I left.'

And I don't know what I'm going to do if you stay.

'They want to start chemotherapy immediately.'

'How long will it take?'

'She'll need a treatment every three weeks for four months.'

Four months.

'Matt has asked me to take a leave of absence. I'm so sorry about all this, honey.'

How did he mean that? Sorry about his job? Sorry about Rachel? Or sorry that our lives are being torn apart? How can I be so selfish? Dana asked herself. *The woman may be dying.*

'I'm sorry, too,' Dana finally said. 'I hope everything turns out all right.' *Turns out all right for whom? For Rachel and Jeff? For Jeff and me?*

When Jeff put down the phone, he looked up and saw Rachel standing there. She was wearing a nightgown and a robe. She looked lovely, with an almost translucent light about her.

'That was Dana?'

'Yes,' Jeff said.

Rachel moved closer to him. 'Poor darling. I know how much this is hurting you both. I – I just couldn't have gone through all this without you. I needed you, Jeff. I need you now.'

Dana arrived at her office early in the morning and logged on to the Internet again. Two items caught her attention. Separately, they were innocuous, but together, they suggested a mystery.

The first item read: 'Vincent Mancino, the Italian minister of commerce, has unexpectedly resigned during trade contract negotiations with Taylor Winthrop, the representative for the United States. Mancino's assistant, Ivo Vale, took over.'

The second item read: 'Taylor Winthrop, special adviser to NATO in Brussels, has asked to be replaced and has returned to his home in Washington.'

Marcel Falcon had resigned, Vincent Mancino had resigned, Taylor Winthrop had quit unexpectedly. Were they connected? Coincidence?

Interesting.

Dana's first call was to Dominick Romano, who worked for the Italia I network in Rome.

'Dana! It's good to hear from you. What's up?'

'I'm coming to Rome, and I'd like to talk.'

'*Bene!* What about?'

Dana hesitated. 'I'd rather discuss it when I get there.'

'When are you coming?'

'I'll be there Saturday.'

'I will bring out the fatted pasta.'

Dana's next call was to Jean Somville, who was working in Brussels at the press headquarters of NATO on the rue des Chapeliers.

'Jean? Dana Evans.'

'Dana! I haven't seen you since Sarajevo. Those were some times. You ever going back there?'

She grimaced. 'Not if I can help it.'

'What can I do for you, *chérie*?'

'I'm coming to Brussels in the next few days. Will you be around?'

'For you? Certainly. Something special going on?'

'No,' Dana said quickly.

'Right. You're just sight-seeing, huh?' There was a skeptical note in his voice.

'Something like that,' Dana said.

He laughed. 'I look forward to it. *Au revoir*.'

'*Au revoir*.'

'Matt Baker would like to see you.'

'Tell him I'll be right there, Olivia.'

Two more phone calls and Dana was on her way to Matt's office.

He said without preamble, 'We may have lucked into something. I heard a story last night that might be a clue to what we're looking for.'

Dana felt her heart quicken. 'Yes?'

'There's a man named' – he consulted a slip of paper on his desk – 'Dieter Zander, in Düsseldorf. He was in some kind of business with Taylor Winthrop.'

Dana was listening intently.

'I don't have the whole story, but apparently something very bad happened between them. They had a violent falling-out, and Zander swore to kill Winthrop. It sounds like it might be worth checking on.'

'It certainly does. I'll look into it right away, Matt.'

They chatted for a few more minutes, then Dana left.

I wonder how I can find out more about it? She suddenly thought of Jack Stone and FRA. *He might know something.* She found the private number he had given her and called it.

His voice came on the line. 'Jack Stone.'

'It's Dana Evans.'

'Hello, Miss Evans. What can I do for you?'

'I'm trying to find something out about a man named Zander in Düsseldorf.'

'Dieter Zander?'

'Yes. You know him?'

'We know who he is.'

Dana registered the *we.* 'Can you tell me anything about him?'

'Is this in connection with Taylor Winthrop?'

'Yes.'

'Taylor Winthrop and Dieter Zander were partners in a business deal. Zander was sent to prison for manipulating some stock, and while he was in prison, his house burned down, killing his wife and three children. He blames Taylor Winthrop for what happened.'

And Taylor Winthrop and his wife had died in a fire. Dana listened in shock. 'Is Zander still in prison?'

'No. I believe he got out last year. Anything else?'

'No. Thank you very, very much.'

'This is just between us.'

'I understand.'

The line went dead.

Now there are three possibilities, Dana thought.

Dieter Zander in Düsseldorf.

Vincent Mancino in Rome.

Marcel Falcon in Brussels.

I'll go to Düsseldorf first.

Olivia said, 'Mrs Hudson is on line three.'

'Thank you.' Dana picked up the phone. 'Pamela?'

'Hello, Dana. I know this is sudden, but a good friend has just come to town and Roger and I are giving him a little party next Wednesday. I know Jeff is still out of town, but we would love to have you come. Are you free?'

'I'm afraid I'm not. I'm leaving for Düsseldorf tonight.'

'Oh. I'm sorry.'

'And, Pamela –'

'Yes?'

'Jeff may be gone for a while.'

There was a silence. 'I hope everything is all right.'

'Yes. I'm sure it will be.' *It has to be.*

Sixteen

That evening at Dulles airport, Dana boarded a Lufthansa jet to Düsseldorf. She had telephoned Steffan Mueller, who worked at Kabel Network to tell him she was on her way. Dana's mind was filled with what Matt Baker had told her. *If Dieter Zander blamed Taylor Winthrop for –*

'Guten Abend. Ich heisse Hermann Friedrich. Ist es das ersten mal das sie Deutschland besuchen?'

Dana turned to look at her seat partner. He was in his fifties, trim, with an eye patch and a full mustache.

'Good evening,' Dana said.

'Ah, you are American?'

'Yes.'

'Many Americans come to Düsseldorf. It is a beautiful city.'

'So I've heard.' *And his family had died in a fire.*

'This is your first visit?'

'Yes.' *Could it have been a coincidence?*

'It is beautiful, beautiful. Düsseldorf is divided by the Rhine River, you know, into two parts. The older part is on the right bank –'

Steffan Mueller can tell me more about Dieter Zander.

'– and the modern part is on the left bank. Five bridges connect the two sides.' Hermann Friedrich moved a little closer to Dana. 'You are visiting friends, perhaps, in Düsseldorf?'

It's beginning to fit together.

Friedrich leaned a little closer. 'If you are alone, I know a –'

'What? Oh. No, I'm meeting my husband there.'

Hermann Friedrich's smile faded. *'Gut. Er ist ein glücklicher Mann.'*

There was a line of taxis out in front of the Düsseldorf International Airport. Dana took one to the Breidenbacher Hof in the center of town. It was an elegant old hotel with an ornate lobby.

The clerk behind the desk said, 'We were expecting you, Miss Evans. Welcome to Düsseldorf.'

'Thank you.' Dana signed the register.

The clerk picked up the telephone and spoke into it. *'Der Raum sollte betriebsbereit sein. Hast.'* He replaced the receiver and turned to Dana. 'I'm so sorry, *Fräulein*, your room is not quite ready. Please have a bite to eat as our guest, and I will call you as soon as the maid is through cleaning it.'

Dana nodded. 'Very well.'

'Let me show you to the dining salon.'

Upstairs in Dana's room, two electronics experts were putting a camera in a wall clock.

Thirty minutes later Dana was in her room, unpacking. Her first telephone call was to Kabel Network.

'I've arrived, Steffan,' Dana said.

'Dana! I could not believe you were really coming. What are you doing for dinner?'

'I hope I'm having it with you.'

'You are. We're going to Im Schiffchen. Eight o'clock?'

'Perfect.'

Dana was dressed and going out the door when her cell phone rang. She hurriedly took it out of her purse.

'Hello?'

'Hello, darling. How are you?'

'I'm fine, Jeff.'

'And where are you?'

'I'm in Germany. Düsseldorf. I think I'm finally onto something.'

'Dana, be careful. God, I wish I were with you.'

So do I, Dana thought. 'How is Rachel?'

'The chemotherapy treatments are draining her. It's pretty rough.'

'Is she going to be – ?' She could not finish the sentence.

'It's too early to tell. If the chemotherapy is effective, she has a good chance of going into remission.'

'Jeff, please tell her how sorry I am.'

'I will. Is there anything I can do for you?'

'Thanks, I'm fine.'

'I'll call you tomorrow. I just wanted to tell you I love you, sweetheart.'

'I love you, Jeff. Good-bye.'

'Good-bye.'

Rachel came out of her bedroom. She had on a robe and slippers, and a Turkish towel was wrapped around her head.

'How is Dana?'

'She's fine, Rachel. She asked me to tell you how sorry she is.'

'She's very much in love with you.'

'I'm very much in love with her.'

Rachel moved closer to him. 'You and I were in love, weren't we, Jeff? What happened?'

He shrugged. 'Life. Or I should say *lives.*' We led separate ones.'

'I was too busy with my modeling career.' She was trying to fight back tears. 'Well, I won't be doing that again, will I?'

He put his arms on her shoulders. 'Rachel, you're

going to be fine. The chemotherapy is going to work.'

'I know. Darling, thank you for being here with me. I couldn't have faced this alone. I don't know what I would do without you.'

Jeff had no answer to that.

Im Schiffchen was an elegant restaurant in a fashionable part of Düsseldorf. Steffan Mueller walked in and grinned as he saw Dana.

'Dana! *Mein Gott*. I haven't seen you since Sarajevo.'

'It seems forever, doesn't it?'

'What are you doing here? Did you come for the festival?'

'No. Someone asked me to look up a friend of his, Steffan.' A waiter came up to the table and they ordered drinks.

'Who's the friend?'

'His name is Dieter Zander. Have you heard of him?'

Steffan Mueller nodded. 'Everyone has heard of him. He's quite a character. He was in a big scandal. He's a billionaire, but he was stupid enough to swindle some stockholders and get caught. He should have gotten twenty years, but he pulled some strings and they let him out in three. He claims he's innocent.'

Dana was studying him. 'Is he?'

'Who knows? At the trial he said Taylor Winthrop

framed him and stole millions of dollars. It was an interesting trial. According to Dieter Zander, Taylor Winthrop offered him a partnership in a zinc mine, supposed to be worth billions. Winthrop used Zander as a front man, and Zander sold millions of dollars' worth of stock. But it turned out the mine was salted.'

'Salted?'

'There was no zinc. Winthrop kept the money and Zander took the fall.'

'The jury didn't believe Zander's story?'

'If he had accused anyone but Taylor Winthrop, they might have. But Winthrop is kind of a demigod.' Steffan looked at her curiously. 'What's your interest in this?'

Dana said evasively, 'As I said, a friend asked me to look up Zander.'

It was time to order dinner.

The meal was delicious. When it was over, Dana said, 'I'm going to hate myself in the morning. But it was worth every bite.'

When Steffan dropped Dana off at the hotel, he said, 'Did you know the teddy bear was invented here by a woman named Margarete Steiff? The cuddly little animal became popular all over the world.'

Dana was listening, wondering where this was leading.

'We have real bears here in Germany, Dana, and they're dangerous. When you meet Dieter Zander, be careful. He looks like a teddy bear, but he's not. He's a real bear.'

Zander Electronics International occupied an enormous building on the industrial outskirts of Düsseldorf. Dana approached one of the three receptionists in the busy lobby.

'I want to see Mr Zander.'

'Do you have an appointment?'

'Yes. I'm Dana Evans.'

'Gerade ein Moment, bitte.' The receptionist spoke into the telephone, then looked up at Dana. *'Fräulein*, when did you make the appointment?'

'Several days ago,' Dana lied.

'Es tut mir leid. His secretary has no record of it.' She spoke into the phone again, then replaced the receiver. 'It is not possible to see Mr Zander without an appointment.'

The receptionist turned to a messenger at the desk. A group of employees was coming in the door. Dana stepped away from the desk and joined them, moving into the center. They got into the elevator.

As it started up, Dana said, 'Oh, dear. I forgot what floor Mr Zander is on.'

One of the women said, *'Vier.'*

'Danke,' Dana said. She got off on the fourth floor and walked over to a desk with a young woman

behind it. 'I'm here to see Dieter Zander. I'm Dana Evans.'

The woman frowned. 'But you have no appointment, *Fräulein*.'

Dana leaned forward and said quietly, 'You tell Mr Zander that I'm going to do a national television broadcast in the United States about him and his family unless he talks to me, and that it would be in his interest to talk to me *now*.'

The secretary was studying her, confused. 'Just a moment. *Bitte*.' Dana watched her get up, open a door marked PRIVAT, and step inside.

Dana looked around the reception office. There were framed photographs of Zander Electronics factories around the world. The company had outlets in America, France, Italy ... *countries where the Winthrop murders had taken place.*

The secretary came out a minute later. 'Mr Zander will see you,' she said disapprovingly. 'But he only has a few minutes. This is most – most unusual.'

'Thank you,' Dana said.

Dana was ushered into a large paneled office. 'This is Fräulein Evans.'

Dieter Zander was seated behind an enormous desk. He was in his sixties, a large man with a guileless face and soft brown eyes. Dana remembered Steffan's story of the teddy bear.

He looked at Dana and said, 'I recognize you. You were the correspondent in Sarajevo.'

'Yes.'

'I do not understand what you want with me. You mentioned my family to my secretary.'

'May I sit down?'

'*Bitte.*'

'I wanted to talk to you about Taylor Winthrop.'

Zander's expression narrowed. 'What about him?'

'I'm doing an investigation, Mr Zander. I believe Taylor Winthrop and his family were murdered.'

Dieter Zander's eyes turned cold. 'I think you had better leave now, *Fräulein.*'

'You were in business with him,' Dana said. 'And –'

'Leave!'

'Herr Zander, I suggest that it would be better for you to discuss this with me privately than for you and your friends to watch it on television. I want to be fair. I want to hear your side of the story.'

Dieter Zander was silent for a long time. When he spoke, there was a deep bitterness in his voice. 'Taylor Winthrop was *scheisse*. Oh, he was clever, very clever. He framed me. And while I was in prison, *Fräulein*, my wife and children died. If I had been home . . . I could have saved them.' His voice was filled with pain. 'It was true I hated the man. But *murder* Taylor Winthrop? No.' He smiled his teddy-bear smile. '*Auf wiedersehen*, Miss Evans.'

*

239

Dana telephoned Matt Baker. 'Matt, I'm in Düsseldorf. You were right. I may have hit pay dirt. Dieter Zander was involved in a business deal with Taylor Winthrop. He claims that Winthrop framed him and sent him to prison. Zander's wife and children died in a fire while he was behind bars.'

There was a shocked silence. 'They died in a *fire*?'

'That's right,' Dana said.

'The same way Taylor and Madeline died.'

'Yes. You should have seen the look in Zander's eyes when I talked about murder.'

'It all fits, doesn't it? Zander had a motive to wipe out the entire Winthrop family. You were right about the murders all the time. I – I can hardly believe it.'

'It sounds good, Matt, but there's no proof yet. I have two more stops to make. I'm leaving for Rome in the morning,' Dana said. 'I'll be home in a day or two.'

'Take care of yourself.'

'Deal.'

At FRA headquarters, three men were watching Dana on a big wall television screen talking on the telephone in her hotel room.

'I have two more stops to make,' she said. 'I'll be home in a few days ... I'm leaving for Rome tomorrow morning.'

The men watched as Dana replaced the receiver, rose, and walked into the bathroom. The scene on the screen switched to a hidden peephole camera in a bathroom medicine cabinet. Dana started to undress. She slipped off her blouse and bra.

'Man, look at those tits!'

'Spectacular.'

'Wait. She's taking off her skirt and panties.'

'Fellows, look at that ass! I want a piece of that.'

They watched Dana get into the shower and close the shower door. The door began to steam up.

One of the men sighed. 'That's it for now. Film at eleven.'

The chemotherapy treatments were hell for Rachel. The chemicals Adriamycin and Taxotere were given intravenously from a bag, and the process took four hours.

Dr Young said to Jeff, 'This is a very difficult time for her. She's going to feel nauseous and drained and she'll suffer a loss of hair. For a woman, that can be the most devastating side effect of all.'

'Right.'

The following afternoon Jeff said to Rachel, 'Get dressed. We're going for a ride.'

'Jeff, I really don't feel up to –'

'No arguments.'

And thirty minutes later they were in a wig shop and Rachel was trying on wigs, smiling and saying to Jeff, 'They're beautiful. Do you like the long one or the short one?'

'I like them both,' Jeff said. 'And if you get tired of these, we'll come back and change you into a brunette or a redhead.' His voice softened. 'Personally, I like you the way you are.'

Rachel's eyes filled with tears. 'I like you the way *you* are.'

Seventeen

Each city has its own rhythm, and Rome's is like that of no other city in the world. It is a modern metropolis cocooned in the history of centuries of glory. It moves at its own measured pace, for it has no reason to hurry. Tomorrow will come in its own good time.

Dana had not been in Rome since she was twelve years old, when her mother and father had taken her there. Landing at the Leonardo da Vinci airport triggered a host of memories. She remembered her first day in Rome when she had explored the Colosseum, where the Christians had been thrown to the lions. She had not slept for a week after that.

She and her parents had visited the Vatican and the Spanish Steps, and she had thrown lire into the Trevi Fountain, wishing that her parents would stop quarreling. When her father disappeared, Dana felt that the fountain had betrayed her.

She had seen a performance of the opera *Otello* at the Terme di Caracalla, the Roman baths, and it was an evening she would never forget.

She had eaten ice cream at the famous Doney's on the Via Veneto and explored the crowded streets of Trastevere. Dana adored Rome and its people. *Who could have imagined that I would return here after all these years, looking for a serial killer?*

Dana checked in at the Hotel Ciceroni, near the Piazza Navona.

'*Buon giorno.*' The hotel manager greeted her. 'We are delighted that you are staying with us, Miss Evans. I understand that you will be here for two days?'

Dana hesitated. 'I'm not quite sure.'

He smiled. 'No problem. We have a beautiful suite for you. If there is anything we can do for you, let us know.'

Italy is such a friendly country. And Dana thought about her former neighbors, Dorothy and Howard Wharton. *I don't know how they heard about me, but they flew a man all the way here just to make a deal with me.*

On an impulse, Dana decided to call the Whartons. She had the operator get her the Italiano Ripristino Corporation.

'I'd like to speak to Howard Wharton, please.'

'Would you spell that?'

Dana spelled it.

'Thank you. One moment.'

One moment turned out to be five minutes. The woman came back on the line.

'I'm sorry. We have no Howard Wharton here.'

The only thing is, we have to be in Rome by tomorrow.

Dana called Dominick Romano, the anchorman at Italia 1 television.

'It's Dana. I'm here, Dominick.'

'Dana! I'm delighted. When can we meet?'

'You name it.'

'Where are you staying?'

'At the Hotel Ciceroni.'

'Take a taxi and tell your driver to take you to Toula. I will meet you there in thirty minutes.'

Toula, on Via Della Lupa, was one of Rome's most famous restaurants. When Dana arrived, Romano was waiting for her.

'*Buon giorno*. It is good to see you without the bombs.'

'You, too, Dominick.'

'What a futile war.' He shook his head. 'Perhaps more than most wars. *Bene!* What are you doing in Roma?'

'I came to see a man here.'

'And the name of this lucky man?'

'Vincent Mancino.'

Dominick Romano's expression changed. 'Why do you want to see him?'

'It's probably nothing, but I'm following up on an investigation. Tell me about Mancino.'

Dominick Romano thought carefully before he spoke. 'Mancino was the minister of commerce. Mancino's background is Mafia. He carries a very big stick. Anyway, he suddenly quit a very important position and no one knows why.' Romano looked at Dana curiously. 'What is your interest in him?'

Dana evaded the question. 'I understand that Mancino was negotiating a government trade deal with Taylor Winthrop when he quit.'

'Yes. Winthrop finished the negotiations with someone else.'

'How long was Taylor Winthrop in Rome?'

Romano thought for a moment. 'About two months. Mancino and Winthrop became drinking buddies.' And then he added, 'Something went wrong.'

'What?'

'Who knows? There are all kinds of stories floating around. Mancino had only one child, a daughter, Pia, and she disappeared. Mancino's wife had a nervous breakdown.'

'What do you mean his daughter disappeared? Was she kidnapped?'

'No. She just kind of' – he tried vainly to find the right word – 'disappeared. No one knows what happened to her.' He sighed. 'I can tell you, Pia was a beauty.'

'Where is Mancino's wife?'

'The rumor is that she's in some kind of sanitarium.'

'Do you know where?'

'No. You don't want to, either.' Their waiter came to the table. 'I know this restaurant,' Dominick Romano said. 'Would you like me to order for you?'

'I would.'

'*Bene.*' He turned to the waiter. '*Prima, pasta fagioli. Dopo, abbacchio arrosta con polenta.*'

'*Grazie.*'

The food was superb and the conversation turned light and casual. But when they got up to leave, Romano said, 'Dana, stay away from Mancino. He is not the kind of man you question.'

'But if he –'

'Forget him. In a word – *omertà.*'

'Thank you, Dominick. I appreciate your advice.'

Vincent Mancino's offices were in a modern building he owned on Via Sardegna. A heavyset guard sat at the reception desk in the marble lobby.

He looked up as Dana entered. '*Buona giorno. Posso aiutarla, signorina?*'

'My name is Dana Evans. I'd like to see Vincent Mancino.'

'You have an appointment?'

'No.'

'Then I'm sorry.'

'Tell him it's about Taylor Winthrop.'

The guard studied Dana a moment, then reached for a telephone and spoke into it. He replaced the receiver. Dana waited.

What in the world will I find?

The phone rang, and the guard picked it up and listened a moment. He turned to Dana. 'Second floor. There will be someone there to meet you.'

'Thank you.'

'*Prego.*'

Vincent Mancino's office was small and unimpressive, not at all what Dana had expected. Mancino sat behind an old, battered desk. He was in his sixties, a medium-size man, with a broad chest, thin lips, white hair, and a hawk nose. He had the coldest eyes Dana had ever seen. On the desk was a gold-framed photograph of a beautiful teenager.

As Dana entered his office, Mancino said, 'You come about Taylor Winthrop?' His voice was raspy and deep.

'Yes. I wanted to talk about –'

'There is nothing to talk about, *signorina*. He died

in a fire. He is burning in hell, and his wife and his children are burning in hell.'

'May I sit down, Mr Mancino?'

He started to say, 'No.' Instead he said, '*Scusi*. Sometimes when I get upset, I forget my manners. *Prego, si accomodi*. Please, have a seat.'

Dana took a chair across from him. 'You and Taylor Winthrop were negotiating a trade deal between your two governments.'

'Yes.'

'And you became friends?'

'For a little while, *forse*.'

Dana glanced at the photograph on the desk. 'Is that your daughter?'

He did not answer.

'She's beautiful.'

'Yes, she was very beautiful.'

Dana looked at him, puzzled. 'Isn't she still alive?' She watched him studying her, trying to make up his mind whether to talk to her.

When he finally spoke, he said, 'Alive? You tell *me*.' His voice was filled with passion. 'I took your American friend, Taylor Winthrop, into my home. He broke bread with us. I introduced him to my friends. Do you know how he repaid me? He made my beautiful virgin daughter pregnant. *She was sixteen years old*. She was afraid to tell me because she knew I would kill him, so she . . . she had an *abortion*.' He spat out the word like anathema. 'Winthrop was afraid of publicity, so he did not send

Pia to a doctor. No. He . . . he sent her to a butcher.' His eyes filled with tears. 'A butcher who tore out her womb. My sixteen-year-old daughter, *signorina . . .*' His voice was choked. 'Taylor Winthrop not only destroyed my daughter, he murdered my grandchildren and all their children and their grandchildren. He wiped out the Mancino family's future.' He took a deep breath to calm himself. 'Now he and his family have paid for his terrible sin.'

Dana sat silent, speechless.

'My daughter is in a convent, *signorina*. I will never see her again. Yes, I made a deal with Taylor Winthrop.' His cold steel-gray eyes bored into Dana's. 'But it was a deal with the devil.'

So there are two of them, Dana thought. *And Marcel Falcon still to meet.*

On the KLM flight to Belgium, Dana was conscious of someone taking the seat next to her. She looked up. It was an attractive, pleasant-faced man, and he had obviously asked the stewardess to switch his seat.

He looked at Dana and smiled. 'Good morning. Permit me to introduce myself. My name is David Haynes.' He had an English accent.

'Dana Evans.'

There was no recognition on his face. 'It's a lovely day for flying, isn't it?'

'Beautiful,' Dana agreed.

He was eyeing her admiringly. 'Are you traveling to Brussels on business?'

'Business and pleasure.'

'Do you have friends there?'

'A few.'

'I'm well acquainted in Brussels.'

Wait until I tell Jeff about this, Dana thought. And then the realization hit her again. *He's with Rachel.*

He was studying her face. 'You look familiar.'

Dana smiled. 'I have that kind of face.'

When the plane landed at the Brussels airport and Dana deplaned, a man standing inside the terminal picked up his cellular phone and reported in.

David Haynes said, 'Do you have transportation?'

'No, but I can –'

'Please allow me.' He led Dana to a waiting stretch limousine with a chauffeur. 'I'll drop you at your hotel,' he told Dana. He gave an order to the chauffeur and the limousine moved into traffic. 'Is this your first time in Brussels?'

'Yes.'

They were in front of a large, skylighted shopping arcade. Haynes said, 'If you plan to do any shopping, I would suggest here – the Galeries St-Hubert.'

'It looks lovely.'

Haynes said to the driver, 'Stop a moment, Charles.' He turned to Dana. 'There's the famous

251

Manneken Pis fountain.' It was a bronze statue of a little boy urinating, placed high in a scallop-shell niche. 'One of the most famous statues in the world.'

While I was in prison, my wife and children died. If I had been free, I could have saved them.

David Haynes was saying, 'If you're free this evening, I'd like –'

'I'm sorry,' Dana said. 'I'm afraid I'm not.'

Matt had been summoned to Elliot Cromwell's office.

'We're missing two of our key players, Matt. When is Jeff coming back?'

'I'm not sure, Elliot. As you know, he's involved in a personal situation with his ex-wife, and I've suggested he take a leave of absence.'

'I see. And when is Dana coming back from Brussels?'

Matt looked at Elliot Cromwell and thought: *I never told him that Dana was in Brussels.*

Eighteen

The headquarters of NATO, the North Atlantic Treaty Organization, is at Building Leopold III, and over the roof the Belgian flag flies, three equal vertical bands of black, yellow, and red.

Dana had been sure it would be easy to find the information about Taylor Winthrop's premature retirement from his post at NATO, and then she would be on her way home. But NATO turned out to be a nightmare of alphabet soup. Beside its sixteen member states, there were offices for NAC, EAPC, NACC, ESDI, CJTF, CSCE, and at least a dozen more acronyms.

Dana went to NATO's press headquarters on rue des Chapeliers and found Jean Somville in the pressroom.

He rose to greet her. 'Dana!'

'Hello, Jean.'

'What brings you to Brussels?'

'I'm working on a story,' Dana said. 'I need some information.'

'Ah. Another story about NATO.'

'In a way,' Dana said cautiously. 'Taylor Winthrop was the United States adviser to NATO here at one time.'

'Yes. He did a fine job. He was a great man. It's such a tragedy about that family.' He looked at Dana, curious. 'What is it you wish to know?'

Dana chose her next words carefully. 'He left his post in Brussels early. I wondered what the reason was.'

Jean Somville shrugged. 'That's very simple. He finished what he had come here for.'

Dana felt a sharp sense of disappointment. 'While Winthrop was serving here, did anything . . . unusual happen? Was there any scandal about him of any kind?'

Jean Somville looked at her in surprise. 'Certainly not! Did someone say that Taylor Winthrop was in a scandal at NATO?'

'No,' Dana offered quickly. 'What I heard was there was a . . . a quarrel, some kind of disagreement between Winthrop and someone here.'

Somville frowned. 'You mean a quarrel of a private nature?'

'Yes.'

He pursed his lips. 'I don't know. I can possibly find out.'

'I would appreciate that very much.'

*

Dana telephoned Jean Somville the following day.

'Were you able to find out anything more about Taylor Winthrop?'

'I'm sorry, Dana. I tried. I'm afraid there is nothing to find out.' Dana had half expected Jean Somville's answer.

'Thanks, anyway.' She felt let down.

'No problem. I'm sorry you wasted the trip.'

'Jean, I read that the French ambassador to NATO, Marcel Falcon, unexpectedly resigned and went back to France. Isn't that unusual?'

'In the middle of a posting, yes. I suppose so.'

'Why did he resign?'

'There's no mystery about that. It was because of an unfortunate accident. His son was killed by a hit-and-run driver.'

'A hit-and-run driver? Did they ever catch him?'

'Oh, yes. Shortly after the accident, he turned himself over to the police.'

Another dead end. 'I see.'

'The man was a chauffeur by the name of Antonio Persico. He was Taylor Winthrop's chauffeur.'

Dana felt a sudden chill. 'Oh? Where is Persico now?'

'St Gilles Prison, here in Brussels.' Somville added apologetically, 'I'm sorry I could not be more helpful.'

*

Dana had a résumé of the story faxed to her from Washington. *Antonio Persico, a chauffeur to Ambassador Taylor Winthrop, was sentenced to life imprisonment by a Belgian court today when he pleaded guilty to the hit-and-run death of Gabriel Falcon, the son of the French ambassador to the United Nations.*

St Gilles Prison is near the center of Brussels, in an old white building with turrets that make it resemble a castle. Dana had telephoned ahead and gotten permission to interview Antonio Persico. Dana walked into the prison courtyard and was escorted to the warden's office.

'You are here to see Persico.'

'Yes.'

'Very well.'

After a brisk search, Dana was led by a guard into the interview room, where Antonio Persico was waiting. He was a small, pale man, with wide-set green eyes and a face that was constantly twitching.

When Dana walked in, Persico's first words were 'Thank God someone has finally come! You'll get me out of here now.'

Dana looked at him, puzzled. 'I – I'm sorry. I'm afraid I can't do that.'

Persico's eyes narrowed. 'Then why have you come? They promised someone would come to get me out.'

'I came to talk to you about the death of Gabriel Falcon.'

Persico's voice rose. 'I had nothing to do with that. I am innocent.'

'But you confessed.'

'I lied.'

Dana said, 'Why would you . . . ?'

Antonio Persico looked into her eyes and said bitterly, 'I was paid. Taylor Winthrop killed him.' There was a long silence.

'Tell me about it.'

The twitching got worse. 'It happened on a Friday night. Mr Winthrop's wife was in London that weekend.' His voice was strained. 'Mr Winthrop was alone. He went to the Ancienne Belgique, a night-club. I offered to drive him, but he said he would drive himself.' Persico stopped, remembering.

'What happened then?' Dana urged.

'Mr Winthrop came home late, very drunk. He told me that a young boy had run in front of the car. He – he ran him down. Mr Winthrop didn't want a scandal, so he kept driving. Then he became afraid that someone might have seen the accident and given the license number to the police and that they would come for him. He had diplomatic immunity, but he said if the news came out, it would spoil the Russian plan.'

Dana frowned. 'The Russian plan?'

'Yes. That's what he said.'

'What is the Russian plan?'

He shrugged. 'I don't know. I heard him say it on the telephone. He was like a crazy man.' Persico shook his head. 'All he kept saying on the phone was "The Russian plan must go on. We've gone too far to let anything stop it now."'

'And you have no idea what he was talking about?'

'No.'

'Can you remember anything else he said?'

Persico thought for a moment. 'He said something like "All the pieces have fallen into place."' He looked at Dana. 'Whatever it was, it sounded very important.'

Dana was absorbing every word. 'Mr Persico, why would you take the blame for the accident?'

Persico's jaw tightened. 'I told you. I was paid. Taylor Winthrop said that if I would confess that I was the one behind the wheel, he would give me one million dollars and take care of my family while I was in prison. He said he could arrange for a short sentence.' He was gritting his teeth. 'Like a fool, I said yes.' He bit down on his lip. 'And now he is dead, and I will spend the rest of my life in this place.' His eyes were filled with despair.

Dana stood there, shocked by what she had heard. Finally she asked, 'Have you told this to anyone?'

Persico said bitterly, 'Of course. As soon as I heard that Taylor Winthrop was dead, I told the police about our bargain.'

'And?'

'They laughed at me.'

'Mr Persico, I'm going to ask you something very important. Think carefully before you answer. Did you ever tell Marcel Falcon that it was Taylor Winthrop who killed his son?'

'Certainly. I thought he would help me.'

'When you told him, what did Marcel Falcon say?'

'His exact words were "May the rest of his family join him in hell."'

Dana thought, *My God. Now there are three.*

I have to talk to Marcel Falcon in Paris.

It was impossible not to feel the magic of Paris, even as they flew over the city, preparing to land. It was the city of light, it was the city of lovers. It was no place to come by oneself. The city made Dana ache for Jeff.

Dana was in the Relais in the Hotel Plaza Athénée talking to Jean-Paul Hubert, with Metro 6 television.

'Marcel Falcon? Of course. Everyone knows who he is.'

'What can you tell me about him?'

'He's quite a character. He's what you Americans call "big time."'

'What does he do?'

'Falcon owns a huge pharmaceutical company. A

259

few years ago he was accused of forcing smaller companies out of business, but he has political connections, and nothing happened. The French premier even made him ambassador to NATO.'

'But he quit,' Dana said. 'Why?'

'It's a sad story. His son was killed in Brussels by a drunk driver, and Falcon couldn't handle it. He left NATO and returned to Paris. His wife had a nervous breakdown. She's at a sanitarium in Cannes.' Jean-Paul looked at Dana and said earnestly, 'Dana, if you're thinking about doing a story on Falcon, be very careful what you write. He has the reputation of being a very vindictive man.'

It took Dana a day to get an appointment with Marcel Falcon.

When she was finally ushered into his office, he said, 'I agreed to see you because I am an admirer of your work, *mademoiselle*. Your broadcasts from the war zone were very courageous.'

'Thank you.'

Marcel Falcon was an imposing-looking man, heavyset, with strong features and piercing blue eyes. 'Please sit down. What can I do for you?'

'I wanted to ask you about your son.'

'Ah, yes.' His eyes looked desolate. 'Gabriel was a wonderful boy.'

Dana said, 'The man who ran him down –'

'The chauffeur.'

Dana looked at him in astonishment.

Think carefully before you answer. Did you ever tell Marcel Falcon that it was Taylor Winthrop who was responsible for his son's death?

Certainly. As soon as I learned that Winthrop was dead.

What did Marcel Falcon say?

His exact words were 'May the rest of his family join him in hell.'

And now Marcel Falcon was acting as though he were unaware of the truth.

'Mr Falcon, when you were at NATO, Taylor Winthrop was also there.' Dana was watching Falcon's face, looking for the slightest change of expression. There was none.

'Yes. We met.' His tone was casual.

That's it? Dana wondered. *Yes. We met. What is he hiding?*

'Mr Falcon, I would like to speak with your wife if –'

'I'm afraid she is away on a holiday.'

She had a nervous breakdown, and she's in a sanitarium in Cannes.

Marcel Falcon was either in a state of complete denial or he was professing ignorance for a more sinister reason.

Dana telephoned Matt from her room at the Plaza Athénée.

'Dana, when are you coming home?'

'I have just one more lead to follow, Matt. Taylor Winthrop's chauffeur in Brussels told me that Winthrop talked about some secret Russian plan that he didn't want interrupted. I have to see if I can find out what he was talking about. I want to speak with some of his associates in Moscow.'

'All right. But Cromwell wants you back in the studio as soon as possible. Tim Drew is our correspondent in Moscow. I'll have him meet you. He can be helpful.'

'Thanks. I shouldn't be in Russia more than a day or two.'

'Dana?'

'Yes?'

'Never mind. Good-bye.'

Thanks. I shouldn't be in Russia more than a day or two.
Dana?
Yes?
Never mind. Good-bye.

Tape ends.

Dana telephoned home.

'Good evening, Mrs Daley – or rather, good afternoon.'

'Miss Evans! It's grand to hear from you.'

'How is everything there?'

'Just lovely.'

'How is Kemal? Are there any problems?'

'None at all. He certainly misses you.'

'I miss him. Will you put him on?'

'He's taking a nap. Would you like me to wake him up?'

Dana said in surprise, 'Taking a nap? When I called the other day, he was taking a nap.'

'Yes. The lad came home from school, and he felt tired, so I thought a nap would be good for him.'

'I see . . . Well, just tell him I love him. I'll call tomorrow. Tell him I'm going to bring him back a bear from Russia.'

'A bear? Well! He'll be that excited.'

Dana called Roger Hudson.

'Roger, I hate to impose, but I need a favor.'

'If there's something I can do . . .'

'I'm leaving for Moscow, and I want to talk to Edward Hardy, the American ambassador there. I was hoping that you might know him.'

'As a matter of fact, I do.'

'I'm in Paris. If you could fax me a letter of introduction, I would really appreciate it.'

'I can do better than that. I'll give him a call and tell him to expect you.'

'Thank you, Roger. I'm very grateful.'

*

It was New Year's Eve. It was a shock to remember that this was to have been her wedding day. *Soon*, Dana told herself. *Soon*. She put on her coat and went outside.

The doorman said, 'Taxi, Miss Evans?'

'No, thanks.' She had nowhere to go. Jean-Paul Hubert was away visiting his family. *This is no city to be alone in*, Dana decided.

She began to walk, trying not to think about Jeff and Rachel. Trying not to think. Dana passed a small church that was open, and on an impulse, she went inside. The cool, quiet vaulted interior gave Dana a sense of peace. She sat down in a pew and said a silent prayer.

At midnight, as Dana was walking the streets, Paris exploded in a cacophony of noise and confetti. She wondered what Jeff was doing. *Are he and Rachel making love? He had not called. How could he have forgotten that this night was so special?*

In Dana's hotel room, on the floor, near the dresser, the cell phone that had fallen from her purse was ringing.

When Dana returned to the Plaza Athénée, it was three in the morning. She walked into her room, got undressed, and crawled into bed. First her father and now Jeff. Abandonment ran through her life like a dark thread in a tapestry. *I'm not going to feel sorry for myself*, she swore. *So what if this was going to be my wedding night. Oh, Jeff, why don't you call me?*

She cried herself to sleep.

Nineteen

The flight to Moscow on Sabena Airlines took three and a half hours. Dana noted that most of the passengers were dressed in warm clothing, and the baggage racks were loaded with fur coats, hats, and scarves.

I should have dressed more warmly, Dana thought. *Well, I won't be in Moscow for more than a day or two.*

She could not stop thinking about Antonio Persico's words. *Winthrop was like a crazy man. All he kept saying on the phone was 'The Russian plan must go on. We've gone too far to let anything stop it now.'*

What important plan was Winthrop working on? What pieces had fallen into place? And soon after, the president had appointed him ambassador to Moscow.

The more information I get, the less sense it makes, Dana decided.

*

To Dana's surprise, Sheremetyevo II, Russia's international airport, was crowded with tourists. *Why would any sane person visit Russia in the winter?* Dana wondered.

When Dana reached the baggage carousel, a man standing nearby was surreptitiously watching her. Dana's heart skipped a beat. *They knew I was coming here*, she thought. *How could they have?*

The man was approaching her. 'Dana Evans?' He had a thick Slovak accent.

'Yes . . .'

He broke into a broad smile and said excitedly, 'You are my biggest fan! You watch me on television all the time.'

Dana felt a surge of relief. 'Oh. Yes. Thank you.'

'I wonder if you would be so pleasant to give me your autograph?'

'Of course.'

He thrust a piece of paper in front of Dana. 'I do not have a pen.'

'I do.' Dana took out her new gold pen and gave him her autograph.

'Spasiba! Spasiba!'

As Dana started to put the pen back in her purse, someone jostled her and the pen fell to the concrete floor. Dana reached down and picked it up. The casing had cracked.

I hope I can get this repaired, Dana thought. And then she looked at it more closely. A tiny wire was showing through the crack. Puzzled, she pulled it out gently. There was a microtransmitter attached to it. Dana stared at it in disbelief. *That's how they always knew where I was! But who put it there and why?* She remembered the card that had come with it.

Dear Dana, have a safe trip. The Gang.

Furious, Dana ripped out the wire, threw it to the ground, and crushed it with her heel.

In an isolated laboratory room, the signal marker on a map suddenly disappeared.

'Oh, shit!'

'Dana?'

She turned. WTN's Moscow correspondent stood there.

'I'm Tim Drew. Sorry I'm late. The traffic out there is a nightmare.'

Tim Drew was in his forties, a tall, red-haired man with a warm smile. 'I have a car waiting outside. Matt tells me that you're here for just a couple of days.'

'That's right.'

They picked up Dana's luggage at the carousel and headed outside.

The drive into Moscow was like a scene from *Doctor Zhivago*. It seemed to Dana that the entire city was wrapped in a mantle of pure white snow.

'This is so beautiful!' Dana exclaimed. 'How long have you been here?'

'Two years.'

'Do you like it?'

'It's a little scary. Yeltsin is always two rolls short of a baker's dozen, and no one knows what to expect from Vladimir Putin. The inmates are running the asylum.' He slammed to a stop to let some jaywalkers pass. 'You're booked at the Sevastopol Hotel.'

'Yes. How is it?'

'It's one of your typical Intourist hotels. You can be sure there will be someone on your floor to keep an eye on you.'

The streets were crowded with people bundled up in furs and heavy sweaters and overcoats. Tim Drew glanced over at Dana. 'You'd better get some warmer clothes or you're going to freeze.'

'I'll be fine. I should be on my way home tomorrow or the next day.'

Ahead of them was Red Square and the Kremlin. The Kremlin itself stood high on a hill that towered over the left bank of the Moskva River.

'My God, that's impressive,' Dana said.

'Yeah. If those walls could talk, you'd hear a lot of screaming.' Tim Drew went on: 'It's one of the most famous buildings in the world. It sits on a plot of land covering Little Borovitsky Hill on the north bank and . . .'

Dana had stopped listening. She was thinking,

What if Antonio Persico lied? What if he made up the story about Taylor Winthrop killing the boy? And lied about the Russian plan.

'That's Red Square outside the east wall. The Kutafya Tower there is the visitors' entrance at the west wall.'

But then why was Taylor Winthrop so desperate to come to Russia? Simply being ambassador would not have meant that much to him.

Tim Drew was saying, 'This is where all the Russian power has been for centuries. Ivan the Terrible and Stalin had their headquarters here, and Lenin and Khrushchev.'

All the pieces fell into place. I have to find out what he meant by that.

They had pulled up in front of an enormous hotel. 'Here we are,' Tim Drew said.

'Thanks, Tim.' Dana got out of the car and was hit by a solid wave of freezing air.

'You go on inside,' Tim called. 'I'll bring your bags in. By the way, if you're free this evening, I'd like to take you to dinner.'

'Thank you very much.'

'There's a private club that has good food. I think you'll enjoy it.'

'Lovely.'

The lobby of the Sevastopol Hotel was large and ornate, and filled with people. There were several clerks working behind the reception desk. Dana walked up to one of them.

He looked up. '*Da?*'

'I'm Dana Evans. I have a reservation.'

The man looked at her a moment and said nervously, 'Ah, yes. Miss Evans.' He handed her a reservation card. 'Would you fill this out, please? And I'll need your passport.'

As Dana began to write, the clerk looked across the lobby at a man standing in the corner and nodded. Dana handed the registration card to the clerk.

'I'll have someone take you to your room.'

'Thank you.'

The room had a vague air of onetime gentility, and the furniture looked worn and shabby and smelled musty.

A heavyset woman in a shapeless uniform brought in Dana's bags. Dana tipped her, and the woman grunted and left. Dana picked up the telephone and called 252–2451.

'American Embassy.'

'Ambassador Hardy's office, please.'

'One moment.'

'Ambassador Hardy's office.'

'Hello. This is Dana Evans. May I speak to the ambassador?'

'Could you tell me what it's concerning?'

'It's – it's personal.'

'Just a moment, please.'

Thirty seconds later Ambassador Hardy was on the phone.

'Miss Evans?'

'Yes.'

'Welcome to Moscow.'

'Thank you.'

'Roger Hudson called to say you were coming. What can I do for you?'

'I wonder if I could come and see you?'

'Certainly. I'm – hold on a moment.' There was a brief pause, and the ambassador came back on the line. 'What about tomorrow morning? Ten o'clock?'

'That will be fine. Thank you very much.'

'Until then.'

Dana looked out the window at the crowds hurrying through the bitter cold and thought, *Tim was right. I had better buy some warmer clothes.*

GUM Department Store was not far from Dana's hotel. It was an enormous emporium, stocked with cheap goods that ranged from clothing to hardware.

Dana walked over to the women's section, where there were racks of heavy coats. She selected a woolen red one and a red scarf to match. It was twenty minutes before she could find a clerk to handle the transaction.

*

When Dana returned to her room, her cell phone was ringing. It was Jeff.

'Hello, darling. I tried to call you on New Year's Eve, but you didn't answer your cell phone, and I didn't know where to reach you.'

'I'm sorry, Jeff.' *So he didn't forget! Bless him.*

'Where are you?'

'I'm in Moscow.'

'Is everything all right, honey?'

'Wonderful. Jeff, tell me about Rachel.'

'It's too soon to say. They're going to try a new therapy on her tomorrow. It's still very experimental. We'll have the result in a few days.'

'I hope it works,' Dana said.

'Is it cold there?'

Dana laughed. 'You wouldn't believe it. I'm a human icicle.'

'I wish I were there to melt you.'

They spoke for another five minutes, and Dana could hear Rachel's voice calling Jeff.

Jeff said on the phone, 'I have to go, darling. Rachel needs me.'

I need you too, Dana thought. 'I love you.'

'I love you.'

The American Embassy at 19–23 Novinsky Bul'var was an ancient, run-down building, with Russian guards standing in sentry booths outside. A long queue of people waited patiently. Dana passed the line and gave her name to a guard. He looked at a roster and waved her in.

Inside the lobby, an American marine stood in a bulletproof glass security booth. An American female guard in uniform checked the contents of Dana's purse.

'Okay.'

'Thank you.' Dana walked to the desk. 'Dana Evans.'

A man standing near the desk said, 'The ambassador is expecting you, Miss Evans. Come with me, please.'

Dana followed him up some marble stairs into a reception office at the end of a long hallway. As Dana entered, an attractive woman in her early forties smiled and said, 'Miss Evans, this is a pleasure. I'm Lee Hopkins, the ambassador's secretary. You may go right in.'

Dana walked into the inner office. Ambassador Edward Hardy rose as she approached his desk.

'Good morning, Miss Evans.'

'Good morning,' Dana said. 'Thank you for seeing me.'

The ambassador was a tall, florid-looking man with the hearty manner of a politician.

'I'm delighted to meet you. Can I get you anything?'

'No thanks, I'm fine.'

'Please have a seat.'

Dana sat down.

'I was delighted when Roger Hudson told me to expect your visit. You've come at an interesting time.'

'Oh?'

'I hate to say this, but between you and me, I'm afraid this country is in free fall.' He sighed. 'To be perfectly frank, I have no idea what's going to happen here next, Miss Evans. This is a country with eight hundred years of history, and we're watching it go down the drain. The criminals are running the country.'

Dana looked at him curiously. 'What do you mean?'

The ambassador leaned back in his chair. 'The law here says that no member of the Duma – that's the lower parliament – can be prosecuted for any crime. The result is that the Duma is filled with men who are wanted for all kinds of felonies – gangsters who have served time in prison, and criminals who are in the process of committing crimes. None of them can be touched.'

'That's incredible,' Dana said.

'Yes. The Russian people are wonderful, but their government . . . Well, what can I do for you, Miss Evans?'

'I wanted to ask you about Taylor Winthrop. I'm doing a story about the family.'

Ambassador Hardy shook his head in sorrow. 'It's like a Greek tragedy, isn't it?'

'Yes.' *That phrase again.*

Ambassador Hardy looked at Dana curiously. 'The world has heard that story over and over. I wouldn't think there's much more to say about it.'

Dana said carefully, 'I want to tell it from a personal angle. I want to know what Taylor Winthrop was really like, what kind of man he was, who his friends were here, if he had any enemies . . .'

'Enemies?' He looked surprised. 'No. Everyone loved Taylor. He was probably the best ambassador we ever had here.'

'Did you work with him?'

'Yes. I was his deputy chief of mission for a year.'

'Ambassador Hardy, do you know if Taylor Winthrop was working on anything where –' She stopped, not sure how to phrase it. ' – all the pieces had to come together?'

Ambassador Hardy frowned. 'You mean some kind of business deal or government deal?'

'I'm not sure what I mean,' Dana confessed.

Ambassador Hardy thought for a moment. 'I'm not, either. No, I have no idea what that could be.'

Dana said, 'Some of the people who are working here in the embassy now – did they work with him?'

'Oh, yes. As a matter of fact, my secretary, Lee, was Taylor's secretary.'

'Would you mind if I talked to her?'

'Not at all. In fact, I'll give you a list of some of the people here who might be helpful.'

'That would be wonderful. Thank you.'

He rose. 'Be careful while you're here, Miss Evans. There's a lot of crime on the streets.'

'So I've heard.'

'Don't drink the tap water. Not even the Russians drink it. Oh, and when you eat out, always specify *chisti stol* – that means a clean table – or you'll find your table loaded with expensive appetizers that you don't want. If you're going shopping, the Arbat is the best place. The shops there have everything. And be careful of the taxis here. Take the older, shabbier ones. The con artists mostly drive new ones.'

'Thank you.' Dana smiled. 'I'll remember.'

Five minutes later Dana was speaking to Lee Hopkins, the ambassador's secretary. They were in a small room alone with the door closed.

'How long did you work for Ambassador Winthrop?'

'Eighteen months. What is it you want to know?'

'Did Ambassador Winthrop make any enemies when he was here?'

Lee Hopkins looked at Dana in surprise. 'Enemies?'

'Yes. In a job like this, I imagine that sometimes you have to say no to people who might resent it. I'm sure that Ambassador Winthrop couldn't please everybody.'

Lee Hopkins shook her head. 'I don't know what you're after, Miss Evans, but if you're intending to write bad things about Taylor Winthrop, you've come to the wrong person for help. He was the kindest, most considerate man I've ever known.'

Here we go again, Dana thought.

In the next two hours, Dana talked to five more people who had worked at the embassy during Taylor Winthrop's term.

He was a brilliant man . . .

He really liked people . . .

He went out of his way to help us . . .

Enemies? Not Taylor Winthrop . . .

I'm wasting my time, Dana thought. She went to see Ambassador Hardy again.

'Did you get what you wanted?' he asked. He seemed less friendly.

Dana hesitated. 'Not exactly,' she said honestly.

He leaned forward. 'And I don't think you will, Miss Evans. Not if you're looking for negative things about Taylor Winthrop. You have everyone upset around here. They loved the man. So did I. Don't try to dig up skeletons that don't exist. If that's all you came here for, you can leave.'

'Thank you,' Dana said. 'I will.'

Dana had no intention of leaving.

The VIP National Club, directly opposite the Kremlin and Manezh Square, was a private restaurant and casino. Tim Drew was waiting there for Dana when she arrived.

'Welcome,' he said. 'I think you'll enjoy this. This place entertains the cream of Moscow's high-society movers and shakers. If a bomb fell on this restaurant, I think the government would be out of business.'

The dinner was delicious. They started with blini and caviar and followed that with borscht, Georgian sturgeon with a walnut sauce, beef stroganoff and *s'loukom* rice, and *vatrushki* cheese tartlets for dessert.

'This is wonderful,' Dana said. 'I had heard that the food in Russia was terrible.'

'It is,' Tim Drew assured her. 'This isn't Russia. This is a special little oasis.'

'What is it like living here?' Dana asked.

Tim Drew was thoughtful for a moment. 'It's like standing near a volcano, waiting for it to erupt. You never know when it's going to happen. The men in power are stealing billions from the country and the people are starving. That's what started the last revolution. God knows what's going to happen now. To be fair, that's only one side of the story. The culture here is incredible. They have the Bolshoi Theater, the great Hermitage, the Pushkin Museum, the Russian ballet, the Moscow Circus – the list goes on and on. Russia produces more books than the rest of the world combined, and the average Russian reads three times as many books a year as the average United States citizen.'

'Maybe they're reading the wrong books,' Dana said dryly.

'Maybe. Right now the people are caught in the middle, between capitalism and communism, and neither is working. There's bad service, inflated costs, and a hell of a lot of crime.' He looked at Dana. 'I hope I'm not depressing you.'

'No. Tell me, Tim, did you know Taylor Winthrop?'

'I interviewed him a few times.'

'Did you ever hear anything about some big project he was involved in?'

'He was involved in a lot of projects. After all, he was our ambassador.'

'I'm not talking about that. I'm talking about something different. Something very complicated – where all the pieces had to fall into place.'

Tim Drew thought for a moment. 'It doesn't ring a bell.'

'Is there anyone here that he had a lot of contact with?'

'Some of his Russian counterparts, I suppose. You might talk to them.'

'Right,' Dana said. 'I will.'

The waiter brought the check. Tim Drew scanned it and looked up at Dana. 'This is typical. There are three separate surcharges on the bill. And don't bother asking what any of them are for.' He paid the bill.

When they were out on the street, Tim Drew said to Dana, 'Do you carry a gun?'

She looked at him in surprise. 'Of course not. Why?'

'This is Moscow. You never know.'. He got an idea. 'I'll tell you what. We're going to make a stop.'

They got into a taxi, and Tim Drew gave the driver an address. Five minutes later they pulled up in front of a gun shop and got out of the taxi.

Dana looked inside the shop and said, 'I'm not going to carry a gun.'

Tim Drew said, 'I know. Just come with me.' The counters of the shop were filled with every type of weapon imaginable.

Dana looked around. 'Can anybody walk in and buy a gun here?'

'All they need is the money,' Tim Drew said.

The man behind the counter muttered something in Russian to Tim. Tim told him what he wanted.

'*Da.*' He reached under the counter and pulled out a small, black, cylindrical object.

'What's this for?' Dana asked.

'It's for you. It's pepper spray.' Tim Drew picked it up. 'All you have to do is press this button at the top and the bad guys will be in too much pain to bother you.'

Dana said, 'I don't think –'

'Trust me. Take it.' He handed it to Dana, paid the man, and they left.

'Would you like to see a Moscow nightclub?' Tim Drew asked.

'Sounds interesting.'

'Great. Let's go.'

*

The Night Flight Club on Tverskaya Street was lavish and ornate and crowded with well-dressed Russians dining, drinking, and dancing.

'There doesn't seem to be any economic problem here,' Dana commented.

'No. They keep the beggars outside on the street.'

At two o'clock in the morning, Dana returned to her hotel, exhausted. It had been a long day. A woman was seated at a table in the hallway, keeping a record of the movements of the guests.

When Dana got to her room, she looked out the window. She had a picture-postcard view of soft snow falling in the moonlight.

Tomorrow, Dana thought determinedly, *I'll know what I've come here for.*

The noise from the jet overhead was so loud it sounded like the plane might hit the building. The man quickly rose from his desk, snatched up a pair of binoculars, and stepped to the window. The tail of the receding aircraft was rapidly descending as it prepared to land at the small airport a half mile away. Except for the runways, everything in the stark landscape was covered with snow as far as his eyes could see. It was winter and this was Siberia.

'So,' he said to his assistant, 'the Chinese are the first to arrive.' His comment did not call for a reply. 'I am told that our friend Ling Wong will not be back. When he returned from our last meeting empty-handed, it was not a happy homecoming for him. Very sad. He was a decent man.'

At that moment, a second jet roared overhead. He did not recognize the make. After it had landed, he trained his high-powered glasses on the men descending from the cabin onto the tarmac. Some of them made no effort to hide the machine pistols they were carrying.

'The Palestinians are here.'

Another jet roared overhead. *Still twelve to go*, he thought. *When we start negotiations tomorrow, it will be the biggest auction yet. Nothing must go wrong.*

He turned again to his assistant. 'Take a memo.'

CONFIDENTIAL MEMO TO ALL OPERATION PERSONNEL: DESTROY IMMEDIATELY AFTER READING.

CONTINUE CLOSE SURVEILLANCE ON SUBJECT TARGET. REPORT ACTIVITIES AND STAND BY FOR HER POSSIBLE ELIMINATION.

Twenty

When Dana awakened, she telephoned Tim Drew.

'Have you heard any more from Ambassador Hardy?' he asked.

'No. I think I offended him. Tim, I need to talk to you.'

'All right. Grab a cab and meet me at the Boyrsky Club at one-fourth Treatrilny Proyez Street.'

'*Where?* I'll never –'

'The cabbie will know. Take one that's beat-up.'

'Right.'

Dana stepped outside the hotel into a freezing, screaming wind. She was glad she was wearing her new red woolen coat. A sign on a building across the street informed her it was – 29 degrees Centigrade. *My God*, she thought. *In Fahrenheit, that's about 20 below zero.*

There was a shiny new taxi in front of the hotel. Dana stepped back and waited until a passenger got into it. The next taxi looked old. Dana took it. The driver looked at her inquiringly in the rearview mirror.

Dana said carefully, 'I want to go to one-quarter Teat –' She hesitated. '– rilny –' She took a deep breath. '– Proyez –'

The driver said impatiently, 'You want the Boyrsky Club?'

'*Da.*'

They took off. They drove along avenues heavy with motor traffic and forlorn pedestrians hurrying along the frozen streets. The city seemed overlaid with a dull, gray patina. *And it isn't just the weather,* Dana thought.

The Boyrsky Club turned out to be modern and comfortable, with leather chairs and couches. Tim Drew was in a chair near the window waiting for her.

'I see you found it all right.'

Dana took a seat. 'The cabdriver spoke English.'

'You're lucky. Some of them don't even speak Russian, they come from so many different distant provinces. It's amazing that this country can function at all. It reminds me of a dying dinosaur. Do you know how big Russia is?'

'Not exactly.'

'It's almost twice as big as the United States. It has thirteen time zones and borders on fourteen countries. *Fourteen countries.*'

'That's amazing,' Dana said. 'Tim, I want to talk to some Russians who had dealings with Taylor Winthrop.'

'That includes about everybody in the Russian government.'

Dana said, 'I know. But there must have been some Russians he was closer to than others. The president –'

'Perhaps someone a little lower in rank,' Tim Drew said dryly. 'I would say that of all the people he dealt with, he was probably closest to Sasha Shdanoff.'

'Who is Sasha Shdanoff?'

'He's the commissar of the Bureau for International Economic Development. I believe Winthrop saw him socially as well as officially.' He looked at Dana closely. 'What are you after, Dana?'

'I'm not sure,' she said honestly. 'I'm not sure.'

The Bureau for International Economic Development was an enormous redbrick building on Ozernaya Street, taking up a full block. Inside the main entrance, two uniformed Russian policemen stood by the door, and a third uniformed guard sat behind a desk.

Dana walked up to the desk. The guard looked up.

'*Dobry dyen*,' Dana said.

'*Zdrastvuytye. Ne –*'

287

Dana stopped him. 'Excuse me. I'm here to see Commissar Shdanoff. I'm Dana Evans. I'm with the Washington Tribune Network.'

The guard looked at a sheet in front of him and shook his head. 'Do you have an appointment?'

'No, but –'

'Then you will have to make an appointment. You are an American?'

'Yes.'

The guard searched through some forms on his desk and handed one to Dana. 'You will fill this out, please.'

'Right,' Dana said. 'Would it be possible to see the commissar this afternoon?'

He blinked. *'Ya ne ponimayu.* You Americans are always in a hurry. What hotel are you at?'

'The Sevastopol. I just need a few min –'

He made a note. 'Someone will inform you. *Dobry dyen.'*

'But –' She saw his expression. *'Dobry dyen.'*

Dana stayed in her room all afternoon waiting for a phone call. At six o'clock, she telephoned Tim Drew.

'Did you get to see Shdanoff?' he asked.

'No. They're going to call me back.'

'Don't hold your breath, Dana. You're dealing with a bureaucracy from another planet.'

*

Early the following morning, Dana went back to the Bureau for International Economic Development. The same guard was at the desk.

'*Dobry dyen*,' Dana said.

He looked up at her, stone-faced. '*Dobry dyen*.'

'Did Commissar Shdanoff get my message yesterday?'

'Your name?'

'Dana Evans.'

'You left a message yesterday?'

'Yes,' she said tonelessly, 'with you.'

The guard nodded. 'Then he received it. All messages are received.'

'May I talk to Commissar Shdanoff's secretary?'

'Do you have an appointment?'

Dana took a deep breath. 'No.'

The guard shrugged. '*Izvinitye, nyet*.'

'When can I –?'

'Somebody will call you.'

On her way back to the hotel, Dana passed Detsky Mir, a children's department store, and she went inside and looked around. There was a section devoted to games. In one corner was a shelf of computer games. *Kemal will like one of those*, Dana thought. She bought a game and was surprised at how expensive it was. She headed back to the hotel to wait for the phone call. At six o'clock she gave up hope. She was about to go downstairs to dinner when the phone rang. Dana hurried over to it and picked it up.

'Dana?' It was Tim Drew.

'Yes, Tim.'

'Any luck yet?'

'I'm afraid not.'

'Well, while you're in Moscow, you shouldn't miss what's great here. The ballet is on tonight. They're doing *Giselle*. Are you interested?'

'Very much, thank you.'

'I'll pick you up in an hour.'

The ballet was held at the six-thousand-seat Palace of Congresses inside the Kremlin. It was a magical evening. The music was wonderful, the dancing was fantastic, and the first act flew by swiftly.

As the lights came on for the intermission, Tim got to his feet. 'Follow me. Quick.'

A stampede was starting up the stairs.

'What's going on?'

'You'll see.'

When they arrived at the top floor, they were greeted by the sight of half a dozen serving tables laden with bowls of caviar and bottles of vodka on ice. The theatergoers who had arrived upstairs first were busily helping themselves.

Dana turned to Tim. 'They really know how to put on a show here.'

Tim said, 'This is how the upper class lives.

Remember that thirty percent of the people live below the poverty line.'

Dana and Tim moved toward the windows, away from the crowd.

The lights started to flash. 'Time for the second act.'

The second act was enchanting, but Dana's mind kept flashing back to snatches of conversations.

Taylor Winthrop was scheisse. *He was clever, very clever. He framed me . . .*

It was an unfortunate accident. Gabriel was a wonderful boy . . .

Taylor Winthrop wiped out the Mancino family's future . . .

When the ballet ended, and they were in the car, Tim Drew said, 'Would you like to have a nightcap at my apartment?'

Dana turned to look at him. He was attractive, intelligent, and charming. But he was not Jeff. What came out was 'Thank you, Tim. But no.'

'Oh.' His disappointment was obvious. 'Maybe tomorrow?'

'I'd love to, but I have to be ready early in the morning.' *And I'm madly in love with someone else.*

Early the next morning Dana was at the Bureau for International Economic Development again. The same guard was behind the desk.

'*Dobry dyen.*'

'*Dobry dyen.*'

'I'm Dana Evans. If I can't see the commissar, can I see his assistant?'

'Do you have an appointment?'

'No. I –'

He handed Dana a sheet of paper. 'You will fill this out . . .'

When Dana returned to her room, her cell phone was ringing, and Dana's heart skipped a beat.

'Dana . . .'

'Jeff!'

There was so much they wanted to say. But Rachel stood between them like a ghostly shadow, and they could not discuss what was uppermost in their minds: Rachel's illness. The conversation was guarded.

The call from Commissar Shdanoff's office came unexpectedly at eight o'clock the following morning. A heavily accented voice said, 'Dana Evans?'

'Yes.'

'This is Yerik Karbava, the assistant to Commissar Shdanoff. You wish to see the commissar?'

'Yes!' She half expected him to say, 'Do you have an appointment?' Instead he said, 'Be at the Bureau for Economic Development in exactly one hour.'

'Right. Thank you very –' The line went dead.

One hour later Dana was entering the lobby of the huge brick building again. She walked up to the same guard seated behind the desk.

He looked up. *'Dobry dyen?'*

She forced a smile. *'Dobry dyen.* I'm Dana Evans, and I'm here to see Commissar Shdanoff.'

He shrugged. 'I'm sorry. Without an appointment –'

Dana held on to her temper. 'I have an appointment.'

He looked at her skeptically. *'Da?'* He picked up a telephone and spoke into it for a few moments. He turned to Dana. 'Third floor,' he said reluctantly. 'Someone will meet you.'

Commissar Shdanoff's office was huge and shabby and looked as though it had been furnished in the early 1920s. There were two men in the office.

As Dana entered, they both stood up. The older man said, 'I am Commissar Shdanoff.'

Sasha Shdanoff appeared to be in his fifties. He was short and compact, with wispy gray hair, a pale, round face, and restless brown eyes that constantly darted around the room as though searching for something. He had a heavy accent. He was wearing a shapeless brown suit and scuffed black shoes. He indicated the second man.

'This is my brother, Boris Shdanoff.'

Boris Shdanoff smiled. 'How do you do, Miss Evans?'

Boris Shdanoff looked totally unlike his brother. He appeared to be about ten years younger. He had an aquiline nose and a firm chin. He was dressed in a light blue Armani suit with a gray Hermès tie. He had almost no accent at all.

Sasha Shdanoff said proudly, 'Boris is visiting from America. He is attached to the Russian embassy in your capital, Washington, DC.'

'I've admired your work, Miss Evans,' Boris Shdanoff said.

'Thank you.'

'What can I do for you?' Sasha Shdanoff asked. 'Do you have a problem of some kind?'

'No, not at all,' Dana said. 'I wanted to ask you about Taylor Winthrop.'

He looked at her, puzzled. 'What is it you wish to know about Taylor Winthrop?'

'I understand that you worked with him, and that you saw him socially, on occasion.'

Sasha Shdanoff said cautiously, '*Da*.'

'I wanted to get your personal opinion of him.'

'What is there to say? I think he was a fine ambassador for your country.'

'I understand he was very popular here and –'

Boris Shdanoff interrupted. 'Oh, yes. The embassies in Moscow have many parties, and Taylor Winthrop was always –'

Sasha Shdanoff scowled at his brother. *'Dovolno!'* He turned back to Dana. 'Ambassador Winthrop sometimes went to the embassy parties. He liked people. The Russian people liked him.'

Boris Shdanoff spoke up again. 'As a matter of fact, he told me that if he could –'

Sasha Shdanoff snapped, *'Molchat!'* He turned. 'As I said, Miss Evans, he was a fine ambassador.'

Dana looked at Boris Shdanoff. He was obviously trying to tell her something. She turned back to the commissar. 'Did Ambassador Winthrop ever get in any kind of trouble while he was here?'

Sasha Shdanoff frowned. 'Trouble? No.' He was avoiding her eyes.

He's lying, Dana thought. She pressed on. 'Commissar, can you think of any reason why someone would murder Taylor Winthrop and his family?'

Sasha Shdanoff's eyes widened. *'Murder?* The Winthrops? *Nyet. Nyet.'*

'You can't think of anything at all?'

Boris Shdanoff said, 'As a matter of fact –'

Sasha Shdanoff cut him off. 'There was no reason. He was a great ambassador.' He took a cigarette from a silver case, and Boris hurried to light it for him.

'Was there anything else you want to know?' Sasha Shdanoff asked.

Dana looked at the two of them. *They're hiding something,* she thought, *but what? This whole thing is like walking through a maze with no exit.* 'No.' She glanced at Boris as she said slowly, 'If you think of anything, I'll be at the Sevastopol Hotel until tomorrow morning.'

Boris Shdanoff said, 'You are going back home?'

'Yes. My plane leaves this evening.'

'I –' Boris Shdanoff started to say something, looked at his brother, and was quiet.

'Good-bye,' Dana said.

'*Proshchayte.*'

'*Proshchayte.*'

When Dana got back to her room, she telephoned Matt Baker.

'There's something going on here, Matt, but I can't find out what it is, damn it. I have a feeling that I could stay here for months and not get any useful information. I'll be home tomorrow.'

There's something going on here, Matt, but I can't find out what it is, damn it. I have a feeling that I could stay here for months and not get any useful information. I'll be home tomorrow.

Tape ends.

Sheremetyevo II Airport was crowded that night. Waiting for her plane, Dana had the same uncomfortable feeling that she was being watched. She scanned the crowd, but she could not single out anyone in particular. *They're out there somewhere.* And the realization made her shiver.

Twenty-one

Mrs Daley and Kemal were waiting at Dulles airport to meet Dana. She had not realized how much she had missed Kemal. She flung her arms around him and hugged him tightly.

Kemal said, 'Hi, Dana. I'm glad you're home. Did you bring me a Russian bear?'

'I did, but darn it, he escaped.'

Kemal grinned. 'Are you going to stay home now?'

Dana said warmly, 'You bet I am.'

Mrs Daley smiled. 'That's good news, Miss Evans. We're that glad you've come back.'

'I'm that glad to be back,' Dana said.

In the car, driving to the apartment, Dana said, 'How do you like your new arm now, Kemal? Are you getting used to it?'

'It's cool.'

'I'm so glad. How are you getting along in school?'

'It's not the pits.'

'No more fights?'

'No.'

'That's wonderful, darling.' Dana studied him a moment. He seemed different somehow, almost subdued. It was as though something had happened to change him, but whatever it was, he certainly seemed a happy child.

When they reached the apartment, Dana said, 'I have to go to the studio, but I'll be back, and we'll have dinner together. We'll go to McDonald's.' *Where we used to go with Jeff.*

When Dana entered the huge WTN building, it seemed as though she had been away for a century. As she made her way to Matt's office, she was greeted by half a dozen fellow workers.

'Glad you're back, Dana. We've missed you.'

'Glad to be back.'

'Well, look who's here. Did you have a good trip?'

'Wonderful. Thanks.'

'The place isn't the same without you.'

When Dana walked into Matt's office, he said, 'You've lost weight. You look terrible.'

'Thank you, Matt.'

'Sit down.'

Dana took a seat.

'You haven't been sleeping?'

'Not much.'

'By the way, our ratings have gone down since you've been away.'

'I'm flattered.'

'Elliot will be glad you've given this up. He's been worried about you.' Matt did not mention how worried he himself had been about Dana.

They talked for half an hour.

When Dana got back to her office, Olivia said, 'Welcome back. It's been –' The phone rang. She picked it up. 'Miss Evans's office . . . Just a moment, please.' She looked at Dana. 'Pamela Hudson on line one.'

'I'll take it.' Dana went into her own office and picked up the phone. 'Pamela.'

'Dana, you're back! We were so worried. Russia is not the safest place to be these days.'

'I know.' She laughed. 'A friend bought me pepper spray.'

'We've missed you. Roger and I would love to have you come by for tea this afternoon. Are you free?'

'Yes.'

'Three o'clock?'

'Perfect.'

The rest of the morning was taken up with preparations for the evening broadcasts.

*

At three o'clock, Cesar was greeting Dana at the door.

'Miss Evans!' There was a big smile on his face. 'I'm so pleased to see you. Welcome home.'

'Thank you, Cesar. How have you been?'

'Just wonderful, thank you.'

'Are Mr and Mrs – ?'

'Yes. They're waiting for you. May I take your coat?'

When Dana walked into the drawing room, Roger and Pamela both exclaimed at once, 'Dana!'

Pamela Hudson gave her a hug. 'The prodigal is back.'

Roger Hudson said, 'You look tired.'

'That seems to be the general consensus.'

'Sit down, sit down,' Roger said.

A maid came in carrying a tray of tea, biscuits, scones, and croissants. Pamela poured tea.

They took seats, and Roger said, 'Well, tell us what's happening.'

'What's happening is I'm afraid I've gotten nowhere. I'm completely frustrated.' Dana took a deep breath. 'I met a man named Dieter Zander who said he was framed by Taylor Winthrop and sent to prison. While he was there, his family was wiped out in a fire. He blames Winthrop for their deaths.'

Pamela said, 'So he had a motive for killing the whole Winthrop family.'

'That's right. But there's more,' Dana said. 'I

302

talked to a man named Marcel Falcon in France. His only son was killed by a hit-and-run driver. Taylor Winthrop's chauffeur pleaded guilty, but the chauffeur now claims that Taylor Winthrop was the driver.'

Roger said thoughtfully, 'Falcon was on the NATO Commission in Brussels.'

'Right. And the chauffeur told him that it was Taylor Winthrop who killed his son.'

'That's interesting.'

'Very. Have you ever heard of Vincent Mancino?'

Roger Hudson thought for a moment. 'No.'

'He's Mafia. Taylor Winthrop got his daughter pregnant, sent her to a quack, and she had a botched abortion. The daughter is in a convent and the mother is in a sanitarium.'

'My God.'

'The point is that all three have strong motives for revenge.' Dana sighed in frustration. 'But I can't prove anything.'

Roger looked at Dana thoughtfully. 'So Taylor Winthrop was really guilty of doing all those terrible things.'

'There's no question about it, Roger. I've talked to those people. Whichever one of them is behind the murders orchestrated them brilliantly. There are no clues – none. Each murder had a different modus operandi, so there is no obvious pattern. Every detail was carefully worked out. Nothing was left to chance. There was not one witness to any of the deaths.'

Pamela said thoughtfully, 'I know this may sound far-fetched, but – is it possible that they're all in this together to get revenge?'

Dana shook her head. 'I don't believe there was collusion. The men I talked to are very powerful. I think each would want to do it on his own. Only one of them is guilty.'

But which one?

Dana suddenly looked at her watch. 'Please excuse me. I promised to take Kemal to McDonald's for dinner, and if I hurry, I can do it before I go to work.'

'Of course, darling,' said Pamela. 'We understand completely. Thank you for stopping by.'

Dana got up to go. 'And thank you both for the lovely tea and for your moral support.'

Driving Kemal to school on Monday morning, Dana said, 'I've missed doing this, but I'm back now.'

'I'm glad.' Kemal yawned.

Dana realized that he had been yawning ever since he had awakened. Dana asked, 'Did you sleep well last night?'

'Yeah, I guess so.' Kemal yawned again.

'What do you do at school?' Dana asked.

'You mean besides horrible history and boring English?'

'Yes.'

'I play soccer.'

'You're not doing *too* much, are you, Kemal?'

'Nah.'

She glanced at the frail figure next to her. It seemed to Dana that all the energy had gone out of Kemal. He was unnaturally quiet. Dana wondered if she should have a doctor look at him. Maybe she could check and see if there were some vitamins that would give him energy. She looked at her watch. The meeting for this evening's broadcast was half an hour away.

The morning went by swiftly, and it felt good to be back in her world. When Dana returned to her office, there was a sealed envelope on her desk with her name on it. She opened it. The letter inside read:

'Miss Evans: I have the information you want. I have made a reservation in your name at the Soyuz Hotel in Moscow. Come immediately. Tell no one about this.'

It was unsigned. Dana read the letter again, unbelievingly. *I have the information you want.*

Of course it was some kind of trick. If someone in Russia had the answer she was looking for, why hadn't whoever it was told her about it when she was over there? Dana thought about the meeting she had had with Commissar Sasha Shdanoff and his brother Boris. Boris had seemed anxious to talk to her, and Sasha had kept cutting him off. Dana sat at her desk, thinking. How had the note gotten on her desk? Was she being watched?

I'm going to forget it, Dana decided. She stuffed the letter in her purse. *I'll tear it up when I get home.*

Dana spent the evening with Kemal. She had thought he would be fascinated by the new computer game she had bought him in Moscow, but he seemed indifferent. At nine o'clock his eyes started to close.

'I'm sleepy, Dana. I'm going to bed.'

'All right, darling.' Dana watched him go into the study and thought, *He's changed so much. He seems like a different boy. Well, from now on we're going to be together. If something's bothering him, I'll find out what it is.* It was time to leave for the studio.

In the apartment next door, the tenant looked at the television set and spoke into a tape recorder.

'The subject has left for the television studio to do her broadcast. The boy has gone to bed. The housekeeper is sewing.'

'We're live!' The camera's red light flashed on.

The announcer's voice boomed out, 'Good evening. This is your eleven o'clock news on WTN with Dana Evans and Richard Melton.'

Dana smiled into the camera. 'Good evening. I'm Dana Evans.'

Seated next to her, Richard Melton said, 'And I'm Richard Melton.'

Dana began, 'We start our news tonight with a terrible tragedy in Malaysia . . .'

This is where I belong, Dana thought, not running around the world on some wild-goose chase.

The broadcast went well. When Dana returned to the apartment, Kemal was asleep. After saying good night to Mrs Daley, Dana went to bed, but she was unable to sleep.

I have the information you want. I have made a reservation in your name at the Soyuz Hotel in Moscow. Come immediately. Tell no one about this.

It's a trap. I'd be a fool to go back to Moscow, Dana thought. *But what if it's real? Who would go to all this trouble? And why? The letter could only have come from Boris Shdanoff. What if he really knows something?* She was awake all night.

When Dana arose in the morning, she telephoned Roger Hudson and told him about the note.

'My God. I don't know what to say.' He sounded excited.

'This could mean that someone is ready to tell the truth about what happened to the Winthrops.'

'I know.'

'Dana, it could be dangerous. I don't like that.'

'If I don't go, we'll never find out the truth.'

He hesitated. 'I suppose you're right.'

'I'll be careful, but I must go.'

Roger Hudson said reluctantly, 'Very well. I want you to stay in close touch.'

'I promise, Roger.'

Dana was at the Corniche Travel Agency buying a round-trip ticket to Moscow. It was Tuesday. *I hope I won't be gone too long*, Dana thought. She left a message for Matt to tell him what was happening.

When Dana returned to her apartment, she said to Mrs Daley, 'I'm afraid I have to go away again. It's just for a couple of days. Take good care of Kemal.'

'You don't have to worry about anything, Miss Evans. We'll be fine.'

The tenant next door turned away from the television set and made a hasty telephone call.

Boarding the Aeroflot plane to Moscow, Dana thought, *It's déjà vu. Maybe I'm making a big mistake. It could be a trap. But if the answer is in Moscow, I'm going to find it.* She settled back for the long flight.

*

When the plane landed the next morning at the now familiar Sheremetyevo II airport, Dana collected her bag and walked outside into a blinding snowstorm. There was a long line of travelers waiting for taxis. Dana stood in the cold wind, grateful for her warm coat. Forty-five minutes later, when it was finally Dana's turn, a burly man tried to push in ahead of her.

'*Nyet!*' Dana said firmly. 'This is my cab.' She got inside.

The driver said, '*Da?*'

'I want to go to the Soyuz Hotel.'

He turned to look at her and said in halting English, 'You sure you wish to go there?'

Dana said, puzzled, 'Why? What do you mean?'

'That is very not nice hotel.'

Dana felt a frisson of alarm. *Am I sure? Too late to back off now*. He was waiting for an answer. 'Yes. I – I'm sure.'

The driver shrugged, put the taxi in gear, and started off into the snowbound traffic.

Dana thought, *What if there is no reservation at the hotel? What if all this is some stupid joke?*

The Soyuz Hotel was located in a working-class district on the outskirts of Moscow on Levoberezhnaya Street. It was an old, unprepossessing building with brown paint peeling off the exterior.

'You want I wait?' the driver asked.

Dana hesitated for only an instant. 'No.' She paid the driver, got out of the taxi, and the icy wind pushed her into the small, shabby lobby. An elderly woman sat behind the desk, reading a magazine. She looked up in surprise as Dana entered. Dana walked up to the desk.

'*Da?*'

'I believe I have a reservation. Dana Evans.' She was holding her breath.

The woman nodded slowly. 'Dana Evans, yes.' She reached behind her and pulled out a key from a rack. 'Four-oh-two, fourth floor.' She handed it to Dana.

'Where do I register?'

The woman shook her head. 'No register. You pay now. One day.'

Dana felt a new sense of alarm. A hotel in Russia where foreigners didn't have to register? Something was very wrong.

The woman said, 'Five hundred rubles.'

'I'll have to get some money changed,' Dana said. 'Later.'

'No. Now. I take dollars.'

'All right.' Dana reached into her purse and took out a handful of bills.

The woman nodded, reached out, and extracted half a dozen of them.

I think I could have bought the hotel with that. Dana looked around. 'Where is the elevator?'

'No elevator.'

'Oh.' A porter was obviously out of the question. Dana picked up her bag and started walking up the stairs.

Her room was even worse than she had antici-
pated. It was small and shabby, the curtains were
torn and the bed unmade. How was Boris going to
contact her? *This could be a hoax*, Dana thought, *but
why would anyone go to this much trouble?*

Dana sat on the edge of the bed and looked out
of the unwashed window at the busy street scene
below.

I've been a bloody fool, Dana thought. *I could be
sitting here for days, and nothing –*

There was a soft rap on the door. Dana took a
deep breath and stood up. She was either going to
solve the mystery now or find out that there was
no mystery. Dana walked over to the door and
opened it. There was no one in the hallway. On the
floor was an envelope. Dana picked it up and carried
it inside. The piece of paper inside said *VDNKh 9:00
PM*. Dana stared at it, trying to make sense of it.
She opened her suitcase and took out the guidebook
she had brought. There it was, *VDNKh*. The text
read *USSR, economic achievements exhibition*, and it
gave an address.

At eight o'clock that evening, Dana hailed a taxi.
'*VDNKh*. The park?' She was not sure of her pro-
nunciation.

The driver turned to look at her. '*VDNKh?* Everything closed.'

'Oh.'

'You still go there?'

'Yes.'

The driver shrugged and the cab leaped forward.

The vast park was in the northeast section of Moscow. According to the guidebook, the lavish exhibitions had been planned as a monument to Soviet glory, but when the economy fell, funds were cut off, and the park had become a decaying monument to Soviet dogma. The grandiose pavilions were crumbling and the park was deserted.

Dana stepped out of the taxi and took out a handful of American money. 'Is this – ?'

'*Da.*' He grabbed the bills and a moment later was gone.

Dana looked around. She was alone in the freezing, windswept park. She walked to a nearby bench and sat down and waited for Boris. She remembered how she had waited at the zoo for Joan Sinisi. *What if Boris – ?*

A voice from behind Dana startled her. '*Horoshiy vyecherniy.*'

Dana turned, and her eyes widened in surprise. She had expected Boris Shdanoff. Instead, she was looking at Commissar Sasha Shdanoff. 'Commissar! I didn't expect –'

'You will follow me,' he said curtly. Sasha Shdanoff started walking rapidly across the park. Dana hesitated an instant, then got up and hurried after

312

him. He walked into a small, rustic-looking café at the edge of the park and took a seat at a back booth. There was only one other couple in the café. Dana crossed over to his booth and sat down.

A slovenly waitress in a soiled apron came up to them. *'Da?'*

'Dva cofe, pozhalooysta,' Shdanoff said. He turned back to Dana. 'I was not sure you would come, but you are very persistent. That can be dangerous sometimes.'

'You said in your note you could tell me what I want to know.'

'Yes.' The coffee arrived. He took a sip, and was silent for a moment. 'You want to know if Taylor Winthrop and his family were murdered.'

Dana's heart began to beat faster. 'Were they?'

'Yes.' It came out in an eerie whisper.

Dana felt a sudden chill. 'Do you know who killed them?'

'Yes.'

She took a deep breath. 'Who?'

He raised a hand to stop her. 'I will tell you, but first you must do something for me.'

Dana looked at him and said cautiously, 'What?'

'Get me out of Russia. I am no longer safe here.'

'Why can't you just go to the airport and fly away? I understand that foreign travel is no longer forbidden.'

'Dear Miss Evans, you are naive. Very naive. True, it is not like the old days of communism, but if I were to try what you suggest, they would kill me before I even got close to an airport. The walls still have ears and eyes. I am in great danger. I need your help.'

It took a moment for his words to sink in. Dana looked at him in dismay. 'I can't get you – I wouldn't know where to begin.'

'You must. You must find a way. My life is in danger.'

Dana was thoughtful for a moment. 'I can talk to the American ambassador and –'

'No!' Sasha Shdanoff's voice was sharp.

'But that's the only way –'

'Your embassy has traitors' ears. No one must know about this but you and whoever is going to help you. Your ambassador cannot help me.'

Dana felt suddenly depressed. There was no possible way she could sneak a top Russian commissar out of Russia. *I couldn't sneak a cat out of this country.* And she had another thought. This whole thing was probably a ruse. Sasha Shdanoff had no information. He was using her as a means to get to America. This trip had been for nothing.

Dana said, 'I'm afraid I can't help you, Commissar Shdanoff.' She got to her feet, furious.

'Wait! You want proof? I will give you proof.'

'What kind of proof?'

It took him a long time to answer. When he spoke, he said slowly, 'You are forcing me to do something

I have no wish to do.' He rose. 'You will come with me.'

Thirty minutes later, they were going up the private back entrance to Sasha Shdanoff's offices at the Bureau for International Economic Development.

'I could be executed for what I am about to tell you,' Sasha Shdanoff said when they arrived. 'But I have no choice.' He made a helpless gesture. 'Because I will be killed if I stay here.'

Dana watched as Shdanoff walked over to a large safe built into the wall. He spun the combination, pulled open the safe, and took out a thick book. He carried it to his desk. On the front of the book it said in red lettering *Klassifitsirovann'gy*.

'This is highly classified information,' Commissar Shdanoff told Dana. He opened the book.

Dana looked closely as he slowly started to turn the pages. Each page contained color photographs of bombers, space launch vehicles, antiballistic missiles, air-to-surface missiles, automatic weapons, tanks, and submarines.

'This is Russia's complete arsenal.' It looked enormous, deadly.

'At this moment, Russia has more than one thousand intercontinental ballistic missiles, more than two thousand atomic warheads, and seventy strategic bombers.' He pointed to various weapons as he turned the pages. 'This is the Awl . . . Acrid . . .

Aphid . . . Anab . . . Archer . . . Our nuclear arsenal rivals that of the United States.'

'It's very, very impressive.'

'The Russian military has grave problems, Miss Evans. We are facing a crisis. There is no money to pay the soldiers, and the morale is very low. The present offers little hope, and the future looks worse, so the military is being forced to turn to the past.'

Dana said, 'I – I'm afraid I don't understand how this –'

'When Russia was truly a superpower, we built more weapons than even the United States. All those weapons are sitting here now. There are dozens of countries hungry for them. They are worth billions.'

Dana said patiently, 'Commissar, I understand the problem, but –'

'This is not the problem.'

Dana looked at him, puzzled. 'No? Then what is?'

Shdanoff chose his next words carefully. 'Have you heard of Krasnoyarsk-26?'

Dana shook her head. 'No.'

'I am not surprised. It is not on any map, and the people who live there do not officially exist.'

'What are you talking about?'

'You will see. Tomorrow I will take you there. You are to meet me at the same café at noon.' He put his hand on Dana's arm, squeezing hard. 'You

316

must not tell anyone about this.' He was hurting her. 'Do you understand?'

'Yes.'

'*Orobopeno*. It is agreed.'

At noon, Dana arrived at the little café in VDNKh Park. She walked in and sat at the same booth, waiting. Thirty minutes later Shdanoff had still not appeared. *What happens now?* she wondered anxiously.

'*Dobry dyen*.' Sasha Shdanoff was standing at the booth. 'Come. We must go shopping.'

'Shopping?' she asked incredulously.

'Come!'

Dana followed him out into the park. 'Shopping for what?'

'For you.'

'I don't need –'

Shdanoff hailed a taxi and they rode in a strained silence to a mall. They got out of the taxi, and Shdanoff paid the driver.

'In here,' Sasha Shdanoff said.

They walked inside the mall past half a dozen stores. When they came to a shop with a display of provocative, sexy lingerie in the window, Shdanoff stopped.

'Here.' He led Dana inside.

Dana looked around at the sleazy garments. 'What are we doing here?'

'You are going to change clothes.'

A saleslady approached them, and there was a rapid exchange in Russian. The saleslady nodded and a few moments later returned with a hot pink miniskirt and a beribboned, very low-cut blouse.

Shdanoff nodded his approval. '*Da.*' He turned to Dana. 'You will put these on.'

Dana recoiled. 'No! I'm not going to wear that. What do you –'

'You must.' His voice was firm.

'Why?'

'You will see.'

Dana thought, *The man is some kind of sex maniac. What the devil have I gotten myself into?*

Shdanoff was watching her. 'Well?'

Dana took a deep breath. 'All right.' She went into a tiny dressing room and put the outfit on. When she came out, she looked in a mirror and gasped. 'I look like a whore.'

'Not yet,' Shdanoff informed her. 'We are going to get you some makeup.'

'Commissar –'

'Come.'

Dana's clothes were stuffed into a paper bag. Dana put on her wool coat, trying to hide her outfit as much as possible. They started walking through the mall again. Passersby were staring at Dana, and men were giving her knowing smiles. A workman winked at her. Dana felt degraded.

'In here!'

318

They were in front of a beauty salon. Sasha Shdanoff went inside. Dana hesitated, then followed him. He walked to the counter.

'*Ano tyomnyj,*' he said.

The beautician showed him a tube of a bright red lipstick and a jar of rouge.

'*Savirshehnstva,*' Shdanoff said. He turned to Dana. 'Put it on. Heavy.'

Dana had had enough. 'No, thanks. I don't know what kind of game you think you're playing, Commissar, but I'm not going to be a part of it. I've had –'

His eyes bored into hers. 'I assure you it is not a game, Miss Evans. Krasnoyarsk-26 is a closed city. I am one of the select few with access to it. They allow a very, very few of us outsiders to bring in prostitutes for the day. That is the only possible way I can get you past the guards. That and a case of excellent vodka as payment for your entry. Are you interested or not?'

Closed city? Guards? How far are we going with this?
'Yes,' Dana reluctantly decided. 'I'm interested.'

Twenty-two

There was a military jet waiting at a private area of Sheremetyevo II airport. Dana was surprised to see that she and Sasha Shdanoff were the only passengers.

'Where are we going?' Dana asked.

Sasha Shdanoff gave her a mirthless smile. 'To Siberia.'

Siberia. Dana felt a knot in her stomach. 'Oh.'

The flight took four hours. Dana tried to make conversation, hoping to get an inkling of what she was facing, but Shdanoff sat in his seat, silent and grim-faced.

When the plane landed at a small airport in what seemed to Dana to be the middle of nowhere, a Lada 2110 sedan was waiting on the frozen tarmac for them. Dana looked around at the most desolate landscape she had ever seen.

'This place we're going to – is it far from here?' *And will I be coming back?*

'It is a short distance. We must be very careful.'
Careful of what?

There was a short, bumpy drive to what looked like a small train station. Half a dozen heavily bundled-up uniformed guards stood on the platform.

As Dana and Shdanoff approached them, the guards were ogling Dana's skimpy outfit. One of them pointed to Dana and smirked. *'Ti vezuchi!'*

'Kakaya krasivaya zhenshina!'

Shdanoff grinned and said something in Russian and all the guards laughed.

I don't want to know, Dana decided.

Shdanoff boarded the train and Dana followed, more confused than ever. *Where could a train be going in the middle of a bleak, frozen tundra?* The temperature in the train was freezing.

The engine started, and a few minutes later the train was entering a brightly lit tunnel cut into the heart of a mountain. Dana looked at the rock on both sides, inches away, and had the feeling she was in some weird, surrealistic dream.

She turned to Shdanoff. 'Will you please tell me where we're going?'

The train jerked to a stop. 'We are here.'

They debarked from the train and started toward an odd-shaped cement building one hundred yards away. In front of the building stood two forbidding-looking barbed-wire fences, patrolled by heavily armed soldiers. As Dana and Sasha Shdanoff approached the gates, the soldiers saluted.

Shdanoff whispered, 'Put your arm in mine and kiss me and laugh.'

Jeff will never believe this, Dana thought. She put her arm in Shdanoff's, kissed him on the cheek, and forced a hollow laugh.

The gates swung open and the two of them went through, arm in arm. The soldiers watched enviously as Commissar Shdanoff walked in with his beautiful whore. To Dana's astonishment, the structure they entered was the top of an elevator station that went below the ground. They stepped into the cab of the elevator and the door banged closed.

As they started down, Dana asked, 'Where are we going?'

'Beneath the mountain.' The elevator was picking up speed.

'How far beneath the mountain?' Dana asked nervously.

He said, 'Six hundred feet.'

Dana looked at him incredulously. 'We're going six hundred feet under a mountain. Why? What's down there?'

'You will see.'

In a few minutes, the elevator began to slow down. Finally, it stopped, and the door opened automatically.

Commissar Shdanoff said, 'We are here, Miss Evans.'

But where is here?

They stepped out of the elevator and had walked no more than twenty feet when Dana stopped in shock. She found herself looking down the street of a modern city, with shops and restaurants and theaters. Men and women were walking along the sidewalks, and Dana suddenly realized that no one was wearing an overcoat. Dana began to feel warm. She turned to Shdanoff. 'We're underneath a mountain?'

'That's right.'

'But –' She looked at the incredible sight spread out before her. 'I don't understand. What is this place?'

'I told you. Krasnoyarsk-26.'

'Is this some kind of bomb shelter?'

'On the contrary,' Shdanoff said enigmatically.

Dana looked again at all the modern buildings around her. 'Commissar, what is the point of this place?'

He gave Dana a long, hard look. 'You would be better off not knowing what I am about to tell you.'

Dana felt a fresh sense of alarm.

'Do you know anything about plutonium?'

'Not very much, no.'

'Plutonium is the fuel of a nuclear warhead, the key ingredient in atomic weapons. Krasnoyarsk-26's sole purpose for existing is to make plutonium. One hundred thousand scientists and technicians live and work here, Miss Evans. In the beginning, they were given the finest food and clothes and housing. But they are all here with one restriction.'

'Yes?'

'They must agree never to leave.'

'You mean –'

'They cannot go outside. Ever. They must cut themselves off completely from the rest of the world.'

Dana looked at the people walking along the warm streets and thought to herself, *This can't be real.* 'Where do they make the plutonium?'

'I will show you.' A tram was approaching. 'Come.' Shdanoff boarded the tram, and Dana followed him. They rode down the busy main street, and at the end entered a maze of dimly lit tunnels.

Dana thought of the incredible work and all the years that must have gone into building this city. In a few minutes, the lights began to get brighter, and the tram stopped. They were at the entrance to an enormous, brightly lit laboratory.

'We get off here.'

Dana followed Shdanoff and looked around in awe. There were three giant reactors housed in the immense cave. Two of the reactors were silent, but the third one was in operation and surrounded by a busy cadre of technicians.

Shdanoff said, 'The machines in this room can produce enough plutonium to make an atomic bomb every three days.' He indicated the one that was working. 'That reactor is still producing half a ton of plutonium a year, enough to make a hundred bombs. The plutonium stockpiled in the next room is worth a czar's ransom.'

Dana asked, 'Commissar, if they have all that plutonium, why are they still making more?'

Shdanoff said wryly, 'It is what you Americans call a catch-twenty-two. They can't turn the reactor off because the plutonium furnishes the power for the city above. If they stop the reactor, there will be no light and no heat, and the people up there will quickly freeze to death.'

'That's awful,' Dana said. 'If –'

'Wait. What I have to tell you gets worse. Because of the state of the Russian economy, there is no longer the money to pay the scientists and technicians who work here. They have not been paid in months. The beautiful homes they were given years ago are deteriorating, and there is no money to repair them. All the luxuries have disappeared. The people here are getting desperate. You see the paradox? The amount of plutonium stored here is worth untold billions of dollars, yet the people who created it have nothing and are starting to go hungry.'

Dana said slowly, 'And you think they might sell some of the plutonium to other countries?'

He nodded. 'Before Taylor Winthrop became ambassador to Russia, friends told him about Krasnoyarsk-26 and asked him if he wanted to make a deal. After he talked to some of the scientists here who felt betrayed by their government, Winthrop was eager to make a deal. But it was complicated, and he had to wait until all the pieces fell into place.'

He was like a crazy man. He said something like 'All the pieces have fallen into place.'

Dana was finding it difficult to breathe.

'Shortly after that, Taylor Winthrop became the American ambassador to Russia. Winthrop and his partner collaborated with some of the rebel scientists and began smuggling plutonium to a dozen countries, including Libya, Iran, Iraq, Pakistan, North Korea, and China.'

After all the pieces had fallen into place! The ambassadorship was important to Taylor Winthrop only because he had to be on hand to control the operation.

The commissar was going on. 'It was easy, because a mass of plutonium the size of a tennis ball is enough to make a nuclear bomb, Miss Evans. Taylor Winthrop and his partner were making billions of dollars. They handled everything very cleverly, and no one suspected a thing.' He sounded bitter. 'Russia has become a candy store – only instead of buying candy, you can buy atomic bombs, tanks, fighter planes and missile systems.'

Dana was trying to digest everything she was hearing. 'Why was Taylor Winthrop killed?'

'He got greedy and decided to go into business for himself. When his partner learned what Winthrop was doing, he had him killed.'

'But – but why murder his whole family?'

'After Taylor Winthrop and his wife died in the fire, his son Paul tried to blackmail the partner, so he had Paul killed. And then he decided he could not take a chance that the other children might know about the plutonium, so he ordered the other two murdered and arranged for their deaths to look like an accident and a burglary gone wrong.'

Dana looked at him, horrified. 'Who was Taylor Winthrop's partner?'

Commissar Shdanoff shook his head. 'You know enough for now, Miss Evans. I will give you the name when you get me out of Russia.' He looked at his watch. 'We must leave.'

Dana turned to take one last look at the reactor that could not be shut off, that was turning out deadly plutonium twenty-four hours a day. 'Is the government of the United States aware of Krasnoyarsk-26?'

Shdanoff nodded. 'Oh, yes. They are terrified of it. Your State Department is working frantically with us to try to find a way to turn these reactors into something less lethal. Meanwhile . . .' He shrugged.

In the elevator, Commissar Shdanoff asked, 'Are you familiar with the FRA?'

Dana looked at him and said cautiously, 'Yes.'

'They are involved in this also.'

'What?' And then the realization hit her. *That's why General Booster kept warning me away.*

They arrived at the surface and stepped out of the

elevator. Shdanoff said, 'I keep an apartment here. We will go there.'

As they started to walk along the street, Dana noticed a woman dressed as she was, clinging to the arms of a man.

'That woman –' Dana started.

'I told you. Certain men are permitted to use prostitutes during the day. But at night the prostitutes must return to a guarded compound. They must know nothing of what goes on below the ground.'

As they walked along, Dana noticed that most of the shops' windows were empty.

The luxuries are gone. The state no longer has money to pay the scientists and technicians who work here. They have not been paid in months. Dana looked at a tall building on the corner and noticed that instead of a clock it had a large instrument mounted on top.

'What is that?' Dana asked.

'A Geiger counter, a warning in case anything goes wrong with the reactors.' They turned into a side street filled with apartment buildings. 'My apartment is in here. We must stay there for a little while so no one will be suspicious. The FSB checks on everyone.'

'The FSB?'

'Yes. It used to be called the KGB. They changed the name, but that is all they changed.'

The apartment was large and was once luxurious, but it had become shabby. The curtains were torn, the carpets were worn, and the furniture needed reupholstering.

Dana sat down, thinking about what Sasha Shdanoff had told her about the FRA. And Jeff had said, *The agency is a cover-up. The real function of the FRA is to spy on foreign intelligence agencies.* Taylor Winthrop had once been the head of FRA, working with Victor Booster.

I would stay as far away as you can from General Booster.

And her meeting with Booster. *Can't you fucking journalists let the dead rest? I'm warning you to stay the hell away.* General Victor Booster had an enormous secret organization to carry out the murders.

And Jack Stone was trying to protect her. *Be careful. If Victor Booster knew I was even talking to you . . .*

FRA spies were everywhere, and Dana felt suddenly naked.

Sasha Shdanoff looked at his watch. 'It is time to leave. Do you know yet how you are going to get me out of the country?'

'Yes,' Dana said slowly. 'I think I know how to arrange it. I need a little time.'

When the plane landed back in Moscow, there were two cars waiting. Shdanoff handed Dana a piece of paper.

'I am staying with a friend at the Chiaka Apartments. No one knows I am there. It is what you call a "safe house". Here is the address. I can't go back to my own place. Come here at eight o'clock this evening. I must know your plan.'

Dana nodded. 'All right. I have a phone call to make.'

When Dana got back to the lobby of the Soyuz Hotel, the woman behind the desk stared at her. *I don't blame her*, Dana thought. *I've got to get out of this dreadful outfit.*

Inside her room, Dana changed into her own clothes before making a phone call. She prayed as the phone kept ringing at the other end. *Please be in. Please be in.* Dana heard Cesar's blessed voice.

'The Hudson residence.'

'Cesar, is Mr Hudson in?' Dana found that she was holding her breath.

'Miss Evans! How nice to hear from you. Yes, Mr Hudson is here. Hold on, please.'

Dana felt her body tremble with relief. If there was anyone who could help her get Sasha Shdanoff into the United States, Roger Hudson would be the one person able to do it.

His voice came on the line a moment later. 'Dana?'

'Roger, oh, thank God I got you!'

'What's the matter? Are you all right? Where are you?'

'I'm in Moscow. I found out why Taylor Winthrop and his family were murdered.'

'*What?* My God. How did you –'

'I'll tell you all about it when I see you. Roger, I hate to impose on you again, but I have a problem. There's an important Russian official who wants to escape to America. His name is Sasha Shdanoff. His life is in danger here. He knows the answers to everything that's happened. We have to get him out, and quickly! Can you help?'

'Dana, neither of us should be involved in anything like this. We could both get in trouble.'

'We have to take that chance. We have no choice. This is too important. It has to be done.'

'I don't like this, Dana.'

'I'm sorry to drag you into this, but I have no one else to turn to.'

'Dammit, I –' He stopped. 'All right. The best thing to do right now is to get him to the American embassy. He'll be safe there until we can work out a plan to get him into the United States.'

'He doesn't want to go to the American embassy. He doesn't trust them.'

'There is no other way. I'll call the ambassador on a secure line and tell him to see that he gets protection. Where is Shdanoff now?'

'He's waiting for me at the Chiaka Apartments. He's staying with a friend. I'm going there to meet him.'

'All right. Dana, when you pick him up, go directly to the American embassy. Don't stop anywhere on the way.'

Dana felt a surge of relief. 'Thank you, Roger. I mean *thank you*!'

'Be careful, Dana.'

'I will.'

'We'll talk later.'

Thank you, Roger. I mean thank you.
Be careful, Dana.
I will.
We'll talk later.

Tape ends.

At seven-thirty, Dana slipped out of the service entrance of the Soyuz Hotel. She went down an alley, ripped by the icy wind. She pulled her coat around her tightly, but the cold was in her bones. Dana walked two blocks, making sure that she was not being followed. At the first busy corner, she hailed a taxi and gave the driver the address Sasha Shdanoff had given her. Fifteen minutes later the taxi stopped in front of a nondescript apartment building.

'Me wait?' the driver asked.

'No.' Commissar Shdanoff would probably have a car. Dana took some dollars from her purse, held

333

out her hand, and the driver grunted and took them all. Dana watched him drive off, and she went inside the building. The hallway was deserted. She looked at the slip in her hand, apartment 2BE. She approached a flight of shabby stairs and walked up to the second floor. There was no one around. A long hallway lay in front of her.

Dana began to walk along it slowly, looking at the numbers on the doors. 5BE . . . 4BE . . . 3BE . . . The door to 2BE was ajar. Dana tensed. Cautiously, she pushed the door open wider and stepped inside. The apartment was dark.

'Commissar . . . ?' She waited. There was no answer. 'Commissar Shdanoff?' A heavy silence. There was a bedroom ahead, and Dana moved toward it. 'Commissar Shdanoff . . .'

As Dana entered the dark bedroom, she tripped over something and fell to the floor. She was lying on something soft and wet. Filled with revulsion, Dana scrambled to her feet. She felt along the wall until she found a switch. She pressed it, and the room was flooded with light. Her hands were covered with blood. On the floor lay the object she had stumbled over: Sasha Shdanoff's body. He was on his back, his chest soaked in blood, his throat slit from ear to ear.

Dana screamed. As she did, she looked at the bed and saw the bloody body of a middle-aged woman with a plastic bag tied around her head. Dana felt her flesh crawl.

Hysterical, she ran down the stairs of the apartment building.

He was standing at the window of an apartment in the building across the street, loading a thirty-shot rifle clip into an AR-7 rifle with a silencer. He was using a 3–6 powered scope, accurate up to sixty-five yards. He moved with the easy, calm grace of a professional. This was a simple job. The woman should be coming out of the building at any minute. He smiled at the thought of how she must have panicked when she found the two bloody bodies. Now it was her turn.

The door to the apartment building across the street flew open, and he carefully raised the rifle to his shoulder. Through the scope, he saw Dana's face as she ran out onto the street, frantically looking around, trying to decide which way to go. He aimed carefully to make sure she was in the exact center of the scope and gently squeezed the trigger.

At that instant, a bus stopped in front of the building, and the spray of bullets hit the top of the bus and blew part of the roof off. The sniper looked down, unbelievingly. Some of the bullets had ricocheted into the bricks of the building, but the target was unharmed. People were pouring out of the bus, screaming. He knew he had to get out of there. The woman was running down the street. *Not to worry. The others would deal with her.*

*

The streets were icy and the wind was howling, but Dana never noticed. She was in a complete panic. Two blocks away she came to a hotel and ran into the lobby.

'Telephone?' she said to the clerk behind the desk.

He looked at her bloody hands and drew back.

'Telephone!' Dana was almost screaming.

Nervously, the clerk pointed to a phone booth in a corner of the lobby. Dana hurried into it. From her purse, she took out a phone card and, with trembling fingers, telephoned the operator.

'I want to place a call to America.' Her hands were shaking. Through chattering teeth, she gave the operator her card number and Roger Hudson's number and waited. After what seemed to be an eternity, Dana heard Cesar's voice.

'The Hudson residence.'

'Cesar! I need to talk to Mr Hudson.' Her voice was choked.

'Miss Evans?'

'Hurry, Cesar, hurry!'

A minute later Dana heard Roger's voice. 'Dana?'

'Roger!' Tears were streaming down Dana's face. 'He's – he's dead. They m-murdered him and his friend.'

'*What?* My God, Dana. I don't know what – are you hurt?'

'No . . . but they're trying to kill me.'

'Now, listen carefully. There's an Air France plane that leaves for Washington at midnight. I'll get you a reservation on it. Make sure you're not followed to the airport. Don't take a taxi there. Go directly to the Hotel Metropol. The hotel has airport buses leaving regularly. Take one of them. Mingle with the crowds. I'll be waiting for you in Washington when you arrive. For God's sakes, watch yourself!'

'I will, Roger. Th – thank you.'

Dana hung up the phone. She stood there a moment, unable to move, filled with terror. She could not get the bloody images of Shdanoff and his friend out of her mind. She took a deep breath and walked out of the booth, past the suspicious clerk, out into the freezing-cold night.

A taxi pulled up to the curb next to her, and the driver said something to her in Russian.

Nyet, Dana said. She began to hurry down the street. She had to go back to her hotel first.

As Roger replaced the phone, he heard Pamela come in the front door.

'Dana's telephoned twice from Moscow. She's found out why the Winthrops were murdered.'

Pamela said, 'Then we must take care of her right away.'

'I already tried. We sent a sniper, but something went wrong.'

337

Pamela looked at him with contempt. 'You fool. Call them again. And, Roger . . .'

'Yes?'

'Tell them to make it look like an accident.'

Twenty-three

In Raven Hill, a red NO TRESPASSING sign and high
iron fence excluded the world from the wooded
acres of the headquarters the FRA had established
in England. Behind the closely guarded base, a series
of satellite-tracking dishes monitored international
cable and microwave communications passing
through Britain. In a concrete house in the center
of the compound, four men were watching a large
screen.

'Beam her up, Scotty.'

They watched the television picture shift away
from a flat in Brighton as the satellite moved. A
moment later an image of Dana came up on the
large screen as she entered her room at the Soyuz
Hotel.

'She's back.' They watched as Dana hurriedly
washed the blood off her hands and started to
undress.

'Hey, here we go again.' One of the men grinned.

They watched as Dana stripped.

'Man, I'd sure like to bonk that.'

Another man hurried into the room. 'Not unless you're into necrophilia, Charlie.'

'What are you talking about?'

'She's about to have a fatal accident.'

Dana finished dressing and looked at her watch. There was still plenty of time to catch the Metropol bus to the airport. With growing anxiety, she hurried downstairs to the lobby. The fat woman was nowhere in sight.

Dana walked out onto the street. Impossibly, it had gotten colder. The wind was a relentless, howling banshee. A taxi stopped in front of Dana.

'Taksi?'

Don't take a taxi. Go directly to the Hotel Metropol. The hotel has airport buses leaving regularly.

'Nyet.'

Dana started walking along the icy street. Crowds were pushing past her, hurrying to the warmth of homes or offices. As Dana reached a busy corner, waiting to cross, she felt a violent shove from behind and she went flying into the street in front of an oncoming truck. She slipped on a patch of ice and fell on her back, looking up in horror as the huge truck sped toward her.

At the last second, the white-faced driver managed to turn his wheel so that the truck passed directly over Dana. For a moment, she lay in darkness, her ears filled with the roar of the engine and the clanking chains flapping against the huge tires.

Suddenly she could see the sky again. The truck was gone. Dana groggily sat up. People were helping her to her feet. She looked around for the person who had pushed her, but it could have been anyone in the crowd. Dana took several deep breaths and tried to regain her composure. The people surrounding her were shouting at her in Russian. The crowd was beginning to press in on Dana, making her panicky.

'Hotel Metropol?' Dana said hopefully.

A group of young boys had approached. 'Sure. We take you.'

The lobby of the Hotel Metropol was blessedly warm, crowded with tourists and businessmen. *Mingle with the crowds. I'll be waiting for you in Washington when you arrive.*

Dana said to a bellman, 'What time does the next bus leave for the airport?'

'In thirty minutes, *gaspazha.*'

'Thank you.'

She sat in a chair, breathing hard, trying to wipe the unspeakable horror from her mind. She was filled with dread. Who was trying to kill her and why? And was Kemal safe?

The bellman came up to Dana. 'The airport bus is here.'

Dana was the first one on the bus. She took a seat at the rear and studied the faces of the passengers. There were tourists from half a dozen countries: Europeans, Asians, Africans, and a few Americans. A man across the aisle was staring at her.

He looks familiar, Dana thought. Has he been following me? She found herself hyperventilating.

One hour later, when the bus stopped at Sheremetyevo II airport, Dana was the last one to disembark. She hurried into the terminal building and over to the Air France desk.

'May I help you?'

'Do you have a reservation for Dana Evans?' Dana was holding her breath. *Say yes, say yes, say yes . . .*

The clerk sorted through some papers. 'Yes. Here's your ticket. It's paid for.'

Bless Roger. 'Thank you.'

'The plane is on schedule. That's flight two-twenty. It will be leaving in one hour and ten minutes.'

'Is there a lounge' – Dana almost said, *with a lot of people* – 'where I can rest?'

'Down the end of this corridor and to the right.'

'Thank you.'

The lounge was crowded. Nothing in there seemed unusual or threatening. Dana took a seat.

In a little while, she would be on her way to America and safety.

'Air France flight two-twenty is now boarding at gate three for Washington, DC. Will all passengers please have their passports and boarding passes ready?'

Dana rose and started toward gate 3. A man who had been watching her from an Aeroflot counter spoke into his cell phone.

'The subject is heading for the boarding gate.'

Roger Hudson picked up the phone and called a number. 'She's on Air France flight two-twenty. I want her met at the airport.'

'What do you want done with her, sir?'

'I would suggest a hit-and-run accident.'

They were flying at a smooth forty-five thousand feet in a cloudless sky. There was not an empty seat on the plane. An American was in the seat next to Dana.

'Gregory Price,' he said. 'I'm in lumber.' He was in his forties, with a long aquiline face, bright gray eyes, and a mustache. 'That's some kind of country we're leaving, huh?'

Krasnoyarsk-26's sole purpose for existing is to

make plutonium, the key ingredient in nuclear weapons.

'The Russians are sure different from us, but you get used to them after a while.'

One hundred thousand scientists and technicians live and work here.

'They sure don't cook like the French. When I come here on business, I bring my own care package.'

They cannot go outside. They cannot have visitors. They must cut themselves off completely from the outside world.

'Were you in Russia on business?'

Dana brought herself back to the present. 'Vacation.'

He looked at her in surprise. 'It's a hell of a time to take a vacation in Russia.'

When the flight attendant came down the aisle with a food cart, Dana started to decline, then realized she was famished. She could not remember when she had eaten last.

Gregory Price said, 'If you'd like a shot of bourbon, I've got the real stuff here, little lady.'

'No thanks.' She looked at her watch. They would be landing in a few hours.

When Air France flight 220 landed at Dulles airport, four men were watching as the passengers began to come through the exit ramp from the plane. The men stood there, confident, knowing there was no way she could escape.

One of them said, 'Do you have the hypodermic?'

'Yes.'

'Take her out to Rock Creek Park. The boss wants a hit-and-run.'

'Right.'

Their eyes turned back to the door. Passengers were streaming out, dressed in heavy woolen clothes, parkas, earmuffs, scarves, and gloves. Finally the flow of passengers stopped.

One of the men frowned. 'I'll go and see what's keeping her.'

He made his way down the ramp into the plane. A cleaning crew was busily at work. The man walked through the aisle. There were no signs of any passengers. He opened the lavatory doors. They were empty. He hurried forward and said to a flight attendant who was just leaving, 'Where was Dana Evans sitting?'

The flight attendant looked surprised. 'Dana Evans? You mean the TV anchorwoman?'

'Yes.'

'She wasn't on this flight. I wish she had been. I would have *loved* to have met her.'

Gregory Price was saying to Dana, 'Do you know what's great about the lumber business, little lady? Your product grows all by itself. Yes, sir, you just sit around and watch Mother Nature make money for you.'

A voice came over the loudspeaker.

'We'll be landing in Chicago's O'Hare Airport in a few minutes. Please fasten your seat belt and return your seat back to the upright position.'

The woman seated across the aisle said cynically, 'Yeah, put your seat back upright. I wouldn't want to be leaning back when I die.'

The word 'die' gave Dana a jolt. She could hear the sound of the bullets ricocheting into the wall of the apartment building and she could feel the strong hand shoving her into the path of the oncoming truck. She shuddered when she thought of the two narrow escapes she had had.

Hours earlier, seated in the waiting lounge at Sheremetyevo II airport, Dana had told herself that everything was going to be fine. *The good guys are going to win.* But there was something bothering her about a conversation she had had with someone. The person had said something disturbing, but it had slipped by. Had it been in a conversation with Matt? Commissar Shdanoff? Tim Drew? The more Dana tried to recall it, the more it eluded her.

A flight attendant announced over the loud-speaker, 'Air France flight 220 is ready to depart for Washington, DC. Please have your passports and boarding passes in hand.'

Dana rose and headed for the gate. As she started to show her ticket to the guard, she suddenly remembered what it was. It was her last conversation with Sasha Shdanoff.

No one knows I am there. It is what you call a 'safe house'.

The only person to whom she revealed Sasha Shdanoff's hide-out was Roger Hudson. And immediately after that, Shdanoff had been murdered. From the very beginning, Roger Hudson had been subtly alluding to some dark connection between Taylor Winthrop and Russia.

When I was in Moscow, there was a rumor that Winthrop was involved in some type of private deal with the Russians. . . .

Shortly before Taylor Winthrop became our ambassador to Russia, he told close friends that he had definitely retired from public life. . . .

It was Winthrop who pressured the president into appointing him ambassador. . . .

She had told Roger and Pamela her every move. They had been spying on her all the time. And there could have been only one reason:

Roger Hudson was Taylor Winthrop's mysterious partner.

When the American Airlines flight landed at O'Hare airport in Chicago, Dana peered out the window looking for anything suspicious. Nothing. It was quiet. Dana took a deep breath and started to deplane. Her nerves were on fire. She managed to keep as many passengers around her as possible as she walked into the terminal, staying with the chattering crowd. She had an urgent call to make. During the flight, something so terrible had occurred to her that it made her own danger seem unimportant. *Kemal.* What if he were in danger because of her? She could not bear the thought of anything happening to him. She had to find someone to protect Kemal. Immediately, she thought of Jack Stone. He was with an organization powerful enough to give her the kind of protection she and Kemal needed, and she was sure that he would arrange it for her. He had been sympathetic to her from the beginning. *He's not really one of them.*

I'm trying to stay outside the loop. I can best help you that way, if you know what I mean.

Dana walked over to a deserted corner of the terminal, reached in her purse, and took out the private number Jack Stone had given her. She called it. He answered immediately.

'Jack Stone.'

'It's Dana Evans. I'm in trouble. I need help.'

'What's going on?'

Dana could hear the concern in his voice. 'I can't go into it all now, but some people are after me, trying to kill me.'

'*Who?*'

'I don't know. But it's my young son, Kemal, I'm worried about. Can you help me get someone to protect him?'

He responded instantly. 'I'll see to it. Is he at home now?'

348

'Yes.'

'I'll send someone over. Now what about you? You say someone is trying to kill you?'

'Yes. They've – they've tried twice.'

There was a momentary silence. 'I'll look into that and see what I can do. Where are you?'

'I'm at American Airlines at O'Hare, and I don't know when I can get out of here.'

'Stay right where you are. I'll get someone there to protect you. Meanwhile, you can stop worrying about Kemal.'

Dana felt a sense of deep relief. 'Thank you. Thank you.' She hung up.

In his office at the FRA, Jack Stone replaced the receiver. He pressed down the intercom button. 'The target just called. She's in an American Airlines terminal at O'Hare. Take her.'

'Yes, sir.'

Jack Stone turned to an aide. 'When is General Booster returning from the Far East?'

'He'll be back this afternoon.'

'Well, let's get the hell out of here before he finds out what's been going on.'

Twenty-four

Dana's cell phone rang.

'Jeff!'

'Hello, darling.' And the sound of his voice was a blanket wrapped around her, warming her.

'Oh, Jeff!' She found that she was trembling.

'How are you?'

How am I? I'm running for my life. But she could not tell him that. There was no way he could help her, not now. It was too late. 'I'm – I'm fine, darling.'

'Where are you now, world traveler?'

'I'm in Chicago. I'll be back in Washington tomorrow.' *When are you going to be with me?* 'How – how is Rachel?'

'She seems to be doing okay.'

'I miss you.'

Rachel's bedroom door opened, and she stepped into the living room. She started to call Jeff's name and stopped when she saw that he was on the phone.

'I miss you more than you can ever imagine,' Jeff said.

'Oh, I love you so much.' A man nearby seemed to be staring at her. Dana's heart began pounding. 'Darling, if – if anything happens to me . . . always remember that I –'

Jeff was instantly alarmed. 'What do you mean if anything happens to you?'

'Nothing. I – I can't go into it now, but – I'm sure everything will be fine.'

'Dana, you can't let anything happen to you! I need you. I love you more than anyone I've ever loved in my life. I couldn't bear to lose you.'

Rachel listened a moment longer, then quietly went back into her bedroom and closed the door.

Dana and Jeff spoke for ten minutes more. When Dana finally hung up, she felt better. *I'm glad I had a chance to say good-bye.* She looked up and saw the man still staring at her. *There's no way one of Jack Stone's men could have arrived so quickly. I need to get out of here.* She felt a rising panic.

Dana's next-door neighbor knocked on Dana's door. Mrs Daley opened it.

'Hello.'

'Keep Kemal home. We're going to need him.'

'I'll take care of it.' Mrs Daley closed the door and called to Kemal. 'Your oatmeal is almost ready, darling.'

Mrs Daley went into the kitchen, took the oatmeal off the stove, and opened a bottom cabinet drawer filled with packets of drugs labeled *BuSpar*. Dozens of empty packets were at the bottom of the drawer. Mrs Daley opened two new packets, hesitated, then added a third. She mixed the powder in with the oatmeal, poured sugar on top, and carried the cereal into the dining room. Kemal came in from the study.

'Here you are, love. Nice, hot oatmeal.'

'I'm not very hungry.'

'You must eat, Kemal.' Her voice was sharp in the way that frightened him. 'We don't want Miss Dana to be disappointed in us, do we?'

'No.'

'Good. I'll bet you can finish every bit of that for Miss Dana.'

Kemal sat down and began to eat.

He should sleep for about six hours, Mrs Daley calculated. *Then I'll see what they want me to do with him.*

Dana raced through the airport until she passed a large dress shop.

I need to hide my identity. She went inside and looked around. Everything seemed normal. Customers were busily buying merchandise and clerks were taking care of them. And then Dana looked out the shop door and she could feel her flesh crawl. Two menacing-looking men were standing there at each side of the entrance. One of them held a walkie-talkie.

How had they found her in Chicago? Dana tried to control her panic. She turned to the clerk. 'Is there another way out of here?'

The clerk shook her head. 'I'm sorry, miss. That's only for the staff.'

Dana's throat was dry. She looked out at the men again. *I have to escape*, Dana thought desperately. *There has to be a way.*

Suddenly, she grabbed a dress off the rack and started to walk to the entrance.

'Wait a minute!' the clerk called. 'You can't –'

Dana was approaching the door, and the two men started to move toward her. As Dana stepped through the door, the sensor on the dress tag triggered an alarm. A store guard came rushing out. The two men looked at each other and stepped back.

'Just a minute, miss,' the guard said. 'You'll have to come back inside the store with me.'

'Why should I?' Dana protested.

'Why? Because shoplifting is against the law.' The guard took Dana's arm and pulled her back inside. The men stood there, frustrated.

Dana smiled at the guard. 'Okay. I admit it. I was shoplifting. Take me to jail.'

Shoppers began to stop to see what was happening. The manager came hurrying over. 'What's the problem here?'

'I caught this woman trying to steal this dress.'

'Well, I'm afraid we'll have to call the pol –' He turned and recognized Dana. 'My God! It's Dana Evans.'

Whispers rippled through the growing crowd.

'It's Dana Evans . . .'

'We watch her on the news every night . . .'

'Do you remember her broadcasts from the war . . . ?'

The manager said, 'I'm so sorry, Miss Evans. Obviously there's been a mistake.'

'No, no,' Dana said quickly. 'I was shoplifting.' She held out her hands. 'You can arrest me.'

The manager smiled. 'I wouldn't dream of it. You can keep the dress, Miss Evans, with our compliments. We're flattered that you like it.'

Dana stared at him unbelievingly. 'You're not going to arrest me?'

His smile widened. 'I'll tell you what. I'll trade you the dress for an autograph. We're big fans of yours.'

One of the women gathered around exclaimed, 'Me, too!'

'Can I have an autograph?'

More people were approaching.

'Look! It's Dana Evans.'

'Can I have your autograph, Miss Evans?'

'My husband and I watched you every night when you were in Sarajevo.'

'You really made the war come alive.'

'I'd like an autograph, too.'

Dana stood there, growing more desperate by the second. She glanced outside. The two men were still there, waiting.

Dana's mind was racing. She turned to the crowd and smiled. 'I'll tell you what I'll do. Let's go outside in the fresh air, and I'll give each of you an autograph.'

There were cries of excitement.

Dana handed the dress to the manager. 'You can keep this. Thank you.' She started toward the door, followed by her fans. The two men outside backed off, confused, as the crowd descended on them.

Dana turned to her fans. 'Who's first?' They were pressing around her, holding out pens and pieces of paper.

The two men stood there, uneasy. As Dana signed autographs, she kept moving toward the terminal exit. The crowd followed her outside. A taxi pulled up at the curb, discharging a passenger.

Dana turned to the crowd. 'Thank you. I have to go now.' She jumped into the cab and a moment later it disappeared into the traffic.

Jack Stone was on the phone with Roger Hudson. 'Mr Hudson, she got away from us, but –'

'Goddammit! I don't want to hear that. I want her taken out of the picture – *now*.'

'Don't worry, sir. We've got the license number of the taxi. She can't get far.'

'Don't fail me again.' Roger Hudson slammed the receiver down.

Carson Pirie Scott & Company, in the heart of Chicago's Loop, was crowded with shoppers. At the scarf counter, a clerk was finishing wrapping a package for Dana.

'Will that be cash or charge?'

'Cash.' *No sense leaving a paper trail.*

Dana took her package and had almost reached the exit when she suddenly stopped, filled with fear. Two different men were standing outside the door with walkie-talkies. Dana looked at them, her mouth suddenly dry. She turned and hurried back to the counter.

The clerk asked, 'Was there something else, miss?'

'No. I –' Dana looked around in desperation. 'Is there another door leading out of here?'

'Oh, yes, we have several entrances.'

It's no use, Dana thought. *They'll have them all covered.* This time there would be no escape.

Dana noticed a woman shopper in a shabby old green coat looking at a scarf in a glass case. Dana studied her a moment, then walked over.

'Beautiful, aren't they?' Dana said.

The woman smiled. 'They certainly are.'

The men outside were watching the two women in conversation. They looked at each other and shrugged. They had every exit covered.

Inside Dana was saying, 'I like that coat you're wearing. It's exactly my color.'

'I'm afraid this old thing is about worn out. Yours is very pretty.'

The two men outside watched as the conversation continued.

'It's damned cold,' one of the men complained. 'I wish she'd get the hell out here and let us get this over with.'

His companion nodded. 'There's no way she can get –' He broke off as he saw the two women in the store start to exchange coats. He grinned. 'Jesus, look what she's trying to get away with. They're swapping coats. What a dumb broad.'

The two women disappeared for a moment behind a clothes rack. One of the men spoke into the walkie-talkie. 'The subject is switching from her red coat into a green coat . . . Hold it. She's heading for exit four. Pick her up there.'

At exit four, two men were waiting. A moment later one of them said into his cellular phone, 'We've got her. Get the car.'

They watched as she came out the door into the cold air. She wrapped her green coat tightly around her and started down the street. They closed in on her. As she reached the corner and started hailing a cab, the men grabbed her arms. 'You don't need a cab. We have a nice car for you.'

She looked at them in astonishment. 'Who are you? What are you talking about?'

One of the men was staring at her. 'You're not Dana Evans!'

'Well, of course I'm not.'

The men looked at each other, let go of her, and raced back to the store. One of the men clicked on his walkie-talkie. 'Wrong target. Wrong target. Do you read me?'

By the time the others piled into the store, Dana had disappeared.

She was caught in a living nightmare, trapped in a hostile world with unknown enemies trying to kill her. She was enmeshed in a web of terror, almost paralyzed with fear. When Dana got out of the taxi, she started walking fast, trying not to run and call attention to herself, having no idea where she was going. She passed a store with a sign that said FANTASY HEADQUARTERS: FANCY DRESS FOR ALL OCCASIONS. On an impulse, Dana went inside. It was filled with costumes, wigs, and makeup.

'Can I help you?'

Yes. Call the police. Tell them someone is trying to kill me.

'Miss?'

'Er – yes. I would like to try on a blond wig.'

'This way, please.'

A minute later Dana was looking at her blond image in the mirror.

'It's amazing how much it changes your appearance.'

I hope so.

Outside the store, Dana flagged down a taxi. 'O'Hare airport.' *I must get to Kemal.*

When the telephone rang, Rachel picked it up. 'Hello ... Dr Young? ... The final results of the test?'

Jeff saw the sudden tension in her face.

'You can tell me over the phone. Just a minute.' Rachel looked at Jeff, took a deep breath, and took the phone into the bedroom.

He could hear her voice, faintly.

'Go ahead, Doctor.'

There was a silence that lasted a full three minutes, and as Jeff, concerned, was about to go into the bedroom, Rachel came out, and she had a glow on her face that he had never seen before.

'It worked!' She was almost breathless with excitement. 'Jeff, I'm in remission. The new therapy worked!'

Jeff said, 'Thank God! That's wonderful, Rachel.'

'He wants me to stay here for another few weeks, but the crisis is over.' Her voice was filled with elation.

'We'll go out and celebrate,' Jeff said. 'I'll stay with you until –'

'No.'

'No, what?'

'I don't need you anymore, Jeff.'

'I know, and I'm glad we –'

'You don't understand. I want you to leave.'

He looked at Rachel, surprised. 'Why?'

'Dear, sweet Jeff. I don't want to hurt your feelings, but now that I'm in remission, it means I can go back to work. It's my life. It's what I am. I'm going to call and see what jobs are available. I've felt trapped here with you. Thanks for helping me, Jeff. I really do appreciate it. But it's time to say good-bye. I'm sure Dana misses you. So please, why don't you just leave, darling?'

Jeff looked at her a moment and nodded. 'Right.'

Rachel watched him go into the bedroom and start to pack. Twenty minutes later, when Jeff came out with his suitcase, Rachel was on the phone.

'. . . and I've come back to the real world, Betty. I'll be able to go back to work in a few weeks . . . I know. Isn't it wonderful?'

Jeff was standing there, waiting to say good-bye. Rachel waved to him and turned back to the telephone. 'I'll tell you what I want . . . get me a shoot on a nice tropical . . .'

Rachel watched Jeff walk out the door. Slowly, she let the phone drop. She walked over to the window and stood there, watching the only man she had ever loved walk out of her life.

Dr Young's words were still ringing in her ears. 'Miss Stevens, I'm sorry, but I have bad news. The treatment didn't work . . . The cancer has metastasized . . . It has spread too far. I'm afraid that it's terminal . . . maybe another month or two . . .'

Rachel remembered the Hollywood director Roderick Marshall saying to her, 'I'm glad you came. I'm going to make you a big star.' And as the excruciating red river of pain began to rack Rachel's body again, she thought: *Roderick Marshall would have been proud of me.*

When Dana's plane landed, Washington's Dulles airport was crowded with passengers waiting for their luggage. Dana walked past the carousels out into the street and climbed into one of the waiting taxis. There were no suspicious-looking men around, but her nerves were screaming. Dana took out her purse and looked in the small mirror for reassurance. Her blond wig did give her a completely different look. *It will have to do for now*, Dana thought. *I've got to get to Kemal.*

Kemal opened his eyes slowly, awakened by the sounds of voices coming through the closed study door. He felt groggy.

'The boy's still asleep,' he heard Mrs Daley say. 'I drugged him.'

A man replied, 'We'll have to wake him up.'

A second man's voice said, 'Maybe it would be better if we carried him there while he's asleep.'

'You could do it to him here,' Mrs Daley said. 'And then get rid of his body.'

Kemal was suddenly wide awake.

'We have to keep him alive for a while. They're going to use him as bait to catch the Evans woman.'

Kemal sat up, listening, his heart pounding.

'Where is she?'

'We're not sure. But we know she'll be coming here for the kid.'

Kemal jumped out of bed. He stood there for a moment, rigid with fear. The woman he had trusted wanted to kill him. *Pizda! It won't be that easy,* Kemal swore to himself. *They couldn't kill me in Sarajevo. They're not going to kill me here.* He began frantically throwing on his clothes. When he reached for his artificial arm on the chair, it slipped out of his hand and fell to the floor with what sounded to Kemal like a thunderous crash. He froze. The men outside were still talking. They had not heard it. Kemal attached his arm and finished dressing quickly.

He opened the window and was hit by a blast of frigid air. His overcoat was in the other room. Kemal moved out onto the window ledge in his thin jacket, his teeth chattering. There was a fire escape leading to the ground, and he climbed onto it, careful to duck out of sight of the living-room window.

As Kemal reached the ground, he looked at his

watch. It was 2:45. Somehow he had slept half the day away. He began to run.

'Let's tie the kid down, just in case.'

One of the men opened the study door and looked around the room in surprise. 'Hey, he's gone!'

The two men and Mrs Daley rushed to the open window in time to see Kemal racing down the street.

'Get him!'

Kemal ran as if in a nightmare; his legs growing weaker and more rubbery with every step. Each breath was a knife in his chest. *If I can get to the school before they close the gates at three o'clock*, he thought, *I'll be safe. They won't dare hurt me with all the other kids around.*

There was a red traffic light ahead. Kemal ignored it and darted across the avenue, dodging cars, oblivious to the outraged sounds of automobile horns and screaming brakes. He reached the other side of the street and kept running.

Miss Kelly will call the police, and they'll protect Dana.

Kemal was beginning to get short of breath and he felt a tightness in his chest. He glanced at his watch again: 2:55. He looked up. The school was just ahead. *Two more blocks to go.*

I'm safe, Kemal thought. *They haven't dismissed classes yet.* A minute later he reached the front gate. He stopped in front of it and stared at it, unbelievingly. *It was locked*. Suddenly, from behind, Kemal felt an iron grip on his shoulder.

'It's Saturday, stupid.'

'Stop here,' Dana said. The taxi was two blocks from her apartment. Dana watched the cab drive away. She walked slowly, her body tense, every sense alert, scanning the streets, looking for anything out of the ordinary. She was sure that Kemal was safe. Jack Stone would be protecting him.

When Dana reached the apartment-house corner, she avoided the front entrance and stepped into the alley that led to the back of the building. It was deserted. Dana went inside the service door and quietly walked up the stairs. She reached the second floor and started down the hall and suddenly stopped. The door to her apartment was wide open. Dana was instantly flooded with fear. She ran toward the door and raced inside. 'Kemal!'

No one was there. Dana dashed through the apartment, frantic, wondering what could have happened. *Where was Jack Stone? Where was Kemal?* In the kitchen, a cabinet drawer had fallen to the floor and its contents had spilled out. There were dozens of small packets, some full, some empty. Curious, Dana picked one up and looked at it. The label said, *BuSpar 15 mg tablets marked NDC D087 D822-32.*

What were they? Was Mrs Daley on drugs, or

had she been giving these to Kemal? Could it have anything to do with the change in his behavior? Dana put one of the packets in her coat pocket.

Filled with dread, Dana slipped out of the apartment. She went out the back way, into the alley, and headed for the street. As Dana turned the corner, a man hidden behind a tree spoke into a walkie-talkie to his confederate standing on the opposite corner.

Ahead of Dana was the Washington Pharmacy. Dana went inside.

The pharmacist said, 'Ah, Miss Evans. Can I help you?'

'Yes, Coquina. I'm curious about this.' She took out the small packet. The pharmacist glanced at it. 'BuSpar. It's an anti-anxiety agent. White crystal, water soluble.'

'What does it do?' Dana asked.

'It's a relaxant. It has a calming effect. Of course, if you overdose, it can cause drowsiness and fatigue.'

He's asleep. Shall I wake him up?

When he came home from school, he felt tired, so I thought a nap would be good for him . . .

So that explained what had been going on. And it had been Pamela Hudson who had sent Mrs Daley.

And I put Kemal in that bitch's hands, Dana thought. She felt sick to her stomach.

She looked at the pharmacist. 'Thank you, Coquina.'

'My pleasure, Miss Evans.'

Dana went out the door back into the street. The two men were approaching her. 'Miss Evans, could we talk to you for a min –' Dana turned and ran. The men were at her heels. Dana reached the corner. A policeman in the middle of the intersection was directing the heavy traffic.

Dana ran out into the street toward him.

'Hey! Go back, miss.'

Dana kept coming.

'You're moving against the light! Did you hear me? Get back!'

The two men were waiting at the corner, watching.

'Are you deaf?' the policeman yelled.

'Shut up!' She slapped the policeman hard across the face. The furious officer grabbed Dana's arm.

'You're under arrest, ma'am.'

He pulled Dana back to the sidewalk and held on to her while he talked into his radio. 'I need a black-and-white.'

The two men stood there looking at each other, uncertain what to do.

Dana looked across at them and smiled. There was the sound of an approaching siren and a few seconds later a police car came to a stop in front of them.

The two men watched helplessly as Dana was put into the backseat of the patrol car and driven away.

*

At the police station, Dana said, 'I'm entitled to one phone call, right?'

The sergeant said, 'Right.'

He handed Dana a phone. She made her call.

A dozen blocks away the man holding Kemal by his shirt collar was pulling him toward a limousine waiting at the curb, its motor running.

'Please! Please let me go,' Kemal pleaded.

'Shut up, kid.'

Four uniformed marines were passing by.

'I don't want to go in the alley with you,' Kemal yelled.

The man looked at Kemal puzzled. 'What?'

'Please don't make me go in the alley.' Kemal turned to the marines. 'He wants to pay me five dollars to go in the alley with him. I don't want to.'

The marines stopped, staring at the man. 'Why, you dirty pervert . . .'

The man backed away. 'No, no. Wait a minute. You don't understand . . .'

One of the marines said grimly, 'Yes, we do, buddy. Get your hands off the kid.' They surrounded the man. He put his hands up to defend himself, and Kemal quickly slipped away.

A delivery boy with a package was getting off a bicycle and starting toward a house. Kemal jumped onto the bicycle and pedaled furiously away. The man watched, frustrated, as Kemal rounded the corner and disappeared. The marines were closing in on him.

At the police station, Dana's cell door clanged open.

'You're free to go, Miss Evans. You're out on bail.'

Matt! The phone call worked, Dana thought happily. *He didn't lose any time.*

As Dana started toward the exit, she stopped in shock. One of the men was standing there, waiting for her.

He smiled at Dana and said, 'You're free, sis. Let's go.' He gripped Dana's arm tightly and started herding her out to the street. As they stepped outside, the man stopped in astonishment. A full television crew from WTN was waiting in front.

'Look this way, Dana . . .'

'Dana, is it true that you slapped a policeman?'

'Can you tell us what happened?'

'Did he harass you?'

'Are you going to press charges?'

The man was shying away, covering his face.

'What's the matter?' Dana called. 'Don't you want your picture taken?'

He fled.

Matt Baker appeared at Dana's side. 'Let's get the hell out of here.'

*

They were in Matt Baker's office at the WTE building. Elliot Cromwell, Matt Baker, and Abbe Lasmann had been listening to Dana for the last half hour in shocked silence.

'. . . and the FRA is involved, too. That's why General Booster tried to stop me from investigating.'

Elliot Cromwell said, 'I'm stunned. How could we all have been so wrong about Taylor Winthrop? I think we should inform the White House about what's happening. Let them call in the attorney general and the FBI.'

Dana said, 'Elliot, so far we only have my word against Roger Hudson's. Who do you think they're going to believe?'

Abbe Lasmann said, 'Don't we have any proof?'

'Sasha Shdanoff's brother is alive. I'm sure he'll talk. Once we pull a single thread, the whole story is going to unravel.'

Matt Baker took a deep breath and looked at Dana admiringly. 'When you go after a story, you go after a story.'

Dana said, 'Matt, what are we going to do about Kemal? I don't know where to look.'

Matt said firmly, 'Don't worry. We'll find him. Meanwhile, we have to get a place for you to hide where no one can find *you*.'

Abbe Lasmann spoke up. 'You can use my apartment. No one will think of looking for you there.'

'Thank you.' Dana turned to Matt. 'About Kemal . . .'

'We'll get the FBI on it right away. I'll have a driver take you to Abbe's apartment. It's in our hands now, Dana. Everything's going to be fine. I'll call you the minute I hear something.'

Kemal pedaled along the icy streets, anxiously looking behind him every few moments. There was no sign of the man who had grabbed him. *I've got to get to Dana*, Kemal thought, desperately. *I can't let them hurt her.* The problem was that the WTN studio was at the other end of downtown Washington.

When Kemal came to a bus stop, he got off the bicycle and pushed it onto the grass. As a bus approached, Kemal felt in his pockets and realized he had no money.

Kemal turned to a passerby. 'Excuse me, could I have a –'

'Get lost, kid.'

Kemal tried a woman who was approaching. 'Excuse me, I need bus fare to –' The woman hurried by.

Kemal stood in the cold, without a coat, shivering. No one seemed to care. *I've got to get bus fare*, Kemal thought.

He yanked off his artificial arm and laid it on the grass. When the next man passed by, Kemal held out his stump and said, 'Excuse me, sir. Could you give me enough money for bus fare?'

The man stopped. 'Of course, son,' he said, and handed Kemal a dollar.

'Thank you.'

When the man walked away, Kemal quickly put his arm back on. A bus was approaching, just a block away. *I've made it*, Kemal thought jubilantly. And at that moment, he felt a sting in the back of his neck. As he started to turn, everything grew faint. Inside his head a voice was screaming, *No! No!* Kemal slumped to the ground, unconscious. Passersby began to gather.

'What happened?'

'Did he faint?'

'Is he all right?'

'My son is diabetic,' a man said. 'I'll take care of him.' He lifted Kemal up and carried him into a waiting limousine.

Abbe Lasmann's apartment was in northwest Washington. It was large and comfortably decorated with contemporary furniture and white rugs. Dana was in the apartment alone, pacing back and forth, panicky, waiting for the phone to ring. *Kemal must be all right. They have no reason to harm him. He'll be fine. Where is he? Why can't they find him?*

When the phone rang, it startled Dana. She snatched it up. 'Hello.' The line was dead. It rang again, and Dana realized it was her cell phone. She felt a sudden sense of relief. She pressed the button. 'Jeff?'

Roger Hudson's voice said quietly, 'We've been looking for you, Dana. I have Kemal here.'

Dana stood there, unable to move, unable to talk. She whispered at last, 'Roger –'

'I'm afraid I can't control the men here much more. They want to cut off Kemal's good arm. Shall I let them?'

'No!' It was a scream. 'What – what do you want?'

'I just want to talk to you,' Roger Hudson said reasonably. 'I want you to come to the house, and I want you to come alone. If you bring anyone, I won't be responsible for what happens to Kemal.'

'Roger –'

'I'll expect you in thirty minutes.' The line went dead.

Dana stood there, numb with fear. *Nothing must happen to Kemal. Nothing must happen to Kemal.* With trembling fingers, Dana punched in Matt Baker's phone number. Matt's recorded voice came on.

'You have reached the office of Matt Baker. I'm not in right now, but leave a message and your call will be returned as soon as possible.'

There was the sound of a beep. Dana took a deep breath and spoke into the phone. 'Matt, I – I just got a call from Roger Hudson. He's holding Kemal at his house. I'm going there now. Please hurry before something happens to Kemal. Bring the police. *Hurry!*'

Dana turned off her cell phone and headed for the door.

Abbe Lasmann was putting some letters on Matt Baker's desk when she saw the message display flashing on Matt's telephone. She dialed Matt's password and played Dana's recording. She stood there a moment, listening to it. Then she smiled and pressed the erase button.

The moment Jeff's plane landed at Dulles airport, he called Dana. All through the flight, he had thought of that strange note in her voice, that disturbing 'If anything should happen to me.' Her cell phone kept ringing. Next Jeff tried her apartment. There was no answer. He got into a taxi and gave the address of WTN.

When Jeff walked into Matt's reception office, Abbe said, 'Well, Jeff! It's good to see you.'

'Thanks, Abbe.' He walked into Matt Baker's office.

Matt said, 'So, you're back. How's Rachel?'

The question threw Jeff for an instant. 'She's fine,' he said tonelessly. 'Where's Dana? She's not answering her phone.'

Matt said, 'My God, you don't know what's been going on, do you?'

'Tell me,' Jeff said tightly.

In the reception office, Abbe pressed her ear against the closed door. She could only hear snatches of the conversation. '... attempts on her life ... Sasha Shdanoff ... Krasnoyarsk-26 ... Kemal ... Roger Hudson ...'

Abbe had heard enough. She hurried to her desk and picked up the telephone. A minute later she was talking to Roger Hudson.

Inside the office, Jeff was listening to Matt, stunned. 'I can't believe it.'

'It's all true,' Matt Baker assured him. 'Dana's at Abbe's. I'll have Abbe try her apartment again.' He pressed down the intercom, but before he could speak, he heard Abbe's voice.

'... and Jeff Connors is here. He's looking for Dana. I think you'd better get her out of there. They're going to be coming over there ... Right. I'll take care of it, Mr Hudson. If –'

Abbe heard a sound and turned. Jeff Connors and Matt Baker were standing in the doorway, staring at her.

Matt said, 'You bitch.'

Jeff turned to Matt, frantic. 'I have to get to the Hudson house. I need a car.'

Matt Baker glanced out the window. 'You'll never get there in time. The traffic is bumper-to-bumper.'

From the heliport on the roof, they heard the sound of the WTN helicopter landing. The two men looked at each other.

Twenty-Five

Dana managed to flag down a taxi in front of Abbe Lasmann's apartment building, but the ride to the Hudsons' home seemed to take forever. The traffic on the slippery streets was horrendous. Dana was terrified she would be too late.

'Hurry,' she pleaded with the driver.

He looked at her in the rearview mirror. 'Lady, I'm not an airplane.'

Dana sat back, filled with anxiety, thinking about what lay ahead. Matt would have gotten her message by now and called the police. *By the time I get there, the police will be there. If they're not there yet, I can stall until they arrive.* Dana opened her purse. She still had the can of pepper spray. *Good.* She did not intend to make it easy for Roger or Pamela.

As the taxi approached the Hudson house, Dana looked out the window for some sign of police activity. There was none. When they went up the driveway, it was deserted. She felt choked with fear.

Dana recalled the first time she had come here. How wonderful Roger and Pamela had seemed to be. And they were Judases, murderous monsters. They had Kemal. Dana was filled with an overpowering hatred.

'You want me to wait?' the taxi driver was asking.

'No.' Dana paid him and walked up the steps to the front door and rang the bell, her heart racing.

Cesar opened the door. When he saw Dana, his face lit up. 'Miss Evans.'

And with a rush of excitement, Dana suddenly realized that she had an ally. She held out her hand. 'Cesar.'

He took it in his huge hand. 'I'm glad to see you, Miss Evans,' Cesar said.

'I'm glad to see *you*.' And Dana meant it. She was sure that Cesar would help her. The only question was when she should approach him. She looked around. 'Cesar –'

'Mr Hudson is waiting for you in the study, Miss Evans.'

'Right.' This was not the time.

Dana followed Cesar down the long hallway, remembering the incredible things that had happened since she first walked down this hall. They reached the study. Roger was at his desk packing some papers.

'Miss Evans,' Cesar said.

378

Roger looked up. Dana watched Cesar walk away. She was tempted to call him back.

'Well, Dana. Come in.'

Dana walked into the room. She looked at Roger, and she was filled with a blinding rage. 'Where is Kemal?'

Roger Hudson said, 'Ah, that dear boy.'

'The police are on their way here, Roger. If you do anything to either of us –'

'Oh, I don't think we have to worry about the police, Dana.' He walked over to her, and before Dana knew what he was doing, he had grabbed her purse and was starting to search through it. 'Pamela told me you have pepper spray. You've been busy, haven't you, Dana?' He took out the can of pepper spray, raised it, and sprayed the contents into Dana's face. She screamed out with the stinging pain.

'Oh, you don't know what pain is yet, my dear, but I assure you, you're going to find out.'

Tears were streaming down Dana's face. She tried to wipe the liquid away. Roger politely waited until she had finished, then sprayed her in the face again.

Dana was sobbing. 'I want to see Kemal.'

'Of course you do. And Kemal wants to see you. The boy is terrified, Dana. I've never seen anyone so terrified. He knows he's going to die, and I told him you're going to die, too. You think you've been clever, don't you, Dana? The truth is that you've been very naive. We've been using you. We knew that someone in the Russian government was aware of what we were doing and was about to expose us. But we couldn't find out who it was. But you found out for us, didn't you?'

The memory of the bloody bodies of Sasha Shdanoff and his friend flashed through Dana's mind.

'Sasha Shdanoff and his brother, Boris, were very clever. We haven't found Boris yet, but we will.'

'Roger, Kemal has nothing to do with any of this. Let him –'

'I think not, Dana. I first began to worry about you when you met poor ill-fated Joan Sinisi. She overheard Taylor talking about the Russian plan. He was afraid to have her killed because she was associated with him. So he fired her. When she sued for unfair dismissal, he made a settlement, on the condition that she never discuss the matter.' Roger Hudson sighed. 'So I'm afraid that you were really responsible for Joan Sinisi's "accident".'

'Roger, Jack Stone knows –'

Roger Hudson shook his head. 'Jack Stone and his men have been watching your every move. We could have gotten rid of you at any time, but we waited until you got us the information we needed. We really have no further use for you.'

'I want to see Kemal.'

'Too late. I'm afraid poor Kemal has had an accident.'

Dana looked at him in horror. 'What have you –'

'Pamela and I decided that a nice little fire is the best way to end Kemal's pitiful little life. So we've

380

sent him back to school. Naughty of him to break into the school on a Saturday. He was just small enough to fit through the basement window.'

She was filled with a blinding rage. 'You cold-blooded monster. You'll never get away with this.'

'You disappoint me, Dana. Resorting to clichés? What you don't understand is that we *have* gotten away with it.' He walked back to his desk and pressed a button. A moment later Cesar appeared.

'Yes, Mr Hudson.'

'I want you to see to Miss Evans. And make sure she's still alive when the accident happens.'

'Yes, Mr Hudson. I'll take care of it.'

He was one of them. Dana could not believe it. 'Roger, listen to me –'

Cesar took Dana by the arm and started leading her out of the room.

'Roger –'

'Good-bye, Dana.'

Cesar tightened his grip on Dana's arm and marched her down the hall, through the kitchen, and out to the side of the house, where a limousine was parked.

The WTN helicopter was approaching the Hudson estate.

Jeff said to Norman Bronson, 'You can set it down on the lawn and –' He stopped as he looked down

381

below and saw Cesar putting Dana into a limousine. 'No! Wait a minute.'

The limousine started moving down the driveway and onto the street.

'What do you want me to do?' Bronson asked.

'Follow them.'

In the limousine, Dana said, 'You don't want to do this, Cesar. I –'

'Shut up, Miss Evans.'

'Cesar, listen to me. You don't know these people. They're murderers. You're a decent man. Don't let Mr Hudson force you to do things that –'

'Mr Hudson isn't forcing me to do anything. I'm doing this for *Mrs* Hudson.' He looked at Dana in the rearview mirror and grinned. 'Mrs Hudson takes good care of me.'

Dana looked at him, stunned. *I can't let this happen.* 'Where are you taking me?'

'To Rock Creek Park.' He didn't need to add: *where I'm going to kill you.*

Roger Hudson, Pamela Hudson, Jack Stone, and Mrs Daley were in a station wagon, heading for Washington National Airport.

Jack Stone said, 'The plane is all ready. Your pilot has the flight plan to Moscow.'

Pamela Hudson said, 'God, I hate cold weather. I

hope that bitch burns in hell for putting me through this.'

'What about Kemal?' Roger Hudson asked.

'The fire at the school is set to go off in twenty minutes. The kid is in the basement. He's heavily sedated.'

Dana was growing more desperate. They were nearing Rock Creek Park, and the traffic was beginning to thin out.

Kemal is terrified, Dana. I've never seen anyone so terrified. He knows he's going to die, and I told him that you're going to die, too.

In the helicopter trailing the limousine, Norman Bronson said, 'He's turning, Jeff. It looks like he's heading for Rock Creek Park.'

'Don't lose him.'

At FRA, General Booster stormed into his office. 'What the hell has been going on here?' he asked one of his aides.

'I told you, General. While you were away. Major Stone recruited a few of our best men, and they're into some big deal with Roger Hudson. They've targeted Dana Evans. Look at this.' The aide pulled up a screen on his computer, and a moment later there was a picture of Dana naked, getting into the shower in the Breidenbacher Hof Hotel.

General Booster's face tightened. 'Jesus!' He turned to his aide. 'Where is Stone?'

'He's gone. He's leaving the country with the Hudsons.'

General Booster snapped. 'Get me the National Airport.'

In the helicopter, Norman Bronson looked down and said, 'They're heading toward the park, Jeff. Once they get there, we won't be able to land because of the trees.'

Jeff said urgently, 'We have to stop them. Can you land in front of them on the road?'

'Sure.'

'Do it.'

Bronson pushed the controls forward and the helicopter began to descend. He passed over the limousine, and then began gently to bring the helicopter down. It landed on the road, twenty yards ahead of the limousine. They watched as the car screeched to a stop.

'Turn off the engines,' Jeff said.

'We can't do that. We'll be at the guy's mercy if –'

'Turn them off.'

Bronson looked at him. 'Are you sure you know what you're doing?'

'No.'

Bronson sighed and turned off the ignition. The huge blades of the helicopter began to slow down until they came to a stop. Jeff looked out the window.

Cesar had opened the back door of the limousine. He said to Dana, 'Your friend is trying to cause us trouble.' His fist shot out and punched Dana in the jaw. She fell back on the seat, unconscious. Then Cesar stood up and started toward the helicopter.

'Here he comes,' Bronson said nervously. 'My God, he's a giant!'

Cesar was approaching the helicopter, his face filled with anticipation.

'Jeff, he's got to have a gun. He's going to kill us.'

Jeff yelled out the window, 'You and your bosses are going to prison, you bastard!'

Cesar started walking faster.

'It's all over for you. You might as well give up.'

Cesar was fifteen yards from the helicopter.

'You'll be jailbait for the boys.'

Ten yards.

'You'll like that, won't you, Cesar?'

Cesar was running now. Five yards.

Jeff pressed his thumb down hard on the start button and the huge vanes of the helicopter slowly began to turn. Cesar paid no attention, his eyes were focused on Jeff, his face was filled with hatred. The vanes began to spin faster and faster. As Cesar ran to the door of the helicopter, he suddenly realized what was happening, but it was too late. There was a loud splash, and Jeff closed his eyes. The outside and the inside of the helicopter were instantly covered with blood.

Norman Bronson said, 'I'm going to be sick.' He turned off the ignition.

Jeff glanced at the decapitated body on the ground, jumped out of the helicopter, and raced to the limousine. He opened the door. Dana was unconscious.

'Dana . . . darling . . .'

Dana slowly opened her eyes. She looked at Jeff and mumbled, 'Kemal . . .'

The limousine was almost a mile from Lincoln Preparatory School when Jeff yelled, 'Look.' Ahead of them in the distance, they could see smoke starting to darken the sky.

'They're burning the school down,' Dana shrieked. 'Kemal is in there. He's in the basement.'

'Oh, my God.'

A minute later the limousine reached the school. A heavy cloud of smoke was rising from the building. A dozen firemen were working to put down the fire.

Jeff jumped out of the car and moved toward the school. A fireman stopped him.

'You can't go any nearer, sir.'

'Has anyone been inside?' Jeff demanded.

'No. We just broke open the front door.'

'There's a boy in the basement.' Before anyone could stop him, Jeff went through the splintered doorway and ran inside. The place was filled with smoke. Jeff tried to yell Kemal's name, but only a cough came out. He put a handkerchief over his nose and ran down the hallway to the steps that led to the basement. The smoke was acrid and thick. Jeff fumbled his way down the stairs, holding on to the banister.

'Kemal!' Jeff called. There was no answer. 'Kemal.' Silence. Jeff made out a vague shape at the other end of the basement. He moved toward it, trying not to breathe, his lungs burning. He almost tripped over Kemal. He shook him. 'Kemal.' The boy was unconscious. With an enormous effort, Jeff picked him up and started carrying him toward the stairs. He was choking and was blinded by the smoke. He lurched drunkenly through the swirling black cloud, carrying Kemal in his arms. When he reached the steps, Jeff half carried him, half dragged him up the stairs. He heard distant voices, and he passed out.

General Booster was on the phone with Nathan Novero, the airport administrator at Washington National Airport.

'Does Roger Hudson keep his plane there?'

'Yes, General. As a matter of fact, he's here now. I believe they've just been cleared for takeoff.'

'Abort it.'

'*What?*'

'Call the tower and abort it.'

'Yes, sir.' Nathan Novero called the tower. 'Tower, abort the takeoff of Gulfstream R3487.'

The air traffic controller said, 'They're already taxiing down the runway.'

'Cancel their clearance.'

'Yes, sir.' The air traffic controller picked up his microphone. 'Tower to Gulfstream R3487. Permission to take off is canceled. You will return to terminal. Abort takeoff. I repeat, abort takeoff.'

Roger Hudson stepped into the cockpit. 'What the hell is this?'

'There must be some kind of delay,' the pilot said. 'We'll have to return to the –'

'No!' Pamela Hudson said. 'Keep going.'

'With all due respect, Mrs Hudson, I'd lose my pilot's license if –'

Jack Stone moved next to the pilot with a gun pointed at the pilot's head. 'Take off. We're heading for Russia.'

The pilot took a deep breath. 'Yes, sir.'

The plane sped down the runway, and twenty seconds later, it was airborne. The airport administrator watched in dismay as the Gulfstream soared higher and higher into the sky.

'Jesus! He went against –'

On the phone, General Booster was demanding, 'What's going on? Did you stop them?'

'No, sir. They – they just took off. There's no way we can make them –'

And at that moment the sky exploded. As the crew on the ground watched in horror, parts of the Gulfstream started raining down through the clouds in fiery pieces. It seemed to go on forever.

At the far edge of the field, Boris Shdanoff watched for a long time. Finally he turned and walked away.

Twenty-six

Dana's mother took a bite of the wedding cake.

'Too sweet. Much too sweet. When I was younger and I used to bake, my cakes would melt in your mouth.' She turned to Dana. 'Isn't that true, darling?'

'Melt in your mouth' would have been the last phrase that came to Dana's mind, but it was not important. 'Absolutely, Mother,' she said with a warm smile.

The wedding ceremony had been performed by a judge at City Hall. Dana had invited her mother at the last minute, after a telephone call.

'Darling, I didn't marry that dreadful man after all. You and Kemal were right about him, so I'm back in Las Vegas.'

'What happened, Mother?'

'I found out that he already had a wife. She didn't like him, either.'

'I'm sorry, Mother.'

'So here I am alone again.'

Lonely was the implication. So Dana had invited her to the wedding. Seeing her mother chatting with Kemal and even remembering his name, Dana smiled. *We'll turn her into a grandmother yet.* Her happiness seemed too immense to absorb. Just being married to Jeff was a blissful miracle, but there was more.

After the fire, Jeff and Kemal had briefly gone to the hospital to be treated for smoke inhalation. While they were there, a nurse talked to a reporter about Kemal's adventures and the story had been picked up by the media. Kemal's photograph was in the newspapers and his story was told on television. A book was being written about his experiences and there was even talk of a television series.

'But only if I get to star in it,' Kemal insisted. Kemal was the hero of his school.

When the adoption ceremony took place, half of Kemal's schoolmates turned out to applaud him.

Kemal said, 'I'm really adopted now, huh?'

'You're really adopted,' Dana and Jeff said. 'We belong to one another.'

'Rad.' *Wait until Ricky Underwood hears about this. Ha!*

The terrible nightmare of the past month was gradually fading away. The three of them were a family now, and home was a safe haven. *I don't need any more adventures*, Dana thought. *I've had enough to last me a lifetime.*

One morning, Dana announced, 'I just found a great new apartment for the four of us.'

'You mean the three of us,' Jeff corrected her.

'No,' Dana said softly. 'The four of us.'

Jeff was staring at her.

'She means she's having a baby,' Kemal explained. 'I hope it's a boy. We can shoot hoops.'

There was more good news to come. *Crime Line*'s opening show, 'The Roger Hudson Story, A Murder Conspiracy,' received both critical acclaim and phenomenal ratings. Matt Baker and Elliot Cromwell were elated.

'You'd better get a place ready to put your Emmy,' Elliot Cromwell told Dana.

There was only one sobering note. Rachel Stevens had succumbed to cancer. The story had been printed in the newspapers, and Dana and Jeff were aware of what had happened. But when the story appeared on the TelePrompTer, Dana looked at it and choked up.

'I can't read it,' she whispered to Richard Melton. So he had read it.

Rest in peace.

*

They were doing the eleven o'clock broadcast.

'. . . And here at home, a guardsman in Spokane, Washington, is charged with the murder of a sixteen-year-old prostitute and is suspected in the deaths of sixteen others . . . In Sicily, the body of Malcolm Beaumont, the seventy-year-old heir to a steel fortune, was found drowned in a swimming pool. Beaumont was honeymooning with his twenty-five-year-old bride. They were accompanied by the bride's two brothers. Now, here's the weather with Marvin Greer.'

When the broadcast was over, Dana went in to see Matt Baker.

'Something is bothering me, Matt.'

'What is it? Name it and I'll slay it.'

'It's the story about that seventy-year-old millionaire who drowned in a swimming pool while he was honeymooning with his twenty-five-year-old bride. Don't you think that was awfully convenient?'

Author's Note

This is a work of fiction, but the secret underground city of Krasnoyarsk-26 is real, one of thirteen closed cities engaged in nuclear production. Krasnoyarsk-26 is located in central Siberia, two thousand miles from Moscow, and since its creation in 1958, it has produced more than forty-five tons of weapons-grade plutonium. Although two of its plutonium-producing reactors were shut down in 1992, one remains active, currently producing half a ton of plutonium a year, which can be used to make atomic bombs.

There have been reported thefts of plutonium, and the United States Energy Department is working with the Russian government on increased security measures to protect nuclear material.